INDIE'S FIRST LOVE

The Cary Street Crew

TRILOGY

BOOK ONE

INDIE'S FIRST LOVE

BEK MINA

MINA
PUBLISHING

Sammi

Satomi Nakamura, better known as Sammi, was just leaving the architecture firm where she worked, and it had been a helluva good day. She had just snagged a huge project, valued at tens of millions of dollars, today was the last day she would be a landlord, and Land's End was having a sale on plaid shirts.

She was feeling relaxed in her SUV, her sleek, shiny black hair slicked back, seat tilted slightly, one hand on the shifter and the other dangling over the top of the steering wheel as she headed toward what used to be her home, six years ago. Even those terrible memories couldn't dim today's high.

It's been six years. Six years since she broke my heart. Haven't had sex in about five years. This will be my last trip to this house. To the place where I got engaged. The place where I saw her in bed with her best friend. The place where she tried to hug me and weasel her way back into my life. I guess I dodged a bullet with that one. It's taken me quite a few years, but I'm becoming me again. Maybe I'm ready to date again, Universe. Just maybe.

As she pulled up to the small, white house she and Ali used to call home, she felt nothing but relief to be signing it away tomorrow to the young family who had bought it from her. She walked in through the front door, took one last look around, and turned the heat up a bit so the new owners would feel comfortable tomorrow as they started their new lives. Sammi stood just inside the front door, looking back, before locking the door for the last time. She was ready. It was time for Sammi to re-enter the world of dating.

She waved goodbye to Mr. Reed, who was sitting on the porch next door, as usual, and he waived back, smiling broadly. She turned to walk back to her vehicle, hands in her pockets, smile on her face. As she walked past the mailbox, she decided to look inside, just in case.

CHAPTER 1

Indie

this is sammi. i got your letter.

As I read the text, my jaw hit the floor. *Holy shit, it worked. It actually worked!*

Pulling me from my shock was my child's voice.

"MOM!"

Her raised brows were aimed at me.

"Yes. Sorry. I was...umm...distracted for a moment."

"You okay, mom? We've both been calling you for a while."

Her once uppity eyebrows furrowed.

"For real, you look like you've seen a ghost."

"Ooooo, who's seen a ghost?" the other offspring chimed in.

"Mom, I think."

"Cool! They have a copy of that dead book from the movie *Beetlejuice* over here, should we get it for the ghost?" my second-born daughter asked.

"No one has seen a ghost. I was just distracted and surprised by a text I got from someone I knew a long time ago. That's all."

I forced a dismissive laugh that cracked towards the end.

I peered at those two faces I loved more than life itself. They echoed the face of my worst mistake, but I wouldn't have changed them for the world. The beings in front of me were far too beautiful and wonderful to ever really remind me of him for more than a split second. Mari, my first born, the worrier, the serious one, still had a furrowed brow. Putting the phone away and giving her a 'no-big-deal-I'm-fine' smile, placated her just enough. She returned her interest to what she wanted to speak with me about.

"So, can we get these?" She gestured towards her sister's hands, which each held a soda can with images from their favorite anime.

"Ummm...sure. Yeah, that's fine."

I replied with the most sincere smile I could muster. I could barely focus. Sixteen years had passed since I'd seen or heard from Sam, but I felt like a giddy eighteen-year-old kid again.

"WOO-HOO!" Veda squealed as she skipped towards the checkout counter, completely oblivious to what was happening between Mari and me.

Her bouncing curls were one of the only obvious differences between her and her older (by three minutes) sister. Only I could tell them apart when Veda straightened her hair, much to their chagrin. The corners of my mouth rose ever so slightly as I watched her. Mari, seeing a genuine smile once again, was appeased and walked after her sister.

Whipping out the phone, I speedily typed a reply.

Great! Call you in about 30 minutes... kids.

———

"Mom, you're fidgeting. You know, distracted driving causes most accidents," Mari stated from the passenger seat, without even glancing in my direction.

I sighed and stopped my fingers from tap dancing their way around the steering wheel. I could feel Mari side-eyeing me. I turned up the music on the radio and started to bop along while Veda belted the lyrics out, violently shaking herself around in the back seat. The song was about lost love, of course. The blood pulsating all too rapidly through my body muffled my hearing. I could feel that pumping organ trying to escape my chest. I was the one who reached out. I was the one who wanted to know how Sam was doing, but what if she hated me? She had reason to, but, then again, so did I. She was the one who had broken things off between us all those years ago.

No, I couldn't let the past pain come roaring back. It had taken me years to get over her, and I was absolutely and completely over her. I just wanted to see how she was doing, that was all. It felt odd to know nothing about someone who was such a huge part of my life. I wanted to make sure she was doing okay. She could have died years ago, and I wouldn't have had a clue.

I just had to get home, bribe the children with some pizza and a streaming movie rental, and make a phone call. Even Mari would be thrilled about pizza and a movie, I hoped.

"Ok, my minions, who wants to place the pizza order?"

The squealing confirmed my hypothesis, and I smiled smugly.

"Hey."

"Oh, hey, hi."

"So, like I said, I got your letter."

"Yeah, no, great. I'm so glad. It was kind of a shot in the dark, ya know? You're not exactly an easy person to find."

"Yeah, I do that on purpose."

"I know."

I was beginning to sweat in the cool autumn air. She definitely didn't sound like she wanted to talk. She could have just ignored the letter. Oh god, why did I write that letter?

"How *did* you find me?" she asked.

"Well, ummm, I just did a Google search one night and a property in Massachusetts popped up with Satomi J. Nakamura as the owner. I had tried to look you up twice before, but never found anything. Then, this time, this address popped up within the first few results. It was a county record of homeowners."

"So, you've been stalking me?"

"What?!? No! I wasn't stalking you. I was trying to find your information so I could reach out and talk to you, not stalk you from afar."

"You've been looking for me for how long?"

"I had looked for you about ten years ago and again about five years ago, but never found anything. I'm not stalking you."

My heart was pounding so loudly by this time, I was certain it could be heard by everyone within a one-mile radius. She must really hate me.

Laughter came pealing through the phone.

"You're still pretty easy to get riled up, you know that?"

"What? Are you...you're mean!" I retorted, which only brought about more laughter. "Yeah, yeah, yeah, make Indie crazy. You know, you're one of the only people who can do that to me."

I finally relaxed. Maybe she wasn't a completely different person from the girl I knew all those years ago.

"So, you still married to that asshole? You know, the one you left me for."

"No. What? Wait just a minute now. No, no, no. I didn't leave you for him. If you recall, you broke up with me right before Christmas."

"Yep, and you waited less than six months to get married."

"Yeah." I confirmed, my voice full of a pain she knew nothing about. "I was young, stupid, and very alone in the world. He promised to take care of me, and I was naive enough to believe him."

There was a long pause, and my mind started to go to dark places. I shook my head, pushing those terrible thoughts back.

"But that was forever ago. So how have you been doing? What have you been up to?" I asked, desperate for another topic.

"Oh, you want to change the subject? Okay. Why did you look me up? Why'd you write me a letter?"

"Well," I paused, realizing she did not share my aversion to reliving the past, "I had dreams for a couple of weeks, and you were in them."

"Oh, so the stalker is dreaming about me, huh?"

I could somehow hear her smile through the phone. My heart stuttered, much to my dismay. I gently reminded that pesky thing we were not going to do any of that ever again. No more lovey-dovey crap. Ever.

"I'm not sure. As soon as you find your stalker, you should ask them, smart ass."

I removed the phone from my ear, so the laughter coming through it wouldn't damage anything important.

"And you're one of the only people who can do that to me."

"Do what?" I didn't even need to feign ignorance.

"Well, two things. One, you're one of the only people I would allow to call me a smart ass, and two, you're one of the only people who's ever been able to make me smile or laugh."

Boom. My heart was a damn puddle.

The next hour and a half was spent tiptoeing around each other on semi-familiar ground. It was weird being so intimately linked to someone, but feeling like you knew nothing about them. We discussed bits and pieces of what had happened over the last sixteen years, why she had moved back to Boston, jobs, school, kids, music, relationships, parents, and people we used to know. I had stayed married for almost ten years, before the cheating caught up with my now ex-husband. She had been engaged six years ago, but that, too, had ended with cheating and leaving. We were both very jaded in the romance department and had each been alone for a long time. I was glad she was on the same page as me when it came to matters of the heart. That would help to keep old feelings in the past where they belonged. We had started out as best friends twenty years ago and it was nice to have that back in my life.

"Well, I've kept my minions at bay as long as I can. I've got to get everyone ready for bed, but this has been great. Really, I'm glad we reconnected." I said with sincerity.

"Oh, yeah, right. You've got kids and stuff. Yeah."

There was a long pause. I knew she had something she wanted to ask me, but I could feel her apprehension.

"Just ask whatever it is you want to ask, Sam."

"Sam, huh? Most people call me Sammi. I haven't heard Sam in a long time. Probably about sixteen years."

"Well, it's what I've always called you. So, go ahead, ask me whatever it is."

"Yes ma'am!"

We both chuckled a bit before she continued.

"Earlier, at the beginning of the conversation, you said you had dreams, and I was in them. What kinds of dreams were they? Why did they prompt you to find me?"

"Oh, well, umm, there were all sorts of dreams. Okay, lemme start by saying, I don't really dream. At least, I haven't for about the last ten years. I've had maybe four or five dreams over the last decade and all of 'em were terrible nightmares. Then, last month, I had dreams almost every night for two weeks straight. Nice dreams. All of them had people from my past. It was like my childhood, teens, and very early twenties all decided to have a dream dinner party. Random groups of people from all different early stages of my life were there. Most of the time, who was there changed every night. The first night, the guest list included my preschool teacher, my great aunt, my cousin, that really skinny manager at the burger joint we worked at in high school, and you."

"Oh, so I was a guest at your dream dinner party one night? Cool."

I didn't say anything back to her. I didn't want to tell her the whole truth.

"Indie? Ind, you still there?"

"Yeah. Yeah, I'm still here."

"You alright?"

"Yeah. I'm good. Sorry, I really do have to go, but please don't be a stranger. I'm glad we got to chat!"

"Me too, me too. G'night, Indie."

"Goodnight, Sam."

As soon as we hung up, I wanted to call her back and tell her all about the rest of the dreams. Fighting the pull she had on me, I put the phone down on the nightstand, closed my eyes, and allowed myself the pleasure of remembering her laughter. Then I shook myself out of my reverie. It must be old feelings, memories coming to the surface after so long. We weren't even the same people anymore and I didn't really know this woman. Yes, fond memories of a simpler time, that was all it was.

CHAPTER 2

Sammi

HUNG UP THE PHONE and fell back on the bed.

Indie.

Indie Woodley, first kiss, first love, first...well...first.

Indie Woodley had looked me up.

Indie Woodley had written to me.

Indie Woodley had just talked to me for an hour and a half on the day I told the universe I was ready to date again. What the hell did that even mean? Did Indie want me like that anymore? Did I want Indie like that anymore?

Gurgling sounds of protest came from an empty stomach. Forcing my body off of the bed, I trudged into the kitchen. The slim pickings in the fridge fortunately provided some eggs and cheese. We had been on the phone for so long, I had forgotten to eat. Just behind the carton of eggs was a half of a tomato.

Score! I thought to myself, *An omelet for dinner!*

My stomach may have been appeased, but my head was spinning. I needed a shower. Pajamas in hand, I gave my cat, Bob, a pet on the head and headed to the bathroom. Hot water did little to clear the head. Thoughts of Indie would not be washed away as easily as the day's dirt.

Bob greeted me in his usual way by nudging my calf with his head as soon as I opened my bathroom door, as did the chilly bedroom air. Giving the cat a quick pet, I dove under the covers. He happily climbed atop the bed and began to nestle in at the foot of the bed, after the customary walking in a circle six or seven times.

"Seriously, Bob, why? It makes no sense. Why do you do that? Why not just, ya know, lay down?"

He replied by turning his face away to complete the circle ritual with his lithe, little body.

"Then again, I'm talking to a damn cat, so who am I to judge?"

I tucked one of the pillows between my legs and the other under my head. One arm underneath the head, bent at the elbow, and the other one fell to touch the other side of the mattress, the bed had never felt emptier. It had been that way for so long. When I said I was ready for dating again, I didn't mean right that instant, and I definitely didn't mean Indie.

There were a lot of feelings around the subject of Indie. Indie had abandoned me and run off to marry some loser she had dated for a few months, way back in the eighth grade. Yes, we were young, but we were so in love. At least I thought we were. How could a person love someone as much as Indie had loved me and then turn around and marry someone else? It had taken over a year to even start dating again, which, for a nineteen-year-old, is practically a decade. Then came the crazy chick who used to punch and scream a lot. I would punch back, and we would end up in bed by the end of it all; a wildly unhealthy relationship which lasted for two years. Many girls came and went over the years, plus a couple of guys, but those never lasted long.

Then came Ali. After that debacle, I was broken. There was nothing left inside that cared. I just wanted to be alone with Bob. Ali had even shown up about a year later, crying, apologizing, wanting to patch things up, but I didn't even flinch. Being used, abused, cheated on, and abandoned one too many times had done its job. Alone was better.

Now, Indie waltzes back in through a letter. I hadn't felt this stirring inside in over six years. There hadn't even been a twinge of anything remotely like this in many more years than that; possibly since Indie was around all those years ago. These feelings were not trickling out of the dam constructed around my heart, they were flooding through a million cracks, and I knew it was only a matter of days before the dam was nothing more than a memory and my heart would, once again, be at the mercy of Indie Woodley. A fact which both terrified and excited me.

Thoughts of first love swam around in my mind as I dozed off in my warm, cozy, solitary bed.

Indie Woodley and Satomi Nakamura.

Indie and Sammi.

Indie's mouth on mine.

Indie's hand on my back.

Indie's giggle in my ear.

Indie's eyes staring at me after we'd made love.

Indie Woodley.

Indie Nakamura.

A family.

I jolted awake. What the heck was I thinking? Wide eyes, adjusted to the dark room and settled on the sleeping cat.

"Hey, if I can't sleep, neither can you, Bobert Nakamura!"

The slight shift of one ear was the only movement from the feline. He was content to ignore the rantings of his human. Following suit, I tried to ignore the rantings of my own mind. Settling back into my usual sleep position, I battled my way into blissful oblivion, eventually.

"Someone is awfully chipper this morning, yet the bags under your eyes are telling a different story. What gives, girl?" Cass asked.

"Nothing. Can't a girl just be in a good mood?" I replied.

"Not you." Cass chuckled. "I have rarely seen you in a truly good mood and it's never for no reason."

"I had a good night, but didn't get much sleep, that's all."

"A good night, or a gooood niiiight?" Cass inquired while raising her eyebrows repeatedly.

I only glared at her.

"Eh, who am I kiddin', you never have a goood niiiiight."

"Shut it. Don't you have work to do?"

"Um, yes, actually. That is precisely why I am here, madame. We need to go over our estimate for that new project. Something is off somewhere. I think Jeff screwed up the furniture cost. It just doesn't seem right, you feel me?"

Rolling my eyes like a bratty teen, I pulled up the estimate on my computer. Cass may be annoying, but when her gut says something is off, it usually is. Almost an hour went by before we both gasped.

"Well, shit," I said.

"Yeah, that's a big boo-boo fo sho. Okay, you email Jeff and Ms. Stanton. He should be able to get it fixed by the time we get back from lunch at Sisco's. Don't forget, it's your turn to treat!" Cass said, already halfway back to her desk.

"Wait, why am I doing the emailing? You're the one who—Cass? CASS!"

"Don't know what you're saying, don't care. Already turned down my hearing aid!"

Reigned to my new duty, I typed away, attaching reports and documents that all had to be altered. As time-consuming as it was tedious, it was leverage that meant Cass would be treating at lunch today. Fifteen minutes into it, the interruption from my phone was welcomed even before I knew who it was.

Good morning, Sam.

morning indie

How is your day going so far?

pretty well just working. yours?

Same, and same. Lol I had a bit of trouble
sleeping last night. It really was so good to
talk to you, though. It's been too long.

same and same

Hahaha, well, good to the second same, boo
to the first. I'll let you get back to work. Good
luck with the closing on your house today!

thanks. i had forgotten all
about that being today. oops

"Wh-hat is that? Is that a real, genuine smile? You are going to have to tell me someday, ya know," said Cass.

My phone was quickly relocated into a pants pocket.

"Leave me be, devil woman. A girl is entitled to her secrets."

"I knew it! So, there *is* a secret? I will get it out of you soon enough, might as well just save yourself the trouble and tell me now."

"I'm glad your hearing aids are working so well now, but you don't need them to understand the language of the eye roll."

My eyes noticed a dark head bobbing along the cubicles. A sharp inhale followed by one word was enough to get Cass's attention.

"Maria!" I whispered.

We both darted to the empty cubicle just past my neighbor Sal's and crawled under the desk. Muffled giggles almost gave us away, but we both managed to pull it together in time. Hearing a huff and some footsteps, I peered out. Maria was briskly walking back towards the main aisle, away from my desk.

"You two have issues, man," Sal said as we passed by his cubicle entrance on our hands and knees.

CHAPTER 3

Indie

"Let's go, let's go, lez gooooooooooo!" I yelled as the three of us were rushing around our light-filled kitchen in the morning. I hadn't slept well and was running behind. Private schools are great until you're running late and can't just put them on a bus. The meeting was at nine. It may be an achievable goal if the girls tucked and rolled as I drove by the school and all of the lights stayed green. I hadn't even remembered to text 'good morning' to Sammi, which I had done every day for over a week now.

"Mom! Your shoes!" Mari yelled, roaring with laughter.

Veda peeked around the corner from the living room and quickly joined in. My confusion was soon quelled as I looked down to see two different shoes on my feet. How that had even happened, I had no idea. I quickly ran down the hall, towards my bedroom, as I yelled back at them to get into the car.

"So, as you can see, moving all production overseas will more than double the profits." Kenny said, pulling me off of memory lane and into the conference room.

"Ummm... overseas." I paused, pondering his words. "Like overseas-overseas? Like a sweat shop in some country on the other side of the world kind of overseas?"

Growing more indignant with each word I spoke, I realized what Kenny had actually proposed during this first quarter meeting, while I was daydreaming and half-asleep. I should have been paying attention and stopped him long ago, evidently.

"W-well, no, b-but, ummm, yes. Not like five-year-olds working in terrible conditions, but an overseas production company would..."

I cut him off mid-sentence, "Since that goes against everything we've built, I'm gonna go with no."

I looked down to discover that I had actually risen up out of my chair and was towering over the table, glaring at poor Kenny. While he was a recent addition to our team, he should have known better.

"Indie," my business partner, Helene, started, "just hear the man out, that's why we pay him."

"Maybe we should send his job overseas then." I retorted as I plopped back down into my chair.

Kenny looked shocked and Helene started laughing, as did a couple of other members of our team. My hot head and quick mouth were famous in our company. No one ever had to wonder what I was thinking and everyone knew where they stood with me. To say I needed to practice tact was an understatement, but I was leaps and bounds better than I was five years ago when Helene and I started this business as two broke, single moms.

Helene was, in a small way, my savior, and I hers. We met at the lowest points in our respective lives and became an unlikely, inseparable duo. She, the super religious, hopeless romantic, southern belle, and I, the lesbian, jaded, northerner who spoke her mind, were a mismatched set that somehow worked. Our cleaning products, which we had started selling at small shops and farmer's markets on the weekends, had turned into quite an operation. With a staff of about thirty people, including the newcomer, Kenny, this business had flourished. We did spend many a night in our respective beds, on our respective laptops, chatting on our respective phones, running a company that neither of us had seen coming.

I looked up at her as soon as she was done thanking everyone and cordially dismissing the meeting. She tilted her head ever so slightly to the side, the way she did when she was about to 'mother' me.

"Indie, sweetie, why are we sending Kenny's job overseas this morning?"

"Because, he pissed me off." I said like a dramatic teenager. I gathered my maturity and continued, more calmly, "We have an ethos at this company. We have a mission statement. He was given all of this information. Direct questions were asked at his interview regarding said ethos and mission statement. He should have known better." Disdain had started to seep back into my words towards the end.

"True, but he is also tasked with finding every possible solution to a problem and presenting them to us."

I huffed and crossed my arms, my last vestige of maturity for the day having been spent.

"Indie." Helene said while I pointedly ignored her. "Indie. What is with you today? Did your morning start badly or something?"

I dropped my hands to my lap and stared at them. She knew me too well to hide anything. Five years of being 'barried', or business married, had a tendency to bring things to the surface most of us prefer to keep hidden from the general public.

"No. It started well, even though I tried to leave the house with two different shoes."

Her eyebrows raised but I shook my head and waved further inquiry off.

"Don't worry, Mari kept me in check. *He* called today."

Helene's usually friendly face took on a very mean look. She always seemed congenial and sweet, but we both knew she had a streak to her that she preferred to keep hidden from the general public.

"What the hell did he want?" she asked flatly, her mouth pressed into a hard line.

"What does he always want?" I replied.

"How long has it been since he last called?"

"Haven't heard from him in just over six months now. Haven't seen him in almost a year."

We both sat there, quietly, for quite a while. Then she reached out to squeeze my hand and, with a twinkle in her eye, said, "Let's give this little problem to Kenny and see what solutions he comes up with. Maybe he'll ship him overseas to work in a sweat shop or something."

I squeezed her hand back as we both started laughing maniacally. People were staring at us through the glass walls, not that either of us cared. If only they knew how crazy their bosses really were.

———

My hands trembled as I picked up the phone. I was free. I had been free for almost ten years now. I had power over myself now. Just like Eleanor Roosevelt had said, no one could make me feel inferior unless I let them. I steeled my resolve and hit the call button.

"Hello?"

"Hello, Zacariah. I am returning your call. What is it that you want?"

"Hey babe! I didn't even look at the phone to see who was calling. I'm so glad it's you and some asshole from work."

"I'm not your babe. Do not call me that." I interrupted.

Zacariah gave no indication that my words were heard or heeded.

"I was wondering when you guys are going on that trip. Veda mentioned a trip. I was thinking about coming out that way to see you guys and didn't want to overlap."

Ah, Veda. The poor thing had no idea about the finer workings of a divorce relationship. I loved her naivete'. He was always fishing for information and, while Mari was very tight lipped on the phone with him, Veda was a giggly open book.

"Yes, Zacariah, I am going on a work trip, but the girls will be here with my neighbor, Sara, so no need to worry about missing them whenever you decide to come visit."

"Well, still, I wouldn't want to stress anyone out. When is the trip again?"

"When and where I go on my own time, without the girls, is not your concern. I have given you all the information you need," I responded coldly.

"Awww come on, Ind, I'm just trying to be friendly. I thought we were being civil to each other."

"Civil and friendly are two different words with two different meanings. We are being civil for the sake of the children you ignore most of the time, but I will not be your friend. We have never been friends, and I don't plan to start now."

"Wow, that's a bit mean, don'tcha think?"

"No, no, I don't. I think it's the truth and, unless you have something else you need to discuss with me about the girls, I have to go."

"Well, I am planning on coming out soon."

"Okay, text me the details of your arrival and I'll make sure the girls are ready when the time comes."

"Umm, yeah, of course. I'll do that."

"Have a good evening, Zacariah."

"Umm, yeah, you too…"

His pet name or whatever else he was going to say to try to get me to converse longer was cut off by the tapping of my finger on the screen. While not as satisfying as a good old-fashioned slamming of a wired phone, it still felt pretty good.

This feeling of power; not power over him, but over myself, would never get old. He would never change. He would always be the selfish asshole he was, but I had grown, started a business, bought a house, and raised the girls all on my own. I would battle with what he did to me for probably the rest of my life, but it had gotten easier with time.

An overwhelming urge to call Sammi swept over me. Pushing it to the back of my mind, I went into Sara's house to collect my children.

CHAPTER 4

Sam

THERE I WAS, presenting to a room full of my peers and superiors, mispronouncing simple words, forgetting things, and looking like a damn fool.

I decided to call a spade a spade and come clean, kind of.

"I apologize to you all. I have not been sleeping well and am not my usual self today."

Nods of understanding and a few head tilts of sympathy flooded the room. I continued on with renewed confidence, not in my abilities, at the moment, but in the knowledge I was not screwing up badly enough to be fired.

"So, as you can see, by utilizing the existing structure on the east side of the site, we can keep this project under budget...or at least have some more cash flow for whatever comes up during construction that we didn't foresee."

Again, nods of understanding, but accompanied by smirks instead of pity. Under budget projects always put my team, and my bosses, in a good mood. Nothing ever went exactly to plan in the world of commercial architecture.

"Excellent as usual, Ms. Nakamura."

I turned to see my boss coming my way.

"Thank you, ma'am. I aim to please."

"Are you in a rush to get home this evening, or do you have a moment to speak with me in private?"

My heart skipped a beat, or ten.

"Ummm, yes, ma'am, no ma'am, yes..." I took a deep breath in, "No ma'am, I'm not in a hurry and yes ma'am, I have time to speak with you."

Mrs. Stanton closed her office door quietly behind us. "I won't keep either of us longer than necessary. You are an amazing architect. I don't think that's a secret. You have been noticed: by me, those below you, and those above both of us."

"Yes, ma'am, uhhhh, thank you."

"I'm going to ask you one more time not to call me ma'am, since I'm only two years older than you, but I know you won't listen."

"Sorry, ma'—Mrs. Stanton, it's ingrained in me from my Navy years. I mean no disrespect at all."

"Oh, I'm sure you don't." she chuckled as she poured herself some water and took two rather large pills. "Prenatal vitamins."

"Oh. Oh!" I repeated as the realization set in. "I know you've been trying; I mean, I know you've wanted to, ummm... congratulations!"

Her smile, in that moment, was the purest I had ever seen.

"Thank you, Satomi. This has been such a long time coming."

Tears filled the kind woman's eyes. She cleared her throat and turned to face me.

"Well, while I am happy to share this news with you, it is not why I asked you into my office. I have decided to leave the firm, once I get closer to the end of my pregnancy, and, like I said before, you have been noticed. The powers that be will bring Mark, from the Dubai office, in to replace me, and they would like you to replace him. You know Mark, right?"

I closed my gaping mouth and nodded.

"Yes, I've worked with Mark a couple of times." The patterns in the carpet got my full attention as I processed what had just been said to me. "I'm sorry, this is a lot to take in. You want me to move? To Dubai? So Mark can come here?"

Mrs. Stanton stared at the shocked architect before her and smiled.

"We want to promote you. You are in the running to head up the office in Dubai."

Phone still in hand, I was still sitting in my car on level four of the parking garage, as I had been for the past fifteen minutes. Going abroad to work in another office had been the goal for many years—so why did my chest feel tight?

Indie.

I couldn't get my old flame off of my mind. All I wanted to do was call her, be near her, so I finally gave in and dialed.

"Hey! Were your ears ringing?"

"W-what?" I asked, confused.

"I was just telling my neighbor, Sara, about you." Indie replied sweetly.

My heart jumped. Indie was telling her friends about me? What was she telling them?

"Okaaaaaay, and what exactly are you saying about me?"

"Hang on, Sam." Indie said as she continued to speak in the background saying her goodbyes. It was much quieter on her end of the phone when she came back on. "What's up? Miss me already?" she asked innocently as her laughter came through the earpiece, making my heart stutter.

"Ha, you wish!" I replied with feigned composure. "Just wanted to check in and see how you're doing. Don't want you falling off something and hurting yourself or anything like that."

"Hey, come on now, I'm not as clumsy as I used to be. And, just so you know, I'm sticking my tongue out at you from afar."

"Real mature."

"I know." Indie said smugly.

"So, Ind, how are you?"

"Better now."

"Better now? Better how? Better because I called, or better because earlier was so terrible and anything is better than that?"

"Both."

"Both?"

"Both. Zacariah called me today."

The anger came in like a tsunami.

"What the hell did he want?"

"Same as always, he was being nosy."

"Nosy about what?"

"Where and when I'm going on a business trip I'm taking."

"Why does he want to know that?"

Indie sighed an exasperated sigh. "I don't know. He's delusional. He thinks we're still...I don't know, something. He wants to know he still has power over me, which he does not. He's just an asshole. I told him he has no right to know."

I smiled. She was stronger than she gave herself credit for.

"So, may I ask where you're going?"

Her laugh made me tingle everywhere.

"Of course you may, madame. I'm heading to Concord, New Hampshire."

My heart thudded in my chest. If there's much more of that, it may just stop all together.

"Concord? I go there often. Wanna have lunch?"

"Oh my gosh, really?"

Indie's excitement was obvious. She was so cute when she couldn't hide her emotions.

"Well, yeah, of course!"

"When are you going?"

"In about three weeks."

"Perfect. Send me the details, and I'll clear my schedule," I said. "So, now that we have that all figured out, what exactly were you telling your friend about me?"

"Hey Bob. How was your day?" I asked the fuzzy being rubbing up on my leg. Purring was all I received in return. "Good, good. My day was quite interesting. Got my dream promotion and the woman I, ummm, used to date is coming to visit. Not you, though, she's gonna visit me. Sorry, Bob," I cooed as I patted him and walked into my kitchen.

The gleaming white counters were soon cluttered with blueprints, a laptop bag, keys, and the like. I looked around. I barely spent any time here, but it was still home. Could I leave it? I walked into the compact living area with its neat gray sofa and gave a loving spritz to Fern; the one plant my mother gave me which I had managed not to kill. It wasn't a fern, but I called her Fern anyway, much to my mother's chagrin.

My mother. What would I even say to her? She knew how badly I had been wanting this promotion and had already planned hypothetical trips to all of the different offices I could possibly be transferred to around the globe.

I couldn't tell her. I couldn't tell her about the promotion, Indie, or the lunch date in Concord, where she lived. I would have to tell her I was there for a business meeting or something. Her peppering questions and meddling could earn her an Olympic medal. The only being on the planet I could tell about my pending date was the most exceptional secret keeper ever: Bob.

A text message notification broke through my thoughts as I was running my fingers lightly across the crisp white linen pillow before me.

> Hey, Sam. Here's my travel info. I'm leaving on the 21st as soon as I drop the girls off at school, so probably 7:45-ish. I should be getting into Concord around 9:30. I have meetings until 2:30 and have nothing going on after those. I have meetings the next day from about 9 a.m. until around 1, followed by a luncheon. All that to say I should be free after the luncheon (on the 22nd) before I drive back home. So, whenever you are free, just let me know.

I smiled as I walked towards my bedroom to take a shower. Another ding rang through my apartment.

> Hope it all makes sense. Am I rambling? I feel like I'm rambling via text, which is sad, because I should read it before I hit send, right? Anyway, excited to see you!!

The glee within me could not be contained. Bob was not used to sounds such as uninhibited laughter emanating from his human, and he jumped at the sound.

I text back a simple reply.

> me too.

By that time, I had reached my white marble bathroom and turned on the shower.

My mind was free to wander to all sorts of wonderful and terrible spaces as the hot water cascaded down my body. What if she hated me? What if she didn't find me attractive after a decade and a half? I was definitely not the same as I was sixteen years ago. Then again, she's had twins! I'm sure she's not the same either. Oh god, what if I don't find her attractive? The mere thought of her touching me was enough to send me into a tailspin, so that scenario was unlikely. I had kept myself from feeling anything for years, ever since Ali. It had been fairly easy to do, but now...now Indie.

I was drying myself off and imagining the towel rubbing my chest was Indie for a moment, then the phone rang. I looked at the name on the screen. My mood instantly changed as I hit the green button in front of me and put the phone up to my ear.

"Hi mom."

CHAPTER 5

Indie

My phone made the tiny trilling sound I had assigned to Sam's texts. My heart fluttered a bit, along with my stomach. I had forgotten to silence my phone before the typical 'good morning' text came through. Mari had gotten inquisitive after the first week of that sound happening every few minutes. Now, she eyed me suspiciously as she walked past. I wished she didn't notice everything so much. Looking up from my book, I smiled sweetly at my eldest twin and pretended to ignore my phone. She went about her Saturday morning and walked into the kitchen. I stealthily lurched at my phone.

good morning

> Morning, Sam. How did you sleep?

ok. you?

> I slept well, woke up around 7, and had some time to read my book. Now, though, I gotta get off my butt and get ready. Helene and I are meeting today, before I go to Concord, to go over some things.

1- why do you use punctuation and grammar and stuff? this is texting

2- what time is the meeting?

> 1- I use those things because it is the proper way to communicate via written language.
>
> 2- It's in 40 minutes, but it only takes me a few minutes to get ready. That's one of the perks of having a very small wardrobe where everything goes with everything else. Plus, it's more of an excuse to go to our favorite breakfast spot than a real business meeting.

1- **insert eyeroll here**

2- wow it takes me like an hour to get ready for work in the morning.

> Hahaha, okay then. I'll communicate with you in a little while, the girls are up and I've got to get dressed.

Ok ttyl

In the kitchen, a very lively conversation about fish skeletons was taking place between two teenagers eating gluten free toast and eggs. They were both so different, but always found something to connect over. Maybe it was a twin thing; maybe it was a sibling thing. My older brothers were ten and twelve years older than me and were only half-brothers, from my dad's first marriage. I was so excited when I found out the girls were twins. My first thought when the doctor told me was that they would never be alone.

I got a pretty mean look when I turned on the blender containing my smoothie ingredients without warning the teens, who were deep in their epic conversation. The evil laugh was drowned out by a whirring machine. I could see Veda's tongue sticking out, making me laugh louder.

"Ind, over here!" Helene called to me as I entered our favorite little breakfast cafe.

I saw her furiously waving hand, which was totally unnecessary in the eight-hundred square foot space.

"Hey girl." I greeted her, hugging her tightly. "Wait, why are you here early? You're never early."

Helene let out a nervous laugh.

"Call it a cosmic screw up. I ordered you some tea already," she stated, steering the conversation away from her unusual punctuality.

"Umm, thanks. So, Concord. I really wanted to get your opinion on a few different things I'm pretty sure will come up."

"Indie." she said softly, not looking up from the table. "I don't think you need my input. I have something to tell you."

I had no idea what my face looked like, but her glance at it brought tears to her eyes. She started tearing at the edges of a paper she was holding. Helene was never this quiet and timid.

"Ooo-kaaay." was the only reply I could force out.

"I'm not one to beat around the bush, and neither are you, so here it is: I'm backing out of the company. It's all yours."

Her words rushed out as she searched my face for clues as to how I was taking this news. I was working very hard to keep my composure and not let anything show, and it must have been working, at least a little bit. Helene looked back down at the piece of paper in her hand, which was slowly being pulverized, before she continued.

"I know this seems sudden, and it kind of is, I guess. Then again, so was starting this business. We came together in our shared pain after our divorces and stayed together because of our shared interests and opposite, yet complimentary, personalities."

That statement caused the corners of her mouth to curl upward, just slightly. Her eyes darted to my unchanged face before she hurried on.

"I just feel like it's time to go back into non-profit. We started this as a way to support our families, and it has been, but natural cleaning products are not where my heart is, Ind."

The shock that had been held at bay showed itself, full force, in the way of my expression.

"Indie? Indie, please, say something." she pleaded.

My eyes met hers.

"I'm not sure what to say."

"I still love you. We'll still be friends, just not business partners. I have the start of an exit strategy which will slowly remove me from the company, so it's not all dumped on you at once. I also had Kenny get..."

"Kenny?!?! You told the new kid before you told me?" I forced out through gritted teeth.

"What? NO! I did not tell Kenny. I didn't even tell Lukas!" she squeaked out.

She cleared her throat and regained control of her voice.

"You are the first person I've mentioned this too."

My forehead fell into my hands.

"Okay, so what about Kenny?"

"I asked Kenny for some specific reports and numbers so I could come up with something before I came to you with this. I'm trying to stress you out as little as possible. Which is, evidently, not working. None of this is set in stone or anything," she said as she passed the half torn up paper to me across the small round table, "it's just my first thoughts on possible ways to do this."

I studied the battered paper for a while. Helene's nervousness was transferred to her napkin after surrendering the paper. Sadness enveloped me after seeing her teary-eyed, worried expression. We had been b-arried for going on seven years now. We had become like sisters, sharing in every aspect of our lives. I felt my own tears gathering. My gaze softened and the swirling haze in my mind cleared just enough for me to make a joke.

"So, my beautiful Helene, you're saying you want a b-ivorce?"

Her laughter shot into the cloud of pain between us, and it dissipated.

"Helene wants out? What?!? Oh girl, I did not see *that* coming," Sara said with genuine shock.

"Yeah, it's kinda crazy. Especially with this Concord thing coming up. If we get into Goodness Goods nationwide, it will exponentially increase... well... everything!"

I pondered exactly how many things would be affected and how much work would be added to me as I sipped on Sara's homemade kombucha.

"You may need something stronger than that right now, chica. You want a brownie? Double chocolate."

I shook my head at her and continued sipping my kombucha.

"Hey, hey, gal pals!" said the Hispanic, slightly flamboyant, gay man walking through the front door. "I got some intel there were brownies on Cary St. And by intel," he said putting air quotes around the word intel, "I mean Sara text me."

Gabriel shot us some quick kisses and went straight to the kitchen.

Sara yelled after him, "Bring me one too."

"Indie, you want one?" Gabriel asked.

"No. And who the hell wears bazillion dollar shoes with sweats? You are shaming gays everywhere," I stated.

"Shush, woman. I'm not trying to impress the two of you," he said, handing Sara her confection.

"Helene wants a b-ivorce," blurted Sara.

"Wait, whaaaaat?" he inquired while chewing a mouthful of chocolatey goodness.

I sighed.

"Oh girl, I'm so sorry. Do we hate her now? I need details!"

"No, we do not hate her." I stated.

"Oh good, I've always liked her. She's funny as hell, and that ass."

He shrugged as we gave him incredulous, accusatory stares.

"What? Guys have asses too, ya know. Just 'cause I don't want the death trap of a sexual organ you ladies possess, doesn't mean I don't know a good ass when I see one."

"Death trap?" Sara asked, choking on the chewy treat.

"Oh yes, those things have teeth. That's the word on the gay street," he replied with a wink.

If laughter could have killed, Sara and I would have been dead. My phone trilled its familiar trill. Drying my tears and catching my breath, I tried to act like it was just another sound my phone makes, but my comrades in laugh-crying didn't buy it.

"So, who's the trill?" Gabriel asked point blank.

"The what? Oh, that? Nothing. No one." I nervously replied.

Sara and Gabriel exchanged glances and came to sit on either arm of my chair.

"I bet it's the old flame that's just a friend," Sara said with emphasis on the word friend.

"Oooo, new love life info and I was not informed?!?! Indie, I'm hurt."

I rolled my eyes at his feigned suffering. "She *is* just a friend. We dated forever ago, like when were kids."

"Yeah, the wistful looks, sighing, and jumpiness at the personal notification tone you gave her really shout 'just a friend'," Sara teased.

"What does 'just a friend' have to say?" Gabriel asked.

I rolled my eyes, let out an overtly exasperated sigh, and picked up my phone to look at the screen.

> **hypothetically speaking, would you
> ever get married again?**

The kombucha sprayed out of my mouth like a fountain.

School pick up lines should come with free entertainment or something. This sitting here left too much time to ponder. Why would she even ask something like that? It had been two days, and I still couldn't get past the marriage question. I had skated around it pretty well, and, in no uncertain terms, made my 'no' as clear as the glass windshield before me. Marriage was a four-letter word wrapped in barbed wire. It did not bring about warm fuzzy feelings. Some called me jaded. I preferred to think of it as warned and informed.

The trill interrupted my matrimonial thoughts. I didn't want to look. Sam wasn't stupid. She knew I was acting weird about her question, and I knew she would not rest until we had discussed this at length. Love and marriage were not mutually exclusive. Marriage was just invented as a way to keep women in check as inventory and to give men the feeling of lording over someone. I remembered reading a lot about it when I was taking all of those anthropology classes in college. Too bad I wasn't warned and informed back then!

"Hey mom." Veda said woefully as she entered the car.

"Hey baby girl. What's up? Everything okay?"

"Ummm, yeah. Why?"

"Well, you just seem a little... umm... off. You know, not quite your usual self."

"It's just been a really long day, that's all. I just wanna go home," she stated, arms crossed, looking out the window.

I stared at her for a moment, strategizing my next mom-move. The other door opened, and in popped Mari.

"Hey mom!" she said cheerfully, flashing a huge grin.

I smiled back and shrugged my shoulders. Perhaps this was like the movie where the mom and daughter switch bodies, but with twins.

Dinner dishes were done, and everyone was doing their own thing. I finally had the mental energy to look at Sam's message. I closed my eyes and took a deep breath.

> So, things have been a bit weird lately.
> What's up? Please tell me. We promised
> to be honest with each other.

I rolled my eyes and threw the phone on my bed, along with myself. Why did she have to pull that? I was the one who insisted we be completely honest with each other, no holding back. Ugh. That was coming back with a proverbial bite to the butt.

> Well, I kind of freaked out
> about the marriage thing.

ok...

> What are the three periods for?

why are you freaked out?

> Because you asked me about
> getting married again.

i said hypothetically

And why would you even ask that question unless you were thinking about it un-hypothetically?

i was just wondering. i've been running from that for decades but lately i just started thinking about it a bit differently and wanted to know where you stood on the matter. i was just trying to figure out what was in your mind and what you were expecting. i didn't want to lead you on in any way. plus with these new to me thoughts popping into my head i wanted to know whether to squash them or entertain them. please don't freak out ind.

Okay

for real you're not freaking out?

No, I'll stop. It's just a difficult subject for me.

what the hell did he do to you?

That's definitely an in-person conversation, Sam.

>:(

It is.

ok. i'm not gonna like this conversation am i?

Nope. And neither will I.

ok let's move on to happier things. how was your day my darling dear?

She had quite a sweet, smart-ass way of changing the subject. A knock at the door interrupted my smirking.

"Yes?" I called out.

"Mom, can I come in?"

"Of course, my darling child."

Veda, still acting weirdly mopey, peered at me in the doorway. I smiled at her and patted the spot on the bed next to me. She plopped down and started to tear up.

"Mom, I don't know what to do."

"It's okay, ya hayati. That's part of the reason you have amazing people in your life like me. We all need help sometimes. So, tell me all about it."

She leaned into my side as my arm wrapped around her.

"Do you know why Mari was so bubbly today?"

"No, that's still as much of a mystery to me as your seriousness. I had an idea involving body switching, but I have a feeling that's not what you're about to tell me."

My little remark managed to get half a smile out of the child.

"Aiden started flirting with her. He's...he's interested in her."

"Aiden? Weren't you and he pretty good friends and then had some sort of a falling out?"

"Yeah, that's the Aiden I'm talkin' about."

"Okaaaayy. I'm sensing there's more to this story."

I urged her onward, feeling her hesitation grow. She looked at me with pained eyes.

"He was.... ummmm..... inappropriate." she forced out, head down, fingers fidgeting.

Anger roared up within me, but I kept it cool and collected on the surface.

"Inappropriate how?"

"Well, like you said, we were friends, right?" She paused and I nodded. "So, yeah, we were friends. Then, out of the blue, he tried to kiss me one day. I dodged him and tried to politely tell him I didn't see him in that way and did not give him permission to kiss me. He kind of scoffed at me and then tried again. His hands were..." she paused again, "He just wouldn't stop, so I pushed him."

"As you had every right to!" I practically shouted before shutting my mouth and letting her continue.

"Then he started calling me terrible names and saying I had been practically begging him for it. He said I was all flirty and stuff. I told him I'm just friendly and thought we were friends. Then he shoved me, and I fell on the floor."

The anger was so incredibly loud in my ears, it sounded like I was in a pool of pudding. His neck was pretty skinny. His was the kind of neck which could be easily wrung. *Deep breaths. She took care of herself. You taught her well. Breathe deeply. Just breathe.*

"Mom? You okay?"

I opened my eyes to see a very worried face in front of me. She was the one that should be asked if she was okay.

"Yes, dear. I'm just—angry." Her brow furrowed. "Not at you. Not at you, kid. You did well, but that Aiden, oh, yeah, I could strangle him with my bare hands."

She let out a snicker. "He's kinda scrawny, mom. I think you could take him."

I smirked and nodded. "So now you're afraid to tell Mari. But why?"

"She's so happy. And excited. Mari is never happy and excited."

"But honey...."

"I know, I know. I have to tell her. I know. I just hate hurting her."

They always had the twin link, and Veda knew better than anyone just how excited Mari was. Veda felt more, saw more, and knew more than her bubbliness let on. I wrapped my arm around this almost-grown woman-child and kissed her head.

"Do you want me to be there or not?"

"No. I'll do it alone." The back of her hand glistened as she ran it across her cheek. "I'll be all mature and stuff," she said with faux bravado.

"Well, today is the day for difficult conversations between people who love each other dearly." Her quizzical look was brushed away by my hand in the air. "It's nothing Earth shattering, just business stuff between Helene and me. Don't stress, kid. You're doing enough of that already. Now go be mature."

She smiled and went to face her sister. That kid was awesome. Miraculously, the girls had both turned out pretty damn well, even with Zacariah and me as parents.

CHAPTER 6

Sam

I WAS DEEP INTO MY SECOND GLASS of whiskey and feeling ways that made parts of me throb. Only one week left until I saw the person responsible for all of the throbbing. How did she still have this effect on me after so many years apart? How can you miss someone you haven't seen in over a decade?

My mind started to dig deep and relish in memories of us 'watching a movie' in her family room as teenagers. I remembered her breasts, so much larger than my own, and the sounds she would make from the slightest touch.

A moan interrupted my reminiscing. Was that me? Did I make that sound? I picked up my phone with shaking hands. I had to see her. Implosion was imminent if I didn't at least talk to her.

hey

> Well, hello there.

wyd?

> Trying to go over reports. Ugh, this Helene thing could not have come at a worse time. We are supposed to be going national with our products. Why did she choose now?

don't know what to tell u. she is just trying
to do what's right for her I guess. from what
you've told me she's a good person.

She is. She is.

just trust her then. so how
are veda and mari?

They're good. They talked out the
whole Aiden situation. Once Mari
heard what Aiden did to her sister, her
infatuation died quickly. I think they
are scheming, but I can't be sure.
That boy is going to rue the day he
messed with the Rufio girls! Lol

what I wouldn't give to be a
fly on the wall for THAT!

I feel you!

yeah i'm feeling things too

Huh?

i miss u. isn't it weird? i haven't
seen u in like 16 years and I can
barely stand to b away from u
anymore.

Yes, it's weird, but, unfortunately,
I understand.

Wait, she understands? Like she can comprehend the feeling,
knows the feeling, or is feeling the same way? To kiss her lips again
would be divine. Does she still shudder when the side of her neck
is kissed? She cannot possibly know how strongly I feel about her,
can she? Could she possibly feel the same? Gotta keep it cool.

Calm down and get some more information before professing undying love.

oh yeah? like comprehend or feel similarly?

Both.

this is all weird for me ind. i haven't felt anything close to this in a long time.
u scare me.

What? I scare you? How?

u make me feel things i never thought i would and it's scary beyond belief

That's fair. Yeah, I have some feelings that won't seem to back down either.

I steeled myself for revealing my secret to this woman who had the power to destroy me with a sentence. Fingers poised above the small screen in front of me, heart ready to swell or shatter. My lungs filled to capacity and my foggy brain didn't have the power to logic its way out of this.

i am a little tipsy right now and i want u so badly. like want u in the way i wanted u back in the day on your parents sofa. i want that and more every day. i want to wake up to u.
i want to grow old with u.

I waited. I had put it out there. I wanted to touch her, to kiss her, to make her scream in ecstasy again, but even more than that. I wanted her—all of her. Every day, for forever; the good, the bad, and the ugly. The tightness in my chest threatened to end me if I couldn't get her to understand how I felt.

10 minutes and no response

30 minutes

40 minutes

An hour

An hour and 10 minutes

Omg, Sam, I'm so sorry! The girls came home and we started chatting, then I got us all some dinner. I want you too. I want everything you just said.

My chest released its grip on my fragile heart and the blood-pumping organ did its job with a renewed gusto. She felt the same way. I could breathe again.

———

Shit! Last night's texting fest, followed by some personal release of sexual frustration, went too far into the night. Bob hissed at me as I threw the blanket on the floor, covering him. His head was soon visible again.

"Sorry, dude. My bad."

He sauntered off into the kitchen to await his breakfast.

I eyed the mess of products on the counter and spots on the mirror and groaned. It would have to wait until I got home, which made me feel unsettled to no end. I smacked the light switch as I ran out of the bathroom, through the bedroom, and into the living room. The beautiful French press was beckoning, wanting to be used. I groaned yet again, grabbed my keys and wallet, and ran out the door.

The one elevator in the building usually takes too long in the morning after 6:45 because everyone and their brother is using it. Stairs it was! After rounding the second landing at breakneck speed, I almost did break my neck, but instead settled for banging my knee into the banister. Hopefully, the Simons kids weren't up and around yet to hear the expletives reverberating around the stairwell.

The door opened to the busy street outside. 7:05. Shit yet again. It takes twenty minutes to get to work on the T on a good day, and today was definitely not shaping up to be a good day. Oh well, there was really no other choice besides trying to fight someone for a taxi. I took off for the T station and crossed my fingers.

"Ms. Nakamura, are you just getting in this morning?"

Of course the boss would be standing there as the elevator doors opened.

"Good morning Mrs. Stanton. Yes, I am. Today has not gone exactly to plan so far."

"Well, it's about to get worse. Mr. Rossi has called a 7:30 meeting for all personnel above level four."

She leaned in a little closer.

"I have no idea why and this was not previously planned."

I glanced at my watch—7:26—No time to even stop by my desk.

"I appreciate the head's up. Missing that meeting would have definitely made my day much worse. I'll just step off quickly and leave my rain jacket with Maria."

"See you up there."

I nodded to her as I squeezed out of the not-fully-open elevator doors towards the floor receptionist's desk. I hated doing this, but I had no other option. Maybe Maria had grown and would not hit on me or see this as a veiled attempt to hit on her. Maybe.

"Gaaaaaahhh!"

The burning pain on my chest cut through my worry. The brown liquid dripped down the front of my starched, pressed, light gray dress shirt. The blazer, at home, on the edge of the sofa, was not doing anyone much good today. I looked up to see none other than Maria.

"Oh my gawd, I'm sorry! I'm so sorry. I didn't see you th– Sammi? Oh hi." Her shocked expression quickly changed to a devious one. "Want me to help you out of that shirt?"

Anger was about to bubble over in a way that could get me fired and it wasn't even eight in the morning yet.

"NO, Maria. I have a 7:30 meeting with Mr. Rossi and it's" I paused to glance at the clock, "7:29!"

I threw my jacket at her and darted towards the stairwell. After running up three flights of stairs with a throbbing knee and a soaked shirt, I arrived at the executive floor. The receptionist up there was a quiet, reserved, useful woman. She took one look at the mess before her, procured a roll of paper towels from one of her desk drawers, and handed them over.

"Thank you so much." I whispered.

She nodded in return, dug in another desk drawer, and handed me a package of baby wipes. I cleaned myself up the best I could and dared to peek at the clock. 7:33. Dammit!!

"Nice of you to join us, Ms. Nakamura." said Mr. Rossi coolly as I entered the executive conference room.

"I apologize, sir. I had a little mishap this morning." I replied, gesturing to my shirt.

In my head, I was thinking I'd had a million mishaps this morning and he should feel grateful I had made it at all. He nodded once, his expression never changing, and I sat down in the only empty seat at the huge table. Cass eyeballed me from across the table, eyebrows raised. I shrugged my shoulders and focused on the boss.

———————

"What the hell was that, girl? Do you want to lose your job and your dignity all in the same day?" said the blonde chick sitting on my desk as I strolled into my cubicle.

"Yeah, Cass, I woke up this morning and thought, 'gee, how can I ruin my life even more?'"

"Even more? What does that mean?" she queried with bright eyes.

Plopping into the squeaky chair, I covered my face with my left hand and leaned into it.

"I am unraveling."

"Unraveling? Ummm ok, that's very... poetic."

Cass paused to allow me to explain, but I just sat there, head in hand.

"Care to expound, milady?"

"Ugh, do I have to?" I glanced at Cass, who was trying to look intimidating. "Fine. Well, on top of my stellar morning which began with waking up very late, running down the stairs and banging the hell out of my knee on the way, showing up to work late, Maria running smack dab into me while holding a cup of coffee, then proceeding to hit on me, AGAIN, and showing up late to Mr. Rossi's meeting looking like a literal hot mess—I think I'm in love."

"What the... hold the phone. What did you, Satomi Nakamura, just say? I think I need to go to my audiologist this afternoon."

She made quite the show of adjusting her hearing aids and putting them back into her ears.

"Could you please repeat yourself, Ms. Nakamura?"

"Shut it. You heard me."

"Well holy shit, girl. I knew something was up! Is it that old flame you've been talking to? I cannot wrap my head around this. It's been –"

"Years, yes I know." I interrupted before she could bring up Ali. "Why the hell do you think I said I'm unraveling? We were up late last night, texting. That's why I was late this morning. I got a little tipsy and started being way too honest."

"Ooo, late night texting, huh? Nice. So, what were you honest about?"

"My feelings, my... needs, everything."

Cass's laugh could not be stifled. Heads everywhere were turning to look.

"Oh girl, your needs haven't been met in a very long time."

"Thank you, Cass," I said, my voice dripping with disdain. "I am well aware of exactly how long it's been. Like I said, that's why I had to rush out of... SHIT! Bob!"

I opened the door to my apartment to find Bob sitting patiently, happy and fed. Luckily, I had gotten in touch with the Simons next door and Jenny fed Bob as soon as she got home from school.

"Sorry, buddy, I didn't mean to forget your food this morning, I swear," I cooed at my oblivious little companion.

He must have already forgiven me. Loving an animal was so much easier. They forgave you no matter what. They don't care about much of anything as long as they're fed and had the basic necessities. Animals are safe, unlike humans. Plants are even safer. Fern could go days without a spritz.

"Fern, you are a trooper, and I appreciate that," I said as I spritzed her beautiful green fronds, before leaning down to pet the ignored being again. "Bob, never fall in love, okay?"

I turned away to pick up the phone and call Indie. I was officially lost.

CHAPTER 7

Indie

"Okay, so you have Sara's number, and Helene's, and Gabriel's, and Amie's. There is plenty of food in the fridge. Amie will be by tonight to take Mari to swimming, then she'll hang out with you guys. Tomorrow, Gabriel is taking Veda to horse riding lessons and you guys are staying at his house. Sara will be with you guys from then on until I get home. And she's taking you all to school this morning and tomorrow morning. Don't forget to put the trash can out by the road tomorrow night."

I was rushing around in every direction shouting whatever popped into my head towards wherever I thought the girls might be.

"Veda, don't forget to take your science project to school today!"

"It's already right next to the door, mom. Weren't you supposed to leave ten minutes ago?" Veda replied.

"Mom is just freaking out like always." Mari shouted back to her from just outside my door. She very calmly said, "We're fifteen, we will be okay for a few days, mom. I promise."

My eyes welled with tears. When did they get this big? I placed my hand on my eldest's cheek.

"Ya hayati."

A tear spilled onto her head as I kissed it.

"Oh my god, Veda, watch out, she's being mushy in Arabic again." Mari shouted as she walked away, grinning like the Cheshire Cat.

"Please, no. Mom, do not come crying and being all touchy-feely. You'll be gone for a couple of days, not years." the usually bubbly child said quietly.

Mornings and Veda had long been enemies, and this morning was no exception.

––––––––––––

The last week had been so much so fast. Flirting had turned quite serious, and we were talking about 'forever'. Sam had even mentioned more kids! I needed this drive time all alone before meeting up with her tonight. We were both so eager to see one another, but both scared as hell too.

As I was jamming to my music, I heard the all-too-familiar trill through my speakers. My heart tried to get out of my chest and run away.

hey i hope your traveling is going well

> Hey there. It's going well.
> I'm about halfway there.

wait are you texting and driving?

> No, my phone is reading me the
> messages through my speakers
> and I am speaking messages back.

complete with punctuation?

> Yes, if I say the word, it places a,
> there.

> Dam it.

> Not that dam, like a beaver.
> The other dam, like a curse word.

> Dam it.

lol nice. this is fun for me

> I'm so glad you are amused, you
> mean person, you. When are you
> leaving?

leaving right now i should be at
my moms in about an hour

> Your mom's?

yeah she lives in concord

> Oh, I did not know. Did you tell
> me that?

i thought i did but who knows. i can't
wait to see you but it also feels like
i might throw up.

> Ditto, Sam.

The hotel was fairly elegant; there was even a chocolate mint on my pillow. Kenny had done well and I kind of hated to admit it. He was doing a decent job, he just seemed to get the brunt of my frustration, and it really wasn't fair to him at all. With Helene leaving, doing some pride swallowing and getting on his good side seemed like the only option.

The voice on the other end of the phone made my heart skip a beat. I answered her moody hello with one of my own.

"Oh, hey! Ind, thank goodness it's you. I'm in the car and didn't look to see who it was before answering. I'm so glad you are not my boss," Sam said, sounding sexier than ever.

"Trouble in paradise?"

"I mean, no, not really. I'm just kinda focused on something else right now and don't really feel like talking to her."

"Focused on something else, huh? Perhaps a meet-up you are attending later?" I suggested.

"Mm-maybe." she teased before turning her voice to a husky whisper. "The things I could do to you in that restaurant tonight and no one would even know anything was happening."

The butterflies in my stomach almost flew away with me as I wobbled on my feet before plopping onto the nicely made bed, complimentary mint tumbling towards the floor. My hands reached out to interrupt its descent to no avail.

"Oh really?" I questioned, my voice shaky and unsure. "We will be in a public place, madame, so perhaps that would not be wise."

"I never said I was wise; I just know what I want. I also know it's going to happen eventually, so why fight it?"

Good god this woman knew how to bring me to my wit's end. I had nothing left, no witty comment, playful retort, or zingy come-back. My brain was mush and the pounding in my chest reverberated through my entire body. I felt a distinct thrumming between my legs, which seemed to happen during every interaction with Sam, that was hard to ignore.

"Indie? You still there?"

"Y-yes, I'm here, sorry, I knocked something onto the floor."

"Uh-huh, and why was that? Getting all hot and bothered? Can't think straight?" she bantered. "I seem to have that effect on you. Don't you worry though, you have a similar effect on me, you're just not mean enough to use it against me."

Before I could defend myself or come up with anything scintillating to say in return, she piped in.

"See you at the 110 Grill tonight at 7:00! Think of me touching you until then!"

The disconnect came at the same time I opened my mouth to try to formulate a response. The chocolate mint was still on the floor. I bent to pick it up and felt a thump on my head. A few expletives rang out in the hotel room. I scurried into the bathroom to find a small bump already beginning to form. Great. This was just what I needed to not only look professional and capable at tomorrow's business meetings, but for my dinner with Sam tonight.

---

110 Grill looked like a decent place. It had a funky vibe, reminiscent of Sam. The slate blue and dark burnt orange color scheme was pleasing to the eye and gave it a slightly masculine feel. Contemporary mixed with industrial... a very Sam-type place if there ever was one.

Finding parking was not difficult but required some looking around. Hopefully it was a sign that the food was good. I took a deep breath and looked at myself in the rearview mirror. The makeup was doing its job the best it could, but the bump would not be completely hidden. It was right there, loud and proud. Well, at least it was off to the side a bit and not front and center.

I picked up the phone and text Sam.

I'm here.

great. running late. my mother is annoying.

Haha, ok. Should I go in and grab a table or wait for you to get here?

just head in. be there in a sec

Ok

The butterflies in my stomach felt desperate to get out. I hoped I wouldn't end up vomiting during dinner. The inside of the restaurant matched the outside, and the hostess was quite polite, assuring me she would lead the striking, thirty-something, Asian woman to my table as soon as she arrived. I started to tear apart my napkin, much like Helene had. I wondered how she was doing. How would the business survive without her? For the first time all day, my thoughts were not on Sam; instead, they were going down a dark spiral. I could feel my lungs tightening and my vision starting to narrow. I closed my eyes and tried to take a deep breath. Just then, someone touched my hand. I looked up to see those beautiful, golden-brown eyes I remembered from so long ago looking at me in a concerned manner.

"Indie, you okay?" Sammi said in an overly-soothing voice like she was talking to a frightened animal.

The breath caught in my throat and the butterflies stilled. Sam. My Sam. She was right here in front of me and it felt right. I almost kissed her right then and there.

"Yes, sorry, my mind was elsewhere. It's so good to see you!" I said as I clumsily got up from the table, knocking my glass of water over, sending water pouring on the floor between us. I hid my face in my hands before bending down to attempt a clean-up with the few napkins on the table.

"Good to know nothing's changed, Ind," Sam laughed heartily.

We exchanged a very awkward hug, which she seemed almost reluctant to be a part of. Spilled drink cleaned up and new drinks ordered, we started to chat about all kinds of things. Some things we had already touched on over our phone and text conversations, some things we had not. Sam kept shifting in her seat, checking her watch. Was this the same woman who had threatened to 'do things' to me in the middle of restaurant just a few hours ago?

The second we had finished eating our dinner, Sam piped up.

"I really should be going. My mother will be waiting for me to come back. I told her I was just meeting up with an acquaintance."

"So, I'm an acquaintance? Hmmm, ok."

"No Indie, but you're someone who I haven't seen in sixteen years, so you're not exactly someone I'm close to, ya know?"

My brows furrowed and my head tilted.

"No, I don't know. Is that why you've been acting aloof all evening?"

"Well, you're... different."

"Yeah, of course I am. We both are. It's been sixteen years. What, did you expect me to look and act like I did when I was twenty?"

"I don't know, it's just a lot for my brain to process right now."

"What does that even mean? Last week you're talking about marriage and today I'm an acquaintance? What are we, Sam?"

"I don't know. I gotta go."

"Yeah, sure. Bye, Sam."

I turned quickly to hide the tears inundating my eyes, threatening to pour over the edges at any moment. As soon as she was out of the restaurant, I walked directly to my car. I had been dismissed. I felt like such an idiot. Relationships came with too much drama, which is why the single life had been so great.

"Case in point!" I shouted aloud in my car as I drove towards my hotel.

Tomorrow morning, I had the biggest meeting of my business life and it had been prefaced with a swift kick to the stomach and the cracking of my heart in a place I thought had healed long ago.

"Ms. Woodley, it is so nice to meet you," an attractive woman with short, dirty blonde, slicked back hair said to me as she rose from her seat at the conference table. Her pants suit perfectly complimented the expensive Italian loafers. I would have to remember to tell Gabriel.

"Ms. Woodley?"

"I'm so sorry, I am a bit tired and, to tell the truth, I was staring at your shoes. Are those Magnanni's?"

She nodded as the left side of her mouth turned up a bit into a half smile.

"I like a woman who knows business and good Italian footwear."

I chuckled. "My friend, Gabriel, has those and is obsessed. He makes sure the rest of us are well educated."

She smiled a full smile at me.

"Every girl needs someone in her life to show her what good taste is. Shall we?" she queried as she gestured towards the conference table.

"I apologize for Helene's absence. Let's just say things are a bit hectic in both work and personal life and we figured both of us didn't need to be here."

I said this as sweetly and nonchalantly as I could muster. I did not want this woman to think we didn't take this seriously and feel led on or blind-sided like I did with Sam last night. *No! No thoughts of Sam. Focus, Indie, FOCUS!*

"Well then, let's get started. I'm Alicia Sadusky."

———————

I got out of the shower and checked my phone for the millionth time that day. Still nothing. After weeks of hundreds of texts per day, nothing. I was irate one second and sobbing the next. Why on Earth had I agreed to dinner with Alicia before going home?

The huge nose and the olive skin reflected in the mirror were familiar, yet alien. Was there a whole group, a family, of people somewhere who looked like the person staring back at me in the mirror?

My musing was interrupted by a text from Alicia. She was on her way. I looked at myself one more time and decided it was going to be a great dinner. I would have fun and remain professional. No personal feelings would seep in tonight. Tonight was all business.

A notification sound rang out. Alicia was out front. I threw my phone into the clutch and another notification came through. I took my phone back out and stared at the screen. There was a text from Sam. After scoffing at the words on my screen, I replied with a simple "okay," squared my shoulders, and headed out the door, but not before I muted Sam on my phone. I had a business to run, kids to raise, and an entire amazing, fulfilling life without Satomi Nakamura.

CHAPTER 8

Sammi

I SAT IN MY TRUCK and watched her drive away. She looked pissed, even though she was trying to hide it. I couldn't even blame her. I had pushed the conversation towards both the past and future of us time and time again. I had wanted to touch her so badly, but then she looked different. Logically, I knew she was older, and so was I, but she hadn't looked exactly like Indie. It threw my brain for a loop. Stranger danger crept into my mind. What the hell was I even thinking trying to rush into something with some chick just because she was my first love? That is not how things are done. Career comes first, and never date women with kids.

My phone felt heavy in my hand. I wanted nothing more than to call or text Indie to explain. I found the name in my contacts that I was looking for and hit the call button. After two rings, a familiar voice came through.

"Hey! So, how did it go?"

"Well, I froze up and she drove off kinda pissed."

"Yep, that sounds about right. Classic Sammi."

"Not funny, Jenn."

"Not meant to be, Sammi. What the hell is wrong with you?

You're still in love with her, that's obvious, always have been. She's right there."

"She's different though. She doesn't look the way I remember. She has children now, and an ex-husband. She is some sort of a businesswoman. I just realized that we're not those kids we once were."

"I think you realized that she makes your cold, dead heart go pitty-pat and that scares the shit out of you. You two were head over heels for each other. We may have all been young, stupid, and inexperienced back then, but we could still recognize true love."

"Yeah right, true love. Like that even exists."

"You can deny all you want to, my friend, but you know you're in love with her. If you weren't, you wouldn't be calling me freaking out."

I couldn't even argue with her. I never called and freaked out before because no one had ever actually mattered. I had gotten my fix here and there with some young thing who was curious or lonely, but even *that* hadn't happened in quite a few years. If I admitted I still loved Indie, that I had never stopped loving Indie, what did it mean for my life? I said I would never fall in love again, but this wasn't falling, this was the first fall that ever happened. She was the OG love. Maybe the only real love. But all of that meant it would hurt even more when it all ended.

"Sammi, you still there?" Jenn interrupted my rapidly spiraling thoughts.

"Yeah. Yeah, I'm here."

"See? You got quiet. You know I'm right and you're scared shitless. Calm yourself down, get your head out of your ass, and don't screw this up."

"Gee, thanks," I said with obvious disdain, "but there's nothing to screw up and there never will be. I cannot, I will not, get involved with a woman who has children, who already broke my heart once before. I'm smarter now. I don't need anyone."

"Yeah, okay, sure. Whatever you say. So, tell me everything from the beginning."

The conversation with Jenn took up most of the long drive home, but I still had too much time to think. I had managed to piss off both my mother, by leaving early, and Indie, by being my anxiety-ridden self. I put my car in park, let my head fall to the steering wheel, sighed, and took out my phone. Indie deserved at least some sort of explanation for my sudden change in demeanor. What the hell could I possibly say that would encompass what was going on in my mind and heart right now?

> hey ind. sorry things got weird. i need time. i am freaking out over here. you scare me. i don't know if i can do this. i just need time. sorry

> okay

Now to call my mother.

Bob was rolling around on the phone at the other end of the sofa. I knew he was simply a cat, but even he seemed to be telling me to contact Indie, meowing and purring and rubbing his little face all over my phone. It had been two days. She must be home by now. Not that it mattered, we weren't together, and we were never going to be. We had a great history, but we were totally different people. I had to stop thinking about her. I had to do something other than sit here and think about this woman and binge watch tv shows.

The fridge had been too long ignored. This was the perfect opportunity to get some things around here done. I got up, a bucket of soapy water, and started to empty the meager contents of the refrigerator when a phone notification sounded. I stumbled over to it, hoping against all hope it was the one person my rational brain didn't want it to be.

Nope. It was Cass.

You're coming back to work tomorrow, right?

yep that is the plan

Ok, good. So... how did it go with the long-lost one?

not good let's leave it at that.

Yikes. Ok then, see you tomorrow.

Yep

I never should have told Cass about this trip at all. She's going to be waiting for the tell-all. I never should have told anyone anything. I never should have gone in the first place. My mother is still mad, Jenn and Cass are concerned and nosy, and Indie is... well, she's Indie. I don't even know how Indie is. All I got back from her was 'okay'. What did that even mean? I was glad she didn't try to smother me and demand deep explanations, but a part of me wondered if she was thinking about me at all. This whole situation was very reminiscent of high school.

"This is ridiculous." I said to Bob, who cocked his head and perked up his ears. "I don't want a relationship. I don't need anyone else in my life. I'm perfectly fine."

Bob meowed in response and went back to grooming his left leg. I put everything back into the still dirty refrigerator and stomped off to my room.

Cass was practically foaming at the mouth when I got to work. I nodded at her as I passed by. She promptly got up from her desk and followed me into my workstation.

"Soooooo?" Cass cooed in my direction, raising her eyebrows expectantly

"So nothing. We met; we parted ways," I replied without even looking at her.

"For fuck's sake. You were all lovey-dovey, ooey-gooey before you left. Something had to happen."

I turned and looked her dead in the eyes.

"Yes. I realized I was just trying to relive the past. I do not date and I sure as hell don't date women with kids!"

I went back to unpacking my backpack. Cass turned around and skulked back to her desk, murmuring, "Well that was anti-climactic."

I looked at all the work to complete in my queue. I had been gone for two days and things were a chaotic mess. I should have just come back sooner so I wasn't this far behind. What was I even thinking taking time off of work? Did I think Indie and I would just pick up right where we left off and end up in bed together for those couple of days? It had been sixteen years! Did I think we were the same people we had been all those years ago? I don't date. Not anymore. Not since Ali. Every woman I had ever loved ended up breaking my heart.

How did I let myself get so caught up with this blast from the past? Yes, she was my first love, my first sexual encounter, my first everything, but that was a long time ago. I am not that love-struck kid anymore. I am Sammi fucking Nakamura, architect, cat-owner, badass, single person. And I have shit to do.

I sat down, focused, and opened the email from my boss about the huge project we were about to take on, the Huntingdon Project.

CHAPTER 9

Indie

A WEEK HAD GONE BY since the meeting at Goodness Goods with Alicia and Helene and I were knee deep in the negotiating phase. How many units, which stores would debut our product, projected sales numbers, and a bunch of fine print stuff were all anyone was talking about.

Mari and Veda thought it would be cool for their mom to have something in a bougee store like Goodness Goods. Mari was interested in some of the finer points of the negotiating process and Veda wanted to know if we could buy a yacht. While neither of them was particularly materialistic, they had both lived through poverty after their father left. He disappeared for over six months, leaving nothing but debt and kids to take care of in his wake. My once voluptuous figure lost almost forty pounds in three months and looked like a skeleton. The electricity and water had been shut off more than once. We walked sometimes because I didn't have enough money for gas. I ate nothing but one piece of bread, and any bits of food the girls left behind on their plates, most days of the week. We had all gone without basic necessities. That may have been years ago, but they each wanted to make sure we were stable in their own ways. Mari asked about the contract, distribution, and profit margins. Veda wanted to know if frivolity was even a possibility.

A week had gone by since I text back an "okay".

A week had gone by since I had heard from Sam, and I was really trying not to care.

CHAPTER 10

Sammi

A WEEK HAD GONE BY since I started working on the Hunting-don Project. This project was the biggest thing I had ever worked on and the opportunity of a lifetime. My boss had put me in charge of the group to see if I was up to the challenge. After all, she had to make sure the person she put up for the promotion could handle a project like this. There were five of us tasked with keeping a fifteen-million-dollar project under budget and on time. We were presenting to the Huntingdon Corporation in three days, the day before Thanksgiving.

I think I slept a few times during that week, but never at my apartment. I ran home twice a day to feed Bob, restock supplies, and grab a shower. Cass hadn't even ventured into the topic of my little vacation again. We talked shop and that was it. Most of the high-level estimates were done and preliminary drawings were being reviewed by the structural engineers. I assigned picking options for finishes to Cass, and she chose Jeff to help. Sal was entrusted with the bid packages from subcontractors and Shay was making sure we could secure the necessary permits. The team was running like a well-oiled machine. I was in my element: high pressure, high stakes. This is where I thrived.

Asian parents tend to pressure their children from the day they're born, maybe even before that. It was all I knew. When things got calm or there wasn't a problem to solve, I got uncomfortable and didn't know how to act. On the other hand, in situations when I had to push myself to the limits, I was unstoppable.

Every hour or so, Indie would pop into my mind, and she'd be pushed out.

Ten days had gone by since Indie had text back "okay".

Ten days had gone by since I'd heard from her, and I was hell-bent on not caring.

CHAPTER 11

Indie

"TWO WEEKS."

"Two weeks?" Sara and Gabriel asked simultaneously.

"Two weeks." I repeated flatly.

"What the hell happened again, exactly? She freaked out when she saw you? Is there something you're not telling us? Something you're leaving out?" Amie queried.

"No. Yes. NO!" I blurted out as I slammed my glass of kombucha on the bar in Sara's kitchen. "I've told you everything. She just said I looked different. We were different and it freaked her out. Maybe I'm just hideous. I mean, I am pretty old. My boobs aren't exactly in the same place they used to be."

Sara, Amie, and I burst out laughing, Gabriel covered his ears and started singing la-la-la over and over.

"Ay-dios mio! I do not want to hear about your breasts, woman. Be still my gay little heart."

"Awww, come on, Gabey, you know you're curious." Sara ribbed our outnumbered friend.

"No thank you, my gal pals. I'll stay far away. Those things squirt milk out of them, and I have it on very good authority that vaginas have teeth or spikes or something in them. You ladies can have them all!" Gabriel retorted, with a disgusted look on his face, as he poked Sara's left breast with a chopstick.

"See, curious." Amie said through her gasps and snorts.

The laughter roared throughout Sara's small kitchen so loudly that the children were soon curious.

"What's going on out here?" Sara's fourteen-year-old daughter, Melonie, asked.

"You do NOT want to know, child." I answered.

"Uncle Gabriel is just being himself, honey," Sara added.

Ethan, Sara's youngest, chimed in with, "Oh, goodness, then we really don't want to know," as he raced past Gabriel and stuck his tongue out.

Gabriel got up to chase Ethan, but was blocked by his own son, Javier. Two twelve-year-old boys, and one old man acting like a twelve-year-old boy, made me forget all about Sam. I smiled at my own children, just emerging from Melonie's room to join in the fun, then around the whole room at all of these people.

"Hey, can the straight people come join this party?" Helene yelled as she came in the side door with her boyfriend, Lukas.

Helene looked right at me, saw the tears in my eyes, and mouthed an *'are you ok'* in my direction. I nodded and smiled broadly at my best friend and soon-to-be-former business partner. She nodded and smiled back.

"Well good, I'm glad everyone is all here and in a good mood."

The ruckus stopped as Helene held up her left hand and revealed a beautiful diamond ring. Everyone stared quietly for two whole seconds before the screaming, shouting, jumping, and clapping started. Hugs were being given left and right. There were so many people all talking at once, it was chaos. But this was my chaos. This was my framily.

———————

The champagne Sara had brought out was good, but my head was feeling a little fuzzy as my children and I stepped out into the perfectly cool night air to walk home. Not eating anything but an apple all day will cause some issues come champagne time.

"Wow, Helene's getting married! We get to go to a wedding!" Veda squealed as she skipped along.

"Do you think she'll ask you to be in the wedding?" Mari asked.

"Oh, umm, I don't know. I guess so, but I'm not sure how big this wedding is going to be or what she wants. I guess we will have to wait and see." I replied.

"Do you think you'll ever have another wedding, mom?" Veda asked, stopping and turning to look at me. Mari froze as well, fear filling her eyes.

"No, ya hayati, definitely not. I've got everything and everyone I need."

———————

I awoke to the sound of an argument in the kitchen and rolled over. It didn't sound like either of them were in a killing mood or anything, making it perfectly acceptable to roll back over. The little trill from the phone meant rolling back over with a groan. The screen seemed out of focus. I rubbed my eyes a bit and yawned deeply.

happy thanksgiving

I replied with, **Happy Thanksgiving to you too!** before looking at who the sender was. Holy shit, it was Sam.

how have you been?

Fine.

> sorry i've been MIA, things got crazy at work. i'm heading up a huge 15 mil $ project.

> Ok. Congrats to you.

> i've been missing our chats.

What did that mean? How the hell was I supposed to answer? I decided it was better to just ignore her and go on with my day. We had to get dressed, bake pies, and go over to Gabriel's for dinner. Besides, it looked like some intervention parenting may be necessary. It was beginning to sound a bit murderous in the kitchen after all.

"What did you say back?" Amie asked, eyes wide as saucers.

"Nothing."

"Nothing?"

Amie shook her head and then quietly started to explain to the newest 'love of her life', Robert, exactly what was going on, since he was quite confused. He seemed nice enough, but quiet. His eyes darted around the room from speaker to speaker, never an emotion crossing his face. It felt like being watched by a psychiatrist doing a study.

"Not a thing. I don't even know what to say. She dropped off the face of the planet after leading me on for weeks on end, then pops right back up? I don't need this aggravation in my life."

"Amen to that, sista!" Sara chimed in. "Single is the way to be. Less shit to deal with."

"Gurl, I know you're right, but I cannot seem to get that through my thick skull," Gabriel sighed.

"It's all the thick, curly hair on your head, it's not letting anything get in," I teased him.

He stuck out his tongue and laughter filled the air before turning back to the serious conversation at hand that I was desperately trying to avoid.

"So, are you going to ever text her again?" asked Helene.

"I have no idea." I replied. "This batch of kombucha is especially tasty, Sara!"

This conversation had to change topics.

Lukas chimed in with his own take on things.

"I figured dating women would be easier if you were one, but I guess that's not the case at all."

The room erupted and Sara shouted above the noise, "Boy, you have no idea how right you are!"

"Ok, enough about me and my drama." I looked squarely at Helene and Lukas. "Do we have dates? Colors? Venue? Anything? Inquiring minds want to know." I stated as my hand made a sweeping motion towards all of the people in the room.

"Well, we're thinking March 22nd," Helene beamed as she relayed the very news I had asked for.

While everyone else was oohing and ahhing, my mind went precisely where I was trying to keep it away from: Sam. March 22nd was her birthday. My chest felt tight, and I excused myself to the bathroom. How had I let myself get so emotionally intertwined with her so quickly? This heart was guarded like Fort Knox. Everyone joked that it had turned to stone. It had been so long since anyone had gotten in, and Sam just strolled right through all of the defenses. Maybe it was because she had already been there long before the walls were built. However she had gotten there, nothing seemed to be able to get her out. The tightening in my chest was squeezing so hard.

Breathe in and out, I told myself. *Slowly. Calmly. Control the breath.* It seemed to be working. The trill on my phone slammed me back to the present moment.

It was her.

I held my breath and stared at the screen. I texted back and quietly made my way to the front door of Gabriel's house and onto the front porch. I loved the cold and reveled in the curling, dancing whisps of white that came and went with each breath, until the phone rang.

"Hello." I answered, watching my breath fade away into the night.

"Hey. How was your Thanksgiving?" The sultry voice on the other line asked, making my knees weaken slightly.

"It has been a nice day. The girls and I went to a Friendsgiving celebration at our friend Gabriel's house. How was yours?"

"Good. Went to my mom's, as usual, then came home and fed Bob some turkey. He was excited."

"That sounds like a good day. Congratulations on your big project at work."

"Oh, yeah, thanks. We literally presented yesterday. I slept at the office for over a week straight. Poor Bob thought I had abandoned him altogether."

"You've been pretty busy lately."

"Yeah, I have."

The silence was awkward. Each millisecond passed with acute awareness. What should I say to the woman who wooed me so tenaciously only to send my hopes crashing down to the ground with her indifference since our meet-up? Only a few seconds had passed, but this conversation had reached its end. Taking a breath to speak, Sam beat me to the punch.

"I'm sorry, Indie. I got overwhelmed. I saw you, in person, like someone who came back from a time long dead, but, well, you looked different. Not bad or anything, just different. My brain started screaming 'stranger danger' at me and I panicked."

Pausing, she allowed a moment for a response, but there was nothing to say.

"Anyway, sorry. Who knew I was such a delicate little bitch, huh?" she joked.

"Ok. Yeah, we *are* different."

"Really? That's all I get for that? I just called myself a delicate little bitch and I receive no snarky comment or anything?!?"

"What do you want me to say?"

"I don't fucking know. I want you to interact with me, to joke, to be... you!"

"Well, this is me."

"No, it's not the *you* you are with me."

"But I'm not with you, Sam. I haven't even heard from you for like two weeks. This is the guarded me most people get to see. I don't even know who you are. I thought I did, but then you just disappeared. You said you needed time and then nothing."

"I know. I said I was sorry, Ind."

"Sorry? We talk and text every day, all day, for weeks and weeks, then you take one look at me and ignore me for almost two weeks. How the hell am I supposed to react to you showing back up? With balloons and confetti?"

"Ind..."

"Don't Ind me. I have been hurt far too many times to put up with any sort of indifference or ignoring from *anyone*." I practically shouted into the phone.

"Wow, ok. Well, I gotta go. Don't wanna ruin your Friendsgiving."

"Have a good night."

"You too. And Indie, I really am sorry."

The phone went dead. Well, if it seemed too good to be true, it was. This was never going to work. She was a workaholic who has no regard for other people's feelings. She freaked out. I couldn't have people freaking out on me. I deserved better: an explanation, communication. Breaking the years-long single streak was a terrible mistake.

My confidence left me as soon as I turned back towards Gabriel's front door. They must have heard everything. The quiet room full of concerned faces confirmed what I already knew. A few of those faces weren't sure where to look or what to say. Sara, however, didn't skip a beat in breaking through the awkward air.

"Fuck her. Literally or figuratively, I don't care, but, fuck her and get her out of your system."

My tear-laden eyes crinkled, spilling their contents as I joined in the merriment which dispelled any awkwardness in the room. These are my people. My heart had never been more thankful than in that moment.

"Hey girl!" I shouted to an empty room as I entered without knocking. I plopped the cookies the girls and I had made onto the counter as they bounded past me, heading into the family room to find their friends.

Raiding the fridge for a pre-dinner juice, I called out, "Sara, come on. I don't want to be late."

As soon as I closed the refrigerator door, Sara's face was cause for concern.

"Oh my god, sweetie, what's wrong?"

"Lisaida. She's taking me to court," she answered, not looking away from a water spot in front of her on the kitchen counter.

"What?!? Why?"

"She doesn't want me to have fifty percent. She wants child support. She wants to take them away from me, Indie. She says I'm not good for them."

Her panicked eyes met mine.

"She wants to take them away!"

The hysterically sobbing woman was not the take-no-shit-from-anyone Sara I knew. When it came to Melonie and Ethan, she was soft and pliable and madly in love. When I first met her and learned she was a mom, I thought that kid to be an unlucky child for sure, but the mother Sara was, was the one we all wanted as a child. She was attentive, kind, allowed them to be themselves and make their own mistakes, was always there for them, expected them to do their best and be respectful at all times, and put her foot down when necessary. She was the parent I tried to be.

Lisaida knew all of that. This court thing was sheer pettiness.

Sara was under my watch for the entirety of the Local Lesbian Leaders dinner. She was her usual, charming, professional self on the surface, but I knew what was lurking beneath. I was available for her if she needed me, which meant I was not my usual, charming, professional self. Sitting at the bar, I watched her every move.

"You know, you should just go talk to her," a voice chimed in.

I looked at the stunning woman standing next to me, getting the bartender's attention to order a drink. Had I imagined this? Didn't she just talk to me?

"What?" I asked her.

"You should talk to that woman you've been eyeing up all night." She gestured towards Sara.

I laughed and shook my head.

"No, that's my friend, Sara. She's, umm, well, she's had a really rough day, and I'm just making sure I'm here if she needs me."

"Ahhh, ok. Well then, in that case, I'm Delia and I've been eyeing you up all night."

She stuck out her hand and I shook it, flabbergasted.

"Uh, nice to meet you, I'm Indie."

Her side smile gave me butterflies and her short, wavy, red hair framed her face perfectly, bringing attention to her amber eyes. She leaned an elbow on the bar and crossed her ankles, looking straight into my eyes.

"So, are you single?"

CHAPTER 12

Sammi

THE NUDGING FURRY FACE could no longer be appeased. It was breakfast time, and he knew it with every fiber of his small body. I groaned and sat up. Taking this as a good sign, he bounded towards the kitchen. Bested by a feline, again, I trudged down the minuscule hall and hissed at the streams of light coming into the window. It had to be past nine a.m., as bright as it was. Sleep had been elusive after the conversation with Indie. The last time I had looked at the clock was somewhere between five and five-thirty. Ugh. It was going to be a long day.

Once Bob was happily chomping down on his breakfast, I slunk back into my room and pulled the covers over my head. My brain was barely functioning. The vibrating on my nightstand felt as loud as a freight train going past my head.

"Hello?" I managed to croak out.

"Sammi? Sammi! Oh my god, guess what?! We got it! We got the Huntingdon Project!"

"That's great, Cass. That's great."

"Ummm, it doesn't sound great. I thought you'd be way more excited. You headed this."

"I know, I know. Sorry, I'm just a little tired. My head is pounding like a damn heartbeat and my eyes hurt."

"Oh," Cass said much more quietly, "I see. Was this a good or bad no-sleep happening?"

"Neither."

"Okay, then bad. Does it have anything to do with a certain first girlfriend?"

"I'm just... she just... I don't even know anymore."

"Well, take a nap or something. We're all going out to celebrate tonight and you are *not* getting out of it. I'll pick you up at eight."

Before I could even inhale to start to argue, the line went dead. There really wasn't any point in arguing with Cass anyway, so I decided to accept my fate and go down to Tony's bakery to grab coffee and a Danish.

The black jeans and hoodie matched my mood as I tried to navigate the streets of Boston on the morning of Black Friday. Thankfully, Tony's bakery was only a block away. The usually busy storefront was eerily empty.

"Hey Tone, how's it going?" I asked.

"H-hey! Well, you know, we opened early today and were swamped, but now, now it's kind of slow."

"'Tis the season," I responded. "Small, no make it a large, coffee, black." Tony's daughter busied herself with my coffee while he awaited further instructions. "Aaaand, ummm, one of the cheese Danishes."

"Sorry, dear, we are out of cheese." Tony shrugged his broad shoulders and grinned. "Busy morning around here."

"Ok, gimme an apple one then. Please, my good sir."

I smiled back at the jovial man and started to look at the displays there to entice the Black Friday shoppers into buying a travel mug or keychain. It looked like it had been picked over a bit and, hopefully, Tony's early morning had been a lucrative one.

Maybe today would be a decent day after all. It really hit me: we had gotten the Huntingdon Project! Yesterday may have ended terribly, but today was a new day.

The little bell above the door rang. A man's voice ordered coffee, telling Tony he heard this was the place to go in this area. The voice sounded vaguely familiar. Not wanting to have to talk to a former client or whoever it was, I pretended to be enthralled with the trinkets before me. Tony and his daughter were both fulfilling orders now, and there was no one left for the man to speak with, unfortunately. Footsteps approached.

"Nice morning, eh?"

"Yep." I answered.

"I heard this was the place in south Boston to get some good coffee and pastries. You come here often?"

I could no longer keep my back to him without seeming rude. There were only a few minutes before my order was ready and I could excuse myself, saying I was late for a meeting or something, so I turned to face this familiar stranger. I froze, my mouth agape.

"Yep, everyone said Tony's bakery was top-notch. I'm here on some business, so I figured I had to check it out." he continued.

He took a good long look at me for the first time.

"Hey, you look kinda familiar. Do I know you? I never forget a face," he said while studying me, head cocked to the side, eyes squinting.

I collected myself quickly, not giving him time to figure out who I was.

"Nope, I don't think so, but maybe we met in business somewhere, sometime. Well, have a great day!" I offered as cheerily as possible.

I grabbed my goodies and thanked Tony before darting out the door and down the block. What the hell was Zacariah even doing in my neighborhood? That had definitely put a damper on the day, but at least he didn't recognize me.

I slammed my back into the door as soon as I entered the safe-haven of my apartment. My body slumped down to the floor. Sipping, chewing, sighing. An hour ebbed away. Anger was oozing out with seemingly no reason. The confusion soon outweighed the anger. I sat motionless, ruminating, as the coffee turned cold.

He hadn't done anything to me, necessarily. He did marry the woman I loved, but he hadn't held a gun to her head. I had broken up with her. I had broken her heart. He rode in on his fake, painted white horse and told her he would take care of her. But then, he hurt her. It was completely natural to feel hatred towards this man, right? But it was so long ago. Did it even matter? He had her and he let her go. He had the life I wanted. He got all those years with her. He had children with her. The anger was beginning to take over.

I found myself pulling out my phone. The anger had taken control, and it needed to contact Indie. She was mine and I was hers. I was not going to allow one more minute of our lives to be without each other. I knew what I had to do and watched my fingers fly across the keyboard at breakneck speed.

> so this is me, laying it all out. this is all happening so fast. you're real. i feel things about you i haven't allowed myself to feel in a long time. possibly ever. it's scaring me to death. my brain wants me to shut it all down but my heart doesn't want to live without you any longer. i have been missing you for over 16 years now, and i never even realized that until now. i want a life with you. i know i'm all over the place, but that's only because what i am feeling is so powerful. if you never want to speak to me again, or if you tell me we can only be friends that's fine. i just needed to get this off my chest and go all in before I regret it again.

There. The heartfelt sentiment had been sent out into the universe, unaccompanied. The fury subsided just a bit and anxiety was waiting patiently to hop into the driver's seat of this suicide mission. My chest was being crushed by some invisible elephant. The words of my therapist echoed in the backseat, just behind anxiety's head. I began breathing with intention and staring at the edge of my coffee table. *Breathe in, breathe out, breathe in, breathe out...*

The flashes of light behind my eyelids flickered slower and slower until they were no longer seizure inducing. I felt the suicide mission begin to turn towards a leisurely drive on a sun-dappled mountain road. Seconds turned into minutes. Self-assurance took the wheel, and everything was right as rain once again.

Panic attack diverted, I stared at the black screen in front of me, trying to wrap my head around the fact that I was still in love with Indie. The soft cushions gave way on the white sofa. Bob nudged and mewed.

"It's ok, buddy. I'm ok." I said, patting his fuzzball of a head. "I mean, I've been on a bit of a roller-coaster, emotionally speaking, lately, but it'll all work out, right, Bobby my boy?"

He mewed again and purred into my outstretched hand. The phone buzzed its silent notification, and I froze. What the hell had I sent to Indie? What was it that I said? Oh. My. God. A shaky hand reached for the phone in front of me, as if it was disconnected from its owner's body. The elephant had also resumed its chest perch once again.

> Umm, yeah, I believe I'm the one who
> said let's get to know each other again.
> You're the one who wanted to have sex in
> the restaurant and avow our love to one
> another, if I remember correctly.

Great. Texts, the most tonally ambiguous form of communication ever invented. Was she being funny or pissy? Well, hope for the best, prepare for the worst, as they say.

i know, you were right milady.

I usually am :-)

Yes! She was joking with me!

yes you are.

So, what exactly is going on? I'm kind of getting whiplash here, Sam.

i know. i truly am sorry. like i said in the first text i just realized i want to be with u in whatever capacity i can have u in my life. my logical side is fighting it but that side can't win when u are involved.

Yeah, I have that effect on people. What did you mean by "regret it again"?

I saw Zacariah this morning.

WHAT? Where? In Boston?

yeah boston. i just went down to my neighborhood coffee/pastry place and he walked in.

Did he recognize you?

no but he did talk to me for a minute and
said i looked familiar. anyway i got super
angry. i got angry for the way he treated u,
for taking u away from me. then I got mad
at myself for letting u go, for missing out on
the life we could have had together if only
i hadn't been so afraid. then i started to
have a panic attack and text u that heartfelt
but rambling text which started this whole
conversation.

Oh. Wow. Ok.

Perhaps that was a bit too transparent? All of this just got dumped on her and she was probably thinking she was talking to a basket case that she should run far, far away from. Which may not be far from the truth, but she had to know how much I loved her.

Ind? u still there?

Yeah, I'm here. Just processing. What
if tomorrow you say you need time
again? You're not the only one with a
warring heart and mind here.

that's fair. how about this: we take it as slow
as u want to. i WILL contact u every day for
as long as you'll allow me to. i swear. if we
are just friends then we are just friends. i
want u to be happy.

Ok. I do still have feelings for you too,
but I think you're right. Let's just get
to know each other all over again. Are
you still lactose intolerant?

nope. i grew out of that after college.

Nice, then I can make you my
famous cheesy chicken tortellini!

i would love that.

Cass and I arrived at Row 34 at the same time and quickly picked out the rest of our team across the room near the seafood on ice behind a glass divider. The cooks behind were busy preparing for our feast, and the raucous crowd in front were waving us down. Weaving our way through the Friday night crowd, Cass leaned in towards me.

"Well, look at you smiling and everything. If I didn't know better, I would say you were in a good mood, Ms. Nakamura."

"Shut it." I replied, grinning like a damn fool.

"Cass! Sammi! The official celebration can now commence!" Sal shouted much too loudly.

"It looks like the celebration started quite a while ago for you, Sal," I teased.

"Nah, that was the pre-celebration celebration, this is the official celebration." he retorted, slurring ever so slightly.

"I think he's been celebrating all damn day." teased Shay. "Jeff had to go pick him up and drive his drunk ass here."

A tap on my shoulder brought my attention away from the scene unfolding in front of me. I turned to see Mrs. Stanton smiling broadly.

"Mrs. Stanton." I said, accepting her outstretched hand.

"Please, call me Geraldine tonight. You did an excellent job, Satomi. This team was led with confidence, and it shows in their performance, and in yours. The success of this entire team did not go unnoticed. Congratulations."

"Thank you so much, Mrs. St– uh, Geraldine. I cannot tell you how much your words mean to me."

She patted my elbow, squeezing my hand one more time before heading past me into the fray, causing Sal to, once again, get all riled up.

I turned to see my team, happy as could be. Things were coming together today. Life was on the path I'd always dreamed of. Promotion, love of my life, feeling accomplished, it was all right there in front of me. Just for tonight, I'm going to just be happy.

Exchanging smiles with Cass, her face suddenly drained of all color. She mouthed something and pointed behind me. After seeing one cheating bastard this morning, I turned to see the other cheating, heartbreaker of a human being. Ali had just walked in.

CHAPTER 13

Indie

THE OFFICE SEEMED DIFFERENT this morning. Perhaps it was the extra day off we gave them in preparation for telling them that Helene was leaving. It would mean more work for some of them over the coming months, plus, we were a tight-knit group. Most people here went through the growing pains of *Not Your Mom's* with Helene and me. Everyone had gotten paid late at times, worked well past normal hours, and handled emergencies like a team, stumbling, but doing what needed to be done. I looked around at these people, each of them smiling, waving, or nodding at me as my eyes met theirs. How did we ever get this lucky?

Luck was really the only word to describe it. Helene and I had no idea what we were doing, sometimes we still didn't. We fumbled our way through the entrepreneurial jungle together, making more mistakes than either of us would care to admit. The beginning was just the two of us, cleaning houses. Less than a year in, when everyone said we would be barely making it, if not completely failing, our business took off. We had fifteen employees, and now, less than three years after starting our endeavor, we were in negotiations with a nationwide retailer about carrying our non-toxic cleaning products.

The genuine smile on my face broadened as my phone chirped. Every day this week, at this time, the good morning text came through. Sam was staying true to her word so far, but that panic still rose anytime I thought about us actually dating. I typed her a quick reply and looked up to see Kenny, rushing towards me.

I beamed at him.

"Good morning, Kenny!"

His usual worried expression not changing, he replied with, "Yes, yes, good morning to you. Where is Helene? Alicia from Goodness Goods is on line two. She would like to speak with both of you."

"Okay."

I glanced down at my shoes before fully comprehending his words and shooting my gaze right back up to eyes, matching his anxious expression almost exactly.

"Oh, right, yes. Okay." I turned toward the conference room and spun back around. "Where is Helene?!"

"I'll go look. You head to the conference room."

I nodded at him.

"I don't want to be tracking you both down." he remarked after turning on his heels.

The yogurt and berries, which had been so tasty that morning, abruptly felt sour in my stomach. Today was the day. I shot off a quick text to the Cary Street Crew and got a few encouraging replies in the mere seconds it took me to open the door and sit down. My fingers tapped on the table in time with my frantic thoughts. This would, without a doubt, bring huge changes within the company. One way or another, Helene would soon be announcing her exit and I would be left to deal with whatever aftermath came after this phone call. We had been awaiting this news before we made the announcement to our staff. We didn't want them, or Goodness Goods, to feel like the business was in any way unsteady. My digits ceased their drumming. I looked up at Helene and Kenny briskly walking across the main office area towards me. My mouth slightly agape, I came to a realization; if Goodness Goods said no to this deal, it would look like Helene jumped ship.

Ever the optimist, Helene burst into the room vibrating with excitement.

"Let's do this!" she exclaimed as she plopped into the chair next to me.

Kenny hit the number two button on the conference phone and squared his slight shoulders. "Good morning, Alicia. Indie, Helene, and I are all here."

"Good morning, Not Your Mom's team!" Alicia enthusiastically replied. "You guys are already familiar with me. I'd like to introduce you to Mr. Rolfe, our CEO, Mr. Williams, our CFO, and Ms. Lee, our COO."

Pleasantries were exchanged among the group of businesspeople. It felt awkward to think of myself as a contemporary of the men and women on the other end of this call. I was a CEO, but I knew I was nowhere near the same level as these people. This was Goodness Goods, a multi-million-dollar corporation with stocks and shareholders. My hands were sweating, and I felt like a kid at the adult's table of life. Somehow, my voice stayed steady during the introductions and hellos. Helene squeezed my hand and smiled at me. I gave her hand a little squeeze back.

"Well, as most of you know, I'm not one to beat around the bush. We here at GG, as we like to call ourselves, are very interested in your product line. We all agree that the products are amazing and, just as importantly, the company has a good look. You guys are just the type of business we can get behind. The female-run, inclusive, rise-from-the-ashes kind of thing markets well. With you two as the face your company will go far, and we'd like to be a part of that ride."

Kenny's face contorted in a foreign way. The corners of his lips rose up. Helene was dancing wordlessly around the room. Shocked, I sat in my chair, feeling overwhelmed and numb at the same time.

The next hour seemed to go by in a blur of words, names, and numbers. Kenny was on top of it all, his stack of papers ever rustling. He seemed like a damn boy scout, but pale and not at all outdoorsy.

"This has truly been a pleasure. We will all be seeing a lot more of each other soon. You guys have a great day!"

Alicia ended the call in both a professional and friendly manner. She was a lot like Helene in that way. Helene was the one to sit down and talk with people; schmooze, as they say. I got things done, but my people skills were sometimes lacking. I glanced over at my friend and business partner. How would I ever do this without her? Tears began to threaten my eyes with their onslaught, but I held them back. This was a good day, dammit. So why did I want to sob so badly?

———————

At our celebratory dinner, Helene and Kenny were all smiles and laughter. Playing the part of happy businesswoman while fighting the urge to cry or scream was exhausting. Helene had already told the Cary Street Crew, in a group text, which resulted in both of us having to mute our phones for the evening. I had told Sam, and she was excited for us. She was currently on a plane, heading to Dubai for a business trip, so I couldn't burden her with my silly, unfounded, infuriating, existential crisis. Plus, I didn't want to get too used to leaning on her. Not yet. The friend group was also out because they would all just tell Helene.

Upon my exit from the restaurant, my exasperated sigh pushed the freshly falling flakes away from my face. The chilly night air was both calming and invigorating. Tonight was the night of oxymoronic emotions, which, in and of itself, fed the overall frustration even more.

"Ok, it's freezing! I'm heading home. Great job team. Love you both so much," Helene cooed.

I accepted her hug gratefully. She was very sincere with her hugs, and you could feel it. Her affection then turned toward Kenny's stiff frame. His pleading eyes met mine and I just shrugged. Eventually, he reached one arm behind her back and patted her, his rigidity never wavering. Helene flitted off into the flurries, leaving a shaken Kenny in her wake.

I couldn't help but laugh aloud. Kenny had shown more sides of himself today than I ever knew existed.

"You'll get used to it." I said.

His eyes looked into mine, head cocked to the side, eyebrows raised.

"Don't worry, I'm not going to hug you or anything, man."

His gaze lowered and a chuckle escaped.

"You are an enigma, Indie Woodley. I can read people pretty well; it's how I got this far in life. While I cannot seem to get a read on you most of the time, this much I know; if *you* ever hug me, one of us must be dying."

Our laughs intermingled as we released them into the night air. His smile was starting to seem less alien as this day wore on.

"Have a good night, Kenny."

"You too, Ms. Woodley." he replied with a melodramatic bow.

The flurries were starting to pick up, but I definitely had a few minutes to have a drink before calling an Uber. I started walking down the block to a nice little lesbian bar. The owner, Kat, was a member of the Local Lesbian Leaders group and she had carved out a safe, low-key space for our community to gather. One of the last lesbian bars in the country.

I entered an almost empty space, except for Kat behind the bar, Suzie waiting tables, and two other patrons who nodded in my direction before continuing their conversation. I went to my usual seat and Kat started pouring me a glass of Blanton's whiskey before I could even ask.

She set the whiskey neat down in front of me and leaned on the bar.

"So, what's up, buttercup? You're..." she eyed me quizzically, "Sad. Lost. Angry. Or all of the above. Oh girl. What the hell happened?"

"Honestly, I'm not even sure. Just been having a week, ya know. I'm confused myself, so I'm not even sure what to tell you, Kat."

"I feel that. Well, drink up. Tonight is on me."

I started to interrupt, but her hand went up in front of me, ending my protest before it began.

"Don't you dare argue with me. Now I gotta go get some stuff done in the back while we're slow and before we get snowed in. Suzie's over there if you need anything."

"Thanks."

I watched her walk over and whisper something to Suzie nodding in my direction. The young waitress gave me a pity smile and a thumbs up. I just looked back at my drink.

"Wow, I go to the bathroom for two minutes and someone takes my seat in an almost empty bar. What are the odds?"

I snapped my head up towards the speaker, ready for an argument, but saw a friendly face with a crooked smile, framed perfectly by short, wavy, red hair.

———

"Damn, girl, that is a lot." said Delia.

"Right? It is, isn't it? I feel like such a whiny baby complaining about landing a deal with a national retail giant, but it comes with so many changes. I already have enough excitement and confusion in my personal life, I don't need it in the business too. Plus," my voice raising ever so slightly in volume as I turned to my companion, "plus I have two teenage girls at home! They have stuff too. Like teenage stuff. And don't even get me started on my ex-husband." I refocused on the empty glass in front of me. "I guess I'm just feeling a bit overwhelmed and alone. Sorry to dump all of this on you. We barely know each other."

"Eh, sometimes that's the best person to dump things on. I have nothing at stake, so anything I say can be taken at face value."

"You're not wrong. I never thought of it that way. I'm usually the one everyone comes to. I guess I never thought about going to anyone else, because I don't want to burden them."

I motioned to Suzie to fill my glass a third time and Delia's a second.

"So, what's the personal stuff? Is it because your business partner is also your friend, or is it something else?" Delia queried.

"Oh, well, that's a whole other long story."

"I've got nowhere to go, and you are wildly interesting, so go ahead."

I chuckled.

"Well, okay then. I'll give you the short version. I dated this girl in high school, she broke my heart, I married a man, had twin girls, and got divorced. Fast forward sixteen years, this girl and I get back into contact. We were texting every day, flirting, healing some old wounds for weeks on end. We meet in person, she freaked out, ignored me for a couple of weeks, then wanted to act like nothing happened and get married and have more kids and stuff."

"Holy shit. No wonder you're a hot mess right now. You're getting things thrown at you on a lot of different fronts."

The tears threatened to spill again, but this time, the alcohol had dulled my senses too much to fight them back. A few escaped and landed on the bar next to a, once again, empty glass. Delia wiped my cheek with a napkin, turned my bar stool towards her, and took my face into her hands. She was standing over me, one leg in between mine, leaning down towards my tear-stained face. She kissed one cheek, then the other. I let out a small sigh. She continued her gentle assault on my forehead, then my chin.

"I think you might need someone to take your mind off of all of this for a while," she whispered, kissing me gently on the lips.

I moaned and felt a familiar throbbing as the blood rushed away from my brain. It had been a very long time since I'd let anyone touch me like this. Years.

"Can I take that as a yes?" she asked in between kisses.

"Yes," I whispered.

We kissed for a few minutes longer and hands started to roam. She reluctantly pulled away from me, put money on the bar, and grabbed my hand. Kissing the back of it, she led us both out onto the snow-dusted street.

CHAPTER 14

Sammi

MY INTERNAL ALARM let me know it was time to send the good morning text to Indie, but I was on a plane, thirty-thousand feet in the air. She was probably still asleep anyway after going out to celebrate last night. I wish I could have been there for her. The need to be with her was getting stronger by the day. I just had to regain her trust, but that may take too much time, and I might explode long before it ever happens.

The flight to Dubai was in hour six, and only at its halfway point. The movie playing was abysmal, allowing my mind the opportunity to overthink everything it possibly could.

What if the Simons forgot about feeding Bob?

What if they didn't spritz Fern?

What if one of the kids left the door open?

What if Indie never opened up to me again?

What if I got promoted?

What if I didn't?

What if I moved to Dubai? Would Indie come with me? Would she find someone else?

Inhale.

Exhale.

Inhale.

Exhale.

I felt a hand gently touch mine and I looked directly into the eyes of the small, old woman next to me. We may not have spoken the same language, but she knew I was spiraling internally. Her tender smile elicited one from me in return. She patted my hand a few more times and turned back to her knitting.

Thank goodness for little old ladies on long flights to Dubai.

———————

The jarring screech of wheels on a tarmac made me jump. I was met once again with a sympathetic smile from my favorite Dubai-ite and a pat of my hand. She said something in Arabic and made hand motions that looked like a plane landing. I answered her with one of the only Arabic words I knew; shukran. She grinned broadly and said many more foreign sounding words. In that moment I was so grateful Indie had taught me a few things from her stint of living in Saudi Arabia while she was married to that asshole.

I picked up my phone to reach out to her, but quickly remembered I needed to buy a local SIM card as soon as we got off the plane if I wanted this phone to actually work. Dammit. I needed to hear from Indie.

The airport itself was an amazing work of design. The people of Dubai were not afraid of chrome. Everything around me gleamed: columns, walls, ceilings. The huge, upside-down-V-shaped windows flooded the space with light. Palm trees, sumptuous curves softening every corner, and elegant Arabic script topped off the feeling of decadence. Luckily, most of the signs also had English translations. I paused my gawking long enough to run into the bathroom. My mind was so enthralled with seeing Brian Broughton's building design in person, I almost forgot about my phone. Ducking into a little shop along the glittering concourse, I paid for and installed a new chip in the phone.

The noises flowed almost immediately. Emails, texts, missed calls, and all sorts of other notifications from the last twelve hours flooded in. I muted the device and went straight to my texts. The sight of Indie's name and message fluttered my heart.

> **Have a safe flight!**

The name below hers caused the fluttering to stop.

> **Hey, I saw you the other night and wanted to come over and say hello. I miss you. I'd love to get together and chat sometime soon.**
> **Love, Ali**

I let Indie know I had landed and would talk to her after I checked into my hotel. Stowing the phone in my pocket, and ignoring everything and everyone else, my attention turned to finding a sign with Nakamura written on it.

If the Dubai International Airport was stunning, this hotel was spectacular. There was a water park and an aquarium inside! The room was bigger than my entire apartment (and possibly the Simons' apartment next door too). A family of four would have fit comfortably in the enormous bathroom alone. Drawing myself a steaming bath, I decided to take full advantage while I could. There would be no more leisure time on this trip. Work was calling.

Sure enough, not five minutes after I was dressed, my phone went off. Mark was on his way to take me to dinner. While we had worked on a few projects together in the last six or seven years, I had only met him in person once. Hopefully two people who met once a few years ago could recognize each other in a crowded hotel lobby.

The lobby looked like a meeting at the U.N. Every society on Earth seemed to converge right here. The internal oohing and ahhing felt like it was overarching every second of this trip so far. Dubai definitely had its charms. I settled into a chair beside a circle of massive, white columns, the bottoms of which were fish whose scales extended all the way up to the wave-like flourishes at the top. Taking center stage among these marble giants was a Chihuly glass sculpture, demanding to be ogled. The tower of delicate glass swirls started at the bottom with shades of blue, the narrowed towards the ceiling before exploding into a flourish of reds and oranges which almost touched the gold-tiled ceiling. The beautiful sound of the water cascading over the scalloped bowl at the base was noticeable even over the din of my fellow travelers. This area's overall design combined with the attention to acoustic comfort astounded my architectural brain. The many curves in the ceiling helped to keep the noises from each distinct area contained, even in this crowded, palatial space.

A strong Bronx accent interrupted my reverie. "Sammiiiiii!"

I turned to see an New York-born, Italian man with outstretched arms. His suit was high quality and his slick, black hair was perfect. I smirked as I ruminated on how long it took him to get ready each morning. Standing up to greet him and his firm handshake, I looked longingly at the space I had been admiring and bid it a silent goodbye.

"Hey there, hope the flight wasn't too terrible. The trip from the East Coast to here is a bitch, man!"

His grip on my hand was exactly how I remembered; unyielding, but friendly.

"And my mother wonders why I don't visit more often," he joked with an exaggerated shrug of his broad shoulders, hair never moving a centimeter in the whole process.

"Hey, Mark. Nah, it wasn't too bad. Luckily, I was seated next to a nice, old grandma. She didn't speak English, but she was a great seatmate," I replied.

"Ready for some good eats?"

My stomach growled almost on command and we both stared at it.

"Evidently, I am! I was so in awe of this place, I totally forgot about food."

"Yeah, Dubai can do that to a person. How the hell do you think they got me to move all the way over here?" he said with a wink. "Just wait until you taste the food here. Almost as good as my mom's"

I shot him a questioning look on behalf of his tiny, Italian mother on the other side of the world.

He raised his hands in defense and replied, "I said almost."

The company car in any other setting would have been impressive, but after what had kept my gaze captive during the previous hours, it seemed lackluster at best. We climbed in and Mark said something to the driver in Arabic. The car slowly inched away from the awe-inspiring accommodation and, I swear, my heart broke just a tiny bit.

"So, they wanna move you out here, huh?"

Mark was never one for subtlety.

"I guess so. And you'll be going to Boston."

"I guess so," he imitated.

We both grinned. His finger found the small button on the door next to him and the glass partition between us and the driver went upward.

"So, ummm, I have something I feel like I need to say to you, but I'm not really sure how to say it."

My nervous laugh would not be contained.

"Mark, I may not know you very well, but I do know you have no trouble speaking your mind."

He joined in my awkward merriment for a moment.

"Well, ya got me there. Okay, I'll just come right out and ask. Are you a lesbian?"

My heart stuttered, my head slowly turning toward my companion. I could not remember anyone outright asking me that question. Ever. I wasn't even sure what to say. I had never been ashamed of who I was, but this definitely caught me off guard.

"Don't be upset. I'm not being an asshole, I swear." He raised his hands in defense, looking me straight in the eye. "I have no problem if you are. My sister is a lesbian. She's married to a wonderful woman whom I adore."

His tone softened as he continued on, looking down at the dark gray carpet at our feet.

"It's just, well, it's illegal here. I'm not talking about frowned upon, I'm talking about illegal. Punishable by imprisonment or death kind of illegal. You don't have to tell me anything, I just thought you should know."

My eyes softened. He was just one human being concerned for the welfare of another human being. The corner of my mouth found its way upward as I responded to his string of words, in an attempt to lighten the mood.

"Well, I was right; you most certainly have no trouble speaking your mind."

He looked at me and smiled, the tension in the drab car melting away.

"Thanks for the heads up. This will undoubtedly play a role in my decision making."

The gurgling in my stomach was no longer due to hunger. The UAE's national dish, Khuzi, had remedied any famine that had existed in my body. I groaned as I patted my stomach like a woman in the late stages of pregnancy. The trill of my phone drew my attention. Whimpering, I eased myself up from the luxurious chair across from the mammoth bed.

A grin spread across my face. The meme Mark had sent echoed my feelings of fullness perfectly. We had eaten way too much and would both be paying for it for at least the next twelve hours.

Indie! Oh god, I forgot to text her! It was 10:37 p.m. In Dubai, which would make it 2:37 p.m. in the U.S.A.

"Thank goodness!" I exclaimed to the empty room.

> hey ind. sorry it took so long, things have been busy over here. it's fucking gorgeous in dubai! for real everywhere i look i'm in awe.

By the time I finished pulling on my pajama shirt over my head, the phone had trilled in response.

> Hey there, Sam. That's nice. I'm glad you're enjoying yourself.

> thanks. so what u been up to?

> Nothing much. Had the celebratory dinner last night, told the employees today, now just working on our asses off to formally seal this deal.

> thats fantastic! did u guys have fun at dinner? did you tell the employees about helene leaving yet?

Dinner was ok. No, not yet.

that's right ur waiting until after
it's all done and stuff.

Yep

well i know ur busy and it's almost 11
over here. i'll let you get back to your deal.
goodnight from the middle east!

Goodnight

My thoughts kept their focus on the businesswoman almost seven thousand miles away as I laid down on the softest sheets ever invented. I wanted a life with her. How on Earth could I accept this position? If it were any other branch in the world, she could come with me. I'd marry her in an instant.

I shot upright, sending those luxurious sheets cascading down my heaving torso. Marriage? Did I just think about marriage?!? What the hell did they put in that food? I must be losing my damn mind.

––––––

"So, this is it. Welcome to Finnick & Douglas, Dubai!" Mark announced as we entered another one of Dubai's glorious buildings.

"Going back to America after this trip is going to feel very dull."

Mark chuckled. "You have no idea how right you are."

We coasted through the sea of people all nodding and smiling at us. The glass work in this monumental space was worthy of marveling. Everyone else around me seemed to barely notice the awe-inspiring space we were all in. To them, the new Asian chick dressed in a fitted gray suit with a crisp white, V-neck collared shirt, leather Oxford's, and slicked back hair, was the novelty to be gawked at.

A striking, dark-skinned woman in a hijab smiled at me in a flirtatious manner. I smiled back, briefly. Fear consumed me. What if someone was watching? If I smiled back too broadly, would they whisk me away? I glanced around frantically. I saw only friendly faces within this glass fortress. Shaking these childish thoughts from my brain, I tried to focus once again on all of the wonderful things around. Everything seemed to be overshadowed by this growing alarm.

---

it's so weird. people like you and me are illegal here. illegal! like they would kill us. i can't stop thinking about it.

Yeah, that's how it is in Saudi too. I mean, I didn't have to worry about it then, because I was married to a man, but there was an underground homosexual world for sure.

i keep feeling like i'm being watched but i know it's just my imagination going crazy.

Well, you'll only be there for a few more days and then you'll be free again. Just don't go picking up some pretty young thing while you're there and you should be good.

haha yeah right. well its late here so i'm gonna go. enjoy your afternoon.

I will. Sleep well.

I fell back on the bed. If only Indie knew what was being asked of me. If I declined this promotion, I would be passed over at best, ignored, and eventually let go at the first chance they got.

Do I give up my life for a few years to get ahead? This was everything I had ever wanted, but Dubai? Death for being a lesbian? I'd gone years without sex before, so I could definitely do it again, but what about Indie? What was she even thinking? She'd been so distant since I ghosted her. While I could understand her reaction, I just wanted her to know how serious I was and, more than that, wanted to know what she was feeling. Did she see a future with me? She was so busy and overwhelmed, it's not like I could just outright ask without seeming selfish.

The backlit tray ceiling with its delicate, ethereal chandelier was captivating. *Breathe in, breathe out, breathe in, breathe out...* I grinned like the Cheshire Cat as I thought about how proud my therapist would be of me. I continued my calming exercise as exhaustion overtook me.

CHAPTER 15

Indie

"INDIE!"

"Huh? Umm, yes. Sorry. What?" I replied to Helene's outcry.

"Girl, you have been spacey all day. The meeting with the law-yer people is in like a week. What in the world is up with you?" she demanded, hands on hips, head cocked, eyebrows raised.

"Oh, well, nothing really."

I shrugged off her inquisition to no avail. My mouth started spewing out more words before she could delve any deeper with her line of questioning.

"It's just, well, it's kinda...it's a lot." This seemed to placate her attitude a tiny bit, so I continued on. "The deal, you leaving, the girls, Sam, peri-menopause, Sara and Lisaida, and whatever else I've forgotten."

"I know, girl, I know. It is a lot on you, on all of us." Sitting next to me, she sighed and took my hands in hers. "It's going to be difficult for a while. There is a lot to... wait... Sara and Lisaida? What's going on with Sara and Lisaida?"

Ahhhh, I'd hit the mother lode. This would keep her from prodding me about my life for at least a day.

Tonight was yet another pizza night. The girls didn't seem to care, but I felt like I was being a terrible mother. At least tonight was Friday, so it seemed more appropriate than it did Tuesday night. Last Friday had been a night of both celebration and breakdown. This one was much more low-key. My psyche felt like it was on a precipice, and I needed this eating pizza and doing nothing night more than I realized. Plopping on the sofa, I was met with the vivacity of Veda.

"Mom, can you do big business-y type deals all the time?" the curly-haired child pleaded through a mouthful of cheese and pepperoni.

"HA! No. If I never talk to another executive or lawyer again, I will be a happy woman." I retorted, much to her chagrin.

"Aren't *you* an executive, Ms. Whiny Woman?" Mari teased.

Mocking her, I replied, "Weren't you the one who was supposed to pick a movie?"

"Yeah, but Veda distracted me." Mari replied.

Veda stuck out her tongue, still covered in gooey cheese.

"Distracted you how?" I challenged, watching both girls look at each other and do their twin grin.

"Well," Veda started, "you remember that idiot boy we told you about?"

I nodded.

"Yeah, we're teaching him a little lesson—twin style."

I eyed both of the smirking girls up and shook my head.

"Okay, just don't get yourselves into any trouble. Now, let's get this thriller that Mari is bound to pick started!"

Thirty minutes later, completely engrossed, the vibration against my leg led to me jumping during a calm scene of the incredibly tense movie. Neither of my offspring appreciated the untimely scare. Glaring, they both tossed popcorn at my head. I expertly ducked out of the line of fire and crawled into the hallway.

"Hello?"

"Hey stranger."

Shock and recognition flooded through me.

"Hey, Delia. How are you?" I replied as calmly as I could muster.

"I'm doing pretty well. Can't complain. I wanted to check in and see what you were up to this weekend. I know your life is crazy, but I'm here if you need a distraction. We could pick up where we left off last Friday night," she suggested.

The palpitations in my chest sped up. The now familiar throbbing between my legs commenced, leaving little to no blood left for sound reasoning.

"Uh, wow. Umm, yeah, I can't. It's movie night here with my girls. But thanks. You sure know how to get a girl's blood pumping." I flattered.

Her laughter had an edge to it.

"You never even got a chance to find out how true that is."

The sultry tease cut right through me, causing me to stifle a groan.

"Well, enjoy your evening, Indie. I'll catch up with you later."

"Yeah, thanks. You too. Bye."

I breathed as my back hit the wall behind me. Sliding to the ground, I finally exhaled. How long had it been? Four years? It never bothered me that whole time; being celibate. All of a sudden, some chick flirting with me is enough to render me practically unconscious with lust? Banging my head lightly against the wall, I glared at the boob light on the ceiling in my hallway. I hated that thing. Boob lights are just lazy design. Boobs, real boobs, on the other hand, those are always exquisite. Big, small, round, long, supple, or firm, they were all simply fantastic. I wondered what Delia's breasts would feel like without her bra on. I closed my eyes and recalled the smooth skin on her stomach, the feel of lace beneath my fingers as they reached upward, kissing, touching, breathing, moaning…

"Mom! You gonna grace us with your presence any time soon?" called Veda.

Her voice snapping me out of my reverie, I replied, "Y-yes, dear child. I'll be there in just a sec."

Last Friday night, it had taken me over an hour and three self-induced climaxes to get any sort of relief from that evening's excitement. I hoped this phone call would not cause history to repeat itself. If I had actually slept with Delia, would it have abated the frenzy within me or caused it to intensify like a drug addict awaiting the next fix?

Rising up off the floor, my phone buzzed once. Sam was back from Dubai and eager to talk to me. What the hell was happening to me? I hadn't felt the need for any sort of sexual or romantic attention in years and now I had two women who made me want to crawl out of my own skin with desire. I pushed it to the back of my mind. For now.

"Hi! Indie? Can you hear me?"

"Yep, I can hear you. You're not halfway across the world anymore."

"Oh yeah, I know. My brain is in a totally different time zone. I am utterly exhausted, but I wanted to talk with you before I crashed for who knows how long. You may not hear from me again until Christmas."

"Well, Christmas is only a couple of weeks away, so I guess that's not too terrible."

"I won't go weeks without talking to you ever again." she said earnestly. "I miss you too much, and I've given up fighting that."

I was silent for longer than felt comfortable, but I wasn't sure how to respond to that.

"Indie? You still there?"

"Yeah, I'm here."

"Oh, okay. I do miss you; ya know."

"So you've said."

"Do you believe me?"

"I'm not sure what to believe. You've said all of that before too."

"That's fair. I'm in it for the long haul, as they say. I messed up and now I have to be patient while I rebuild your trust. I've waited for you for over sixteen years, another couple of trips around the sun won't hurt me. So how have you been over the last couple of days? Anything new and exciting?"

"Uh, yes, no, kind of." I vacillated.

New? She wanted to know what was new? How the hell was I supposed to tell her everything going on inside of me right now?

"Well, we're officially in lawyer-y type meetings all the damn time now. Helene, Kenny, and I are planning her exit strategy. Umm, lemme see," I hesitated. "The girls are going after that Aiden kid with some sort of plan to humiliate him and teach him a lesson. And I got hit on and kissed."

There. I had said it. I threw it out into the universe and was going to let the chips fall where they may.

"Wow, umm, that's a lot to take in. Let's just start with the biggest one. Someone kissed you?" she asked me, attempting to sound calm.

"Umm, yes. It was a girl from my networking group. We had met before through the networking stuff, then she saw me the night that I went to that celebration dinner with Helene and Kenny."

"And she just kissed you?"

"Well, yes. No. Not exactly. I was feeling really overwhelmed that night, so after dinner, I walked down to Kat's bar and got a glass of whiskey. Delia recognized me..."

"Delia. The girl who kissed you?"

"Yes. So anyway, she recognized me and sat at the bar with me. We started chatting and ended up having three whole glasses of whiskey. By the end of the night, we were both a bit drunk and she kissed me."

I decided, in that moment, to leave out the part where we felt each other up, I went home with her, and we almost had sex.

"Did you kiss her back?"

"Yes."

"Okay, I see."

The silence that permeated the conversation felt tangible, like it was a wall. My nervous heartbeat evened out. I had done nothing wrong. Sam and I weren't anything, technically. She had run away when I came close. We had only been talking and I was a single woman in every sense of the word. Squaring my shoulders and steeling my resolve, I walked over and looked at myself in the mirror. The woman in front of me no longer allowed anyone to make her feel badly about herself. I had almost forgotten that.

"We are not officially anything, but I also didn't want to keep it from you. So now you know. Anyway, so how was the trip to Dubai?"

I heard the inhalation of her resignation once she realized the cutting truth of my statement.

"It was so beautiful and amazing, and I got some major brownie points with the bosses, just for going to check it out. They wanted me to see it and meet the people who might be working under me if they give me this promotion."

Promotion? My steely resolve crumbled under the weight of that word.

"Oh, wow, a promotion. That's good news. Really good news. So, you're moving to Dubai. Well, okay then." I sputtered.

Was this whole thing just a ruse to lead me on? She couldn't care all that much about me if she ghosted me and then decided to move to Dubai. How could she be so concerned about me being guarded when she was the one not even taking my feelings into account? I had been open since the beginning, even about Delia! She was the one who kept springing things on me.

"I mean, I'm not moving. I didn't get the promotion yet or anything; it's just a possibility."

"How long have you known about this possibility?"

"Umm, a little while. I guess it's been a few weeks. I just didn't really believe it. I'm not the only one up for this promotion, just a candidate. I probably won't even get it, but it's nice to even be nominated, as the stars say on awards shows."

"Oh, okay. Well, I guess that's good then. I really gotta go now. We're doing movie night, and the girls are wondering where I am."

"Yeah, I should get to sleep; reacclimate myself to this side of the world. Goodnight."

"Goodnight."

The movie, once again, had everyone's attention for the next hour. Once we each went to our own rooms at the end of the night, I could work on easing some tension. Throwing the phone, and myself, across my bed, I released all of my frustration into my pillow through a high-pitched scream. Maybe I should have slept with Delia! I was so riled up; I couldn't even think about sleep. Turning on my computer, I got to work on some *Not Your Mom's* tasks I'd been putting off.

An hour into working the frustrations out of my mind, my phone dinged. The expectation was to see Helene or Kenny's name, since we had all been working late nights recently. Instead, my heart thrummed with excitement. It was Delia.

You still up? Can't stop thinking about
the other night.

My fingers fumbled picking up the phone, almost causing me to drop it, and the now-familiar throbbing between my legs resumed its onslaught. It was like I was starving before, but content with the familiar feeling, and, now, I had a taste of food and realized my ravenous hunger.

> **Yeah, I'm up. Me either, to be honest.**

Weekends were no longer weekends, that much was certain. Helene and Kenny arrived promptly at ten a.m. and we got down to business. The work involved in a deal this big was unlike anything encountered before. Helene and I were soon overwhelmed. Kenny seemed to take it all in stride. His neat stacks of papers, daily agenda, spreadsheets, iPad, and phone splayed out on my table like soldiers at the ready. None of them were out of line for fear of Kenny's wrath. I couldn't help but smile at the scene before me.

"What are you smiling about, woman? This has got to be one of the circles of hell. I've been thinking, maybe I should just bow out now?" Helene offered.

I let out a chuckle and Kenny's head snapped up.

"Oh no you don't, Ms. Smart ass. I have put too much work into this already," he scolded, his serious expression never faltering.

Helene and I burst into laughter. Kenny's minuscule head shake was all he gave in the way of acknowledgment of our hysterics.

"I'm pretty sure Kenny will kill you, Hel." I warned the woman shrugging her shoulders next to me.

"Meh, I ain't skeered." she goaded, leaning in towards Kenny and winking. He barely looked up from his pile of paperwork to give her a glare. "See? He loves me. Just loves me."

"Yeah, that's it," I teased.

"So, since Kenny is in his little zone, let's take a moment and focus on you, Indie darling dearest."

"W-what? Me?!? Why are you picking on me? I'm not the one who glared at you,"

Crossing her legs, Helene took on the air of a therapist with me as her unwilling patient.

"I know you. Something is up. Now spill, or I will bother you to no end, which will then annoy Kenny, and he'll turn on you, making your situation even worse with both of us nagging you."

I looked at the aforementioned employee and I swear I saw the flash of a grin. Feeling surrounded, outnumbered, and hopeless, I gave in.

"Fine. Remember the other night when we had our celebratory dinner?" I queried before going on. Helene nodded to keep me talking. "Well, after you guys left, I went down to Kat's for a quick drink. She and I chatted while I sat at the bar, then she went to the backroom to do some stuff, since it was such a slow night with the snow and everything. You know." I said with a wave of my hand.

Helene's nodding prodded me onward.

"I ran into that new girl from LLL, the redhead, and, well, we started talking. Then we drank. A lot. Too much. Things started, umm, happening."

"Happening?" inquired Helene.

I glanced up at her expectant face, only to realize Kenny had also become interested in the conversation. His head was still down, but his inquisitive stare was directed at me. I lowered my gaze and became engrossed in the fidgeting of my fingers.

"Yes, happening. We started kissing and there may have been some groping. I can't remember all of it because I was three glasses deep by that point."

"Indie Woodley had a torrid affair in a lesbian bar!!" Helene exclaimed.

"Shhhh! The girls will hear you!" I chastised, glancing around for signs of teenage life. "It was NOT a torrid affair, for Pete's sake! It was two, grown, single, women having a little bit of passion," I continued on with a sigh.

"Passion? Girl, I didn't think you remembered what that was anymore. Evidently Ms.... umm, what's her name?"

"Delia." I stated.

"Ms. Delia has helped to jog your memory. Bless her sweet soul."

Kenny dropped all pretense of working.

"Exactly how long has it been since *passion* has been a part of your life?"

"Way too long." Helene interjected. "You don't even want to know."

"Don't even want to know what?" boomed a male voice from the living room.

I turned to see Gabriel in all his finery making his way toward our huddle. I tried to make my eyes plead, but he was far too interested in whatever gossip was happening to care if it was about me and throw me a proverbial bone.

"Since Indie got some!" jested Helene.

"Oh my, yes, it has been *quite* a while for that. Why exactly are we bringing it up, though?" Gabriel inquired, entering the kitchen and seeing a brand-new face. "And, follow up question; who is this?"

His gesture toward a stunned Kenny ended in a side hug for me, followed by one for Helene.

"This is our admin guy, Kenny. Kenny, Gabriel; Gabriel, Kenny."

Helene raised her eyebrows expectantly at me as Gabriel went past us towards Kenny. I shrugged at her and turned my attention back to the flirtatious men in front of us, glad to have a reprieve from the previous line of questioning.

"Pleased to meet you, my good sir." crooned Gabriel, out-stretching his hand. "I'm Gabriel, a friend of these two fabulous, crazy women."

"Uh, yes, pleased to meet you too. I'm Kenny, their businessy person; their assistant. The crazy ladies, that is," he sputtered as he grasped Gabriel's hand. "I'm an employee of them, not that they're crazy." Kenny corrected, staring at us.

Helene and I burst out laughing again. This was turning out to be quite an eventful and interesting morning. I had never seen Kenny so flustered, but, then again, Gabriel seemed to ave that effect on men and women. His charm never ceased to amaze.

My business partner leaned in towards me and whispered, "Don't think, for one second, we are done with the conversation we were having before Gabriel got here." She patted my shoulder for good measure.

CHAPTER 16

Sammi

"DAMN, GIRL. Let me check my hearing aids. I cannot believe what I'm hearing. Dubai? Indie? Ali? Stolen kisses? It's like a damn telenovela up in here! So, let's start with the whole Indie thing." Cass rose from her seat at the corner of my desk and started pacing in my cubicle. "You ghosted her, you told her you might be moving to Dubai, and now you're pissed because she's guarded and kissed some other woman, right?"

"Yeah, I guess that about sums the situation up in an overly simplistic way."

"It is that simple. How did you expect her to react when you ghosted her? How would you have reacted? I mean, I don't know 'bout you, but I'd be guarded like Fort Knox." Cass stopped pacing and looked directly at me. "When did you tell her about Dubai?"

"Last night." I answered.

"Last night? So you kept that from her too? Guuuurl. You say you want a future with this woman, but you keep her out of your life's decisions?"

"Really, Cass? I thought you were *supposed* to be my friend. It's not like she cares. She's the one going around kissing random women."

"You need to decide what the hell you want, Sammi. Don't play these fuck-fuck games with a woman you've been hung up on for going on two decades now," she countered, glaring into my soul. "You are the master of self-sabotage in every area of your life except work and it's exhausting to watch."

I watched as Cass turned on her heels and walked down the aisle between our cubicles. She was right, and I hated that. I was a force to be reckoned with in the workplace, but definitely faltered at every turn in my personal life. I did need to decide what the hell I wanted. Work was all I'd ever had, really. Besides Bob and Cass, there wasn't much else in my life. I looked at the mottled reflection staring back at me in the computer screen in front of me. She looked tired, frazzled, and confused. None of these words were what Sammi Nakamura was or ever wanted to be. Sammi Nakamura was a woman of decision and action.

My eyes closed; *Breathe in, breathe out, breathe in, breathe out.*

When they opened again, I knew exactly what I wanted, or rather, who I wanted. Indie and I needed to spend some real time together. Not on the phone, not through text or dreams, but in real life. I picked up my phone to make plans with the woman I couldn't seem to be able to live without.

My fingers sped across the keypad, typing,

> hey come to my house this weekend. i have a guest room. i want to spend some time together. really get to know each other again.

I hit send before I could overthink myself out of doing it.

———

Bob was confused, to say the least. Through all of my cleaning and furniture moving, he had become concerned and was lying by the front door, since that was the only place that seemed safe from my whirlwind. His small head darted back and forth, following my movements in and out of the main living area.

The last week had been full of promises, talking candidly about feelings, and lots of other things that did not come naturally to me, but it had worked. Indie would be here any moment. Indie, in my house. Alone, with me. She had told that other chick that they were just friends, and she warned me that this was my chance. No more freak outs or ghosting of any sort.

The buzz from downstairs startled us both, causing Bob to bolt into the bedroom. Even the cat was abandoning me in my time of need.

"Traitor!" I hissed at his receding shadow.

"Hey, George, I'm expecting an Indie Woodley today, if that's what this is about." I revealed to my doorman as I pressed the intercom button.

"Yes, Ms. Nakamura, I'll send the lovely young lady up." George gushed, unabashedly.

"Thanks." I added before changing my house shoes and dashing out of the door towards the elevator.

Would this seem too forward? I wondered to myself, darting back inside my humble abode and shutting the door behind me. Awkwardly walking around my living area, I tried to figure out where to stand. Then I realized that I would be answering the door. She wasn't going to just waltz in and see me standing confidently in a pose by my sofa.

Sweat beads formed above my top lip, I decided to go back out to the elevator and be calm, cool, and collected as I ushered her into my apartment. I took off my house shoes, yet again, replacing them with the nicest loafers I owned. The door closed behind me just as Indie stepped off the elevator into the hallway. My fast-beating heart felt altogether immobilized. There she was, the love of my life, standing just outside my door. She looked down the hall away from me, then toward me, smiling as her eyes found me. The beating heart started again, accelerating past its former rate, edging ever closer to actual cardiac arrest.

Her swaying hips were accentuated perfectly by the cut of her knee length, deep red dress, as were other things a bit further north. She stopped two feet in front of my stunned frame, coat over one arm and a small overnight bag over the other.

"Well, are you going to invite me in?" she teased.

"Wha? Oh, yeah, yes, of course! Come in, madame." I replied, finally getting my charm to turn on. "You look fantastic, by the way." I flattered in her ear, turning to reopen the door that just slammed behind me. My head lightly thumped on the barrier in front of me. Turning to Indie, smiling, I cooed, "But first, let's go say hi to George again. I think he really likes you."

Although she did her best to suppress her giggles, she was openly snickering by the time we meandered the short distance back to the elevator. I just shrugged and led her back into the elevator.

"So, you're a bit nervous and you locked yourself out, huh?" she joshed.

"Me? Nah. I'm cool as a cucumber. This happens all the time, really," I explained.

"Suuuure it does." jested Indie, bumping my shoulder with hers. "It's ok, I'm nervous too. And, by the way," she whispered, leaning in, "I'm allergic to cucumbers."

I glanced at her and her lopsided smile, undoing any calming my heart had done. She was going to be the death of me, literally.

Thai food containers splayed around the normally pristine living room. We were sitting across from each other, me on the sofa, Indie on the floor like the hippie she was at heart.

"I think I'm going to have a food baby," she moaned, patting her stomach. "I'll name it Thai."

I almost spit the last of my pad see ew on the coffee table between us. "Listen, lady, I'm not giving you child support!"

"That's ok, I'll take care of Thai all by myself." she joked, feigning indignation. "I'm used to it anyway."

She oohed over a tiny bit of mango sticky rice that was left in the bottom of a container.

I looked at her, truly seeing the woman she had become for the first time.

"What do you mean by you're used to it?"

"Huh?" she mumbled through a mouth full of food. "Oh, nothing. It's just that Zacariah hasn't exactly been a model father or anything. He's been paying regularly for the past couple of years, but before that, it was sporadic at best."

"What about the girls?" I asked, indignation rising.

Shrugging her shoulders, she responded, "I always made sure they had enough, no matter what," still nibbling on leftover food.

"What about you?"

Her nibbling ceased. She swallowed hard and looked me in the eye, defiantly. "I always made sure the girls had enough, no matter what."

I looked away from her stare. I knew that she had had some rough spots, but, in that moment, I grasped the concept that I had never known existed.

"I have no doubt about that. Someday I hope you tell me more."

"Eh, not much to tell. I did what I had to and did without quite a lot of things for a long time." Her hollow eyes quickly filled with fire. "But you know what? I made it. Me. All by myself."

"Yes, you did." I replied.

"You have quite a few books about Egypt." She flipped through one such book on my coffee table.

"Yeah, I became a little obsessed with their architecture when I was in the Navy. They sent us over there during a deployment to do some desert training. How they ever succeeded in building half the structures they did is beyond me. It's mind boggling. They may have been jerks to the slave population, but you gotta respect their architecture."

"So," she said, shutting the book and coming around the coffee table until she was right in front of me, hands on my knees, "what are we doing this evening?"

My thundering heartbeat only got louder as she smiled and tilted her head inquisitively.

"We could watch that movie we always used to watch back in the day."

Her eyes widened in recognition. "You still have that?!" she squealed, her hands clapping together.

"Of course. Well, no, but as soon as I invited you here last week, I found a copy online and had it shipped." I admitted.

She kissed my cheek and stunned my heart into stillness once more before turning around.

"You get the movie in, Nakamura, I'll clean up dinner."

"Yes ma'am!"

I was sitting on my sofa with Indie Woodley after sixteen years. It felt so comfortable, yet scary. Ours was a relationship of oxymorons. Indie's feet found their way onto my lap, and I rested my hands on top of her shins, lightly rubbing them. I glanced at her grin as she was all cozied up at the other end of the sofa with my fuzzy blanket. Starting to gently rub her feet elicited a small moan.

I remembered those moans all too well. Memories of some very intimate times came flooding back to me.

Indie was, by far, the best lover I'd ever had. We may have both been very inexperienced, but we worked well together. I could only imagine how it would be now that we were both older and wiser. The pulsation in my groin felt like my heart had earlier. With her being so near, it was hard to keep my body in check. I was affected by her, whether I liked it or not, and there was nothing I could do about it. Betrayed by my own body.

"Okay, this side is done, time to turn me over." Indie declared as she flipped over, putting her head in my lap and her feet at the opposite end of the sofa.

My entire body was throbbing at this point. Her head was in my crotch, for heaven's sake. Engrossed in the movie, she was oblivious to my internal plight. My hands searched for a place to rest, awkwardly flailing about. I finally rested one on the side of her ribs, dangerously close to the breasts I remembered so well. The other found its way to her scalp, caressing and extracting yet another moan. I bit my lip and tried to concentrate on the movie. After what seemed like an hour, but in earnest was closer to five minutes, I decided to just go for it. I brought my thumb to her jawline, going up and down the bone and onto her sensitive neck. Subsequently, I brought it towards her lips, tracing them as they parted and kissed the pad of my roving thumb. My hand found its way down her neck to her collarbone. She shifted to give me a little more access, and I smirked. Her skin felt like butter beneath my fingertips. I rested my hand there for a while before inching the fingers just below the neckline of her shirt, where they stayed for the remainder of the movie.

"Well," she declared, breaking the silence, "that was just how I remembered it. Seeing bits and pieces of the movie while being felt up by Sam Nakamura."

I couldn't hold back my laugh. "You call that being felt up? Good god woman, how long has it been for you?"

"Long enough, but you were feeling me, that's for sure," she teased. "I don't think you got to where you wanted to go."

Raising my eyebrows, I replied with, "Oh really?"

"Yep. Guess you're just not as brave as you used to be."

"How dare you!" I jested. "I am quite brave. If you recall, Madame, I am the one who invited you here. I am the one who started rubbing your body in various places. I am the one who used to eat your terrible food, without care for my own health and safety!"

Her arm punches were more powerful than I recalled. "I'm not saying that's not a true statement, but it's not very nice! And I cook way better now," she rebutted, on her hands and knees, inches away from my shocked face. Her smile had a bit of a wicked quality. Brushing my lips with hers drew a moan out of me. "Still got it." she breathed into my ear.

"Yes, you do." I swooned, leaning in to fully envelop her.

Our lips touched gingerly, then pressed together with more urgency. Grabbing her at the waist, I flipped her onto my lap. Her hands reached up to pull my head down closer to her eager mouth. My thumb felt the hardness of her nipple through her shirt as I brushed over it, causing her to whimper beneath me.

When we came up for air, I remarked, "Your kisses taste exactly the way I remember."

"Yeah, yours do too. I wonder if other things still taste the same."

"Indie!" I chastised light-heartedly. "What are you implying?"

"Oh, I think you know," she said before diving back into our make-out session.

Just as things started to get very interesting, Indie's phone rang. She immediately pulled away.

"I have to get that. Everyone but the girls are on silent."

I released my hold on her and watched her enter mom mode. It was a side of her I had never seen and couldn't really imagine. She was a mother. She was responsible for other human beings. Her life was not entirely her own. I had Bob, but that was extremely different. I stared at this woman who held my heart and realized I had to be cautious. She was more than just her. I had to be ready for a family if I was going to continue down this road. We had to tread carefully. It wasn't just about us anymore.

Was I really ready to take this on?

CHAPTER 17

Indie

SITTING UP IN BED, I wondered where the hell I was. As I looked around at the modern design around me, the memories of last night came flooding back. I plopped right back down onto the bed. Sam and I had made out. Then she just backed off after that call from Mari and I went to bed alone, across the hall from the woman who said she wanted to be with me. Was she pissed that my child called me? Was she turning around and running the other way just like before?

I had believed her. I had believed she wanted to try to have a future together so much that I cleared my insanely busy schedule and abandoned my children for the weekend to come here and see if we were still compatible. I laid there for a few more minutes, ruminating. What the hell was I supposed to do now? This was not ghosting over text or phone; this was pushing me away while I was staying in her goddamn guest bedroom.

I bolted upright and flung my feet over the side of the bed. I knew right then and there; I had to leave. I picked up my phone; five in the morning. Do I just sneak out now, or wait? I started to quietly pack my things. I was grateful I traveled lightly. If I left now, I would be just as bad as her. *No*, I thought to myself, *I'm better than that.*

My head whipped toward the door, where whispered swearing was drifting through from the hall. Sam was awake. I could say my curt goodbye and leave. As I opened the door, I saw coffee grounds spilling out of the kitchen into the hallway and couldn't help but laugh. Sam's head poked around the corner.

"Oh, sorry! Did I wake you?" she inquired.

"No, I've been awake for about half an hour." I responded matter-of-factly.

"Oh good! I was trying to be so quiet and then I stubbed my toe and dropped the coffee grounds." she explained, gesturing to the mess on the floor. "Anyway, you want some coffee? I do have more than what is currently on the floor before you."

Her smile was so wide, and she seemed sincerely happy to see me. I eyed her up for a moment, but her look never wavered.

"Thanks, but, actually, I don't drink coffee. I'll take tea if you have any."

"Pfft, if I have any? I am Japanese, of course I have tea!" she gushed, grabbing my hand and pulling me past the sea of black on the floor.

Heat starting building in my body as soon as she touched me. I tried to keep it at bay, but I didn't seem to have control over myself anymore, especially in her presence. She whipped open a cabinet door to reveal a veritable tea store. My mouth dropped open as I perused the vast selection before me. The spiced chai leapt out at me and I inhaled its aroma.

Looking over my shoulder, Sam commented in a bad, fake British accent, "Excellent choice, madame. Hints of vanilla in that one. Might I recommend just a bit of honey and a splash of milk?"

Placing her hands on my hips, she gave me a quick peck on the side of my neck before turning around to grab a mug for me.

Noticing my facial expression upon handing me a beautiful, hand-made vessel, she asked, "Everything alright?" and cocked her head to the left.

"Yeah, yeah, just tired." I lied. "I'm not exactly used to being up at this hour."

Her resounding laugh was pure sunshine to this dark morning. I hadn't heard that laugh in so long. I melted just a little bit, but then pulled myself together. I could not let my guard down yet.

"Yeah, I'm always up at this time. Sometimes I forget this is, in fact, early."

Mugs in hand of our respectively chosen drinks, mine chai, hers green tea, we adjourned to the living room, as we had the night before. She sat right next to me, facing my direction, arm over the back of the sofa.

"Did you sleep well?" she asked.

"Yes, thank you." I answered, after swallowing my first sip of tea. "Mmmm, you were right, this is quite a tasty combination," I reveled.

She smiled so broadly it was once again like sunshine melting my resolve. I had to tell her I was leaving now, or I may lose the resolve to do so.

"I think I'm going to head out in a little while here."

Her face fell. She seemed to be genuinely disappointed.

"Oh, ok. Why?"

"Well, I'm not sure if leaving the girls this weekend was such a good idea." I lied, once again.

"I see. Well, they do come first. Let me make you breakfast first," she offered, disappointment gone.

She quickly rose from her seat next to me and bounded into the kitchen. I guessed she was happy to see me go after all. I stood and went back into the guest room to get dressed and pack up what remained of my belongings. With each thing I shoved into my bag, my anger deepened. Why would she invite me here, have me drive all of that way, just to push me away? I had things to do. I did not have time to play games. This was why I had remained single for so long. It was such a complete waste of my time to be dealing with any sort of dating.

I exited the guest room and placed my bag by the front door. I would be polite, eat my breakfast, and head out, never to return.

Sam came out of the kitchen carrying a breakfast burrito wrapped in foil.

"I didn't want to keep you from your children, so I made it to-go." She beamed as if she had done me a favor by kicking me out even earlier.

"Gee, thanks." I scoffed.

Her quizzical look returned, as did the left-sided head tilt. "You sure you're okay?"

I waved off her concern. "Yeah, just peachy. Thanks for the tea and the burrito." I said, turning to get my bag.

Sam gently grabbed my arms and came in for a kiss. I was so surprised I almost slapped her, but instead just backed up.

"Ok, what is wrong? You're acting weird," she accused.

"I'm acting weird?!?! You are the one who just randomly pushes me away whenever you feel like it. I'm not here to play games, Satomi. I am a businesswoman and a mother. I have responsibilities and shit to do!" I fumed, voice squeaking with choked back tears.

"Hey, hey," she cooed, taking my chin in her hand and lifting my face up to hers, "I know you are. I know you do. I'm trying to be sensitive to that."

"What?" The tears spilled over the boundaries of my eyes.

"Last night, when your daughter called, I realized it's not just you and me. You are a mother. I have to be careful and respectful of that. You are not just a woman; you are a family. I have to be ready for a family. I have to be sure of every move I make. If we rush, if we're not right for each other, I could hurt not only you, but two innocent children," she said softly, wiping the tears from my cheeks.

I couldn't believe what I was hearing. She cared. That's why she backed off physically last night. I threw my arms around her neck and pressed my lips to hers. She wrapped her arms around my torso and pulled me in. I intertwined my fingers in her hair and softly bit her lower lip. Her verbal response was followed by her hands going down my back, finding the bottom of my shirt. In one swift movement, my former covering was lying on the floor next to us. I hadn't bothered to put on a bra earlier and her shocked, but pleased expression made me giggle.

"What a lovely surprise," she stated before lowering her head to flick one of my taut peaks with her tongue.

I grasped the sides of her face and pulled her back up to my lips, kissing her deeply before returning the favor of disrobing her top half. Her perky breasts were a bit fuller than I remembered, but still similar enough to recognize them. I greeted them hungrily as one of my hands found its way to her thighs. They eagerly parted, allowing me to feel the wetness through her pajama pants. She moaned as I slowly pulled what was left of her clothing down to the floor and brought my attention to her stomach, kissing slowly and softly. I looked up, seeing Sam in all of her glory. My god, she was the sexiest woman I had ever seen.

I hitched her leg up onto my shoulder and continued my slow onslaught of kissing, extending from her knee to the fold where her leg met the rest of her body. Her hands were bracing herself against the wall I was leaning against, mid-section undulating, begging me to go further. I was all too happy to oblige. I thrust my tongue in-between her lips, touching the swollen pleasure peak buried there. Sam let out an audible gasp. She looked down, placing one hand aside my upturned face.

"You do taste exactly the same," I purred before diving back in with a new sense of urgency. I wrapped my arms around her hips, palms cupping her buttocks, pulling her closer. She moved her hand to the back of my head while the other held onto the door frame to keep us both from being knocked over. I wanted nothing more, in that moment, than to hear her cry out in ecstasy. My tongue never paused in its assault on her clitoris. Within minutes, I felt the sinewy muscles of her inner thigh tense. The involuntary convulsions of her body as she cried out in rapture reminded me of many years ago, when we had to be quiet, for fear of being found out. This, however, was now, and I didn't want her to be quiet. I ground the tip of my tongue against her pleasure point faster and harder for just a few more seconds, bringing her up to and over the edge of her satisfaction.

She released her grip on my head as I started peppering her gorgeous thighs with kisses. I slowly rose up from my knees and paid homage to her breasts one more time. I smiled broadly and licked my lips which elicited yet another moan from the spectacular creature in front of me.

"Your turn," breathed Sam, pinning me against the wall and biting my neck.

Blood rushed away from my head, leaving me dizzy, but wanting more. Her onslaught of affection moved further south to my stretch-marked breasts. The playful, sweet Sam was gone. This version was hungry and would not stop until she got exactly what she wanted.

"I'm going to make you scream my name," she whispered in my ear before returning to the nape of my neck.

Bringing her hand down my side and under the waistband of my linen pants, she found the lack of any undergarments appealing and snickered at her unencumbered access. Her hand cupped me, palm pressing into my clit, making slow, small circles. Unable to hold back my groans of pleasure, I let loose, which emboldened Sam to go harder.

My breathing became shallower. As I felt the pressure start to build, Sam stopped. A small whimper escaped my lips.

"Good girl. Just allow me to do my work," she ordered, slipping a finger into my slit. "I will make sure you get everything you want, and then some."

My hips began to writhe under her expert work and my moans of delight grew louder and louder. I heard myself whispering her name and telling her not to stop, but didn't recall intending to do so. I was no longer in control, she was.

I arched my back, the moans turning into screams, and felt a hand cover my mouth while a tongue flicked, once again, at my nipple. A wave of gratification swept over me, consuming all I was. I almost collapsed right then and there.

Sam's finger brushed against my pulsating summit, causing me to shudder once more. Her lips came back to mine and we kissed tenderly. Pressing her full body against mine, she wrapped her arms around me and smiled.

"Well, this has been a very interesting morning. Twenty minutes ago, I thought you didn't want to be here anymore, and, now, I'm naked by my front door. You are very full of surprises, milady."

"Haha, yes, that's a bit of a story." I said, receiving raised eyebrows in return.

"You can tell it to me in my bed. Which is where I plan on staying the rest of the day." she purred, removing my now soaked pants and leading me to her bedroom.

By evening we were both spent. The entire day had been bouts of sex, with long talks in between. We had caught up on a decade and a half of news, not once getting dressed.

"You do realize this weekend changes everything, right?" Sam offered, propping herself up on one elbow, facing me.

"What?"

"I will never again be able to live without you. I lost you once and I know, without a doubt, I cannot go through that again."

I kissed her pouty lips, confessing, "Me either. So, what's with all of the scissors?"

She looked at the glassed-in display on the far wall of her bedroom and laughed. Her naked form headed towards it.

"This one, you may remember, is an antique pair of scissors that was a family heirloom," she stated, pointing to an intricately carved silver pair in the middle. "All the rest are a collection I have procured over the years. It started with that one pair, then became kind of a lesbian joke, if you get my drift, and snowballed. Soon people were getting me cool antique scissors left and right. Then I even got into it, and here we are, seventy-two pairs later, with this display. Each of them has a story."

"Ooo, very cool. Do I get to hear any of them?"

"Well, you know the one in the middle already. How about this, for each round of sex in this bed, I give you one story?"

"Are you trying to bribe me into having sex with you?" My feigned indignance was marred by the stifled laugh that came out with it.

"Gotta keep you coming back." Sam winked as she slid back under the covers, hand roaming. Interrupted by the doorbell, she jumped out of bed and threw on her robe. "More Thai food!"

"What?" I asked, getting out of bed trying to find something suitable to throw on in her closet.

I found a kimono way in the back and put it on.

"When did you order Thai food?" I inquired, walking out into the living room.

Sam's face dropped when she saw me, losing all color and life.

"What's wrong?" I asked, rushing over to her.

"Where did you get that?" she questioned, motioning to the kimono.

"Sorry, I found it in the back of your closet. Is it an antique or a family heirloom or something?"

"No. It is—was Ali's. I got it for her in Japan. I didn't even realize it was still here."

"Oh god, Sam, I'm sorry. I didn't know, I'm sorry." I apologized, shuffling out of the offending robe and handing it to her.

She took it without a word. I watched as she walked into the kitchen and threw it into the trash can. She came out, smiling meekly.

"No worries. That's from a whole different life. The one before you came back around. It doesn't even matter now."

Her eyes traveled up and down my nakedness.

"I like you better with no robe anyway."

Walking over to me, she untied her robe and beckoned me forward. Tying both of us up in its fuzzy warmth, we held each other, content just to be together.

"Umm, Sam, the doorbell?"

"Oh, right!"

The robed bandit fled the kitchen, once again leaving me buck naked without a robe.

Sammi

THE MONTH FOLLOWING our second first time together was a blur of lovey-dovey texts, phone calls, and rendezvous. I was in love, completely out of my element, and couldn't get Indie off my mind. Opening a new browser on my computer, I typed "bohemian engagement rings" into the search bar. Indie would never be happy with some run-of-the-mill ring.

She had just left my apartment that morning, but the rest of this week was going to be hell. Between the business stuff and her best friend's wedding, I knew I would barely get to talk with her.

"This is still weird."

Startled at the unknown speaker, I jerked my head up, exiting the tab I had just opened.

"Cass, geez! You scared the shit out of me. What the hell are you doing here just staring at me, ya creeper?"

"You look like Sammi Nakamura, you even swear like her, but I'm just not convinced."

"Oh my god, girl, let it go. I'm in love, big deal. You're acting like I've had some sort of lobotomy."

"A lobotomy! Maybe that's it!" exclaimed Cass, ducking to

avoid the balled-up paper I just threw in her direction. "A month ago, you took a long weekend and came back all different and stuff. You had a lobotomy! It all makes sense, really."

"Shut it, crazy lady," I scolded the giggling lunatic standing at the entrance to my cubicle. "So, what's going on, you know, work wise. We are supposed to be working, just fyi."

"Oh riiiight, work. Yeah. Well," she replied, her mocking tone disappearing, "we've got the Huntingdon Project assessment coming up, that meeting with the Delaney group, and the lobby furniture is delayed. Again."

I threw my arms up. "What? Why? HOW? I could have driven to Milwaukee and picked them up myself, one at a time, by now. This is ludicrous."

"Yeah, it really is, at this point. So, ummm, what was that I saw on your computer screen a minute ago?" prodded Cass.

My piss-poor job of hiding my shock and discomfort made for a hilarious exit for Cass. Yet another paper ball sailed her way, knocking her on the back of her head.

Glancing around, nervously, I reopened the tab.

Just a few days ago I was looking at rings, and then I was focusing intently on three little words that may be the end of everything I know. *Can. We. Talk.*

The text had chimed in just moments after I left work. As soon as I entered my apartment, Bob could sense my stress and did his are-you-ok head bumping thing, over and over. I realized I could not wait forever to answer, and I was really only prolonging my own suffering. I pressed the call symbol next to the name "First" in my phone.

One ring

Two rings

"Hello?"

"Hi, babe. Sorry it took me so long. I was literally just walking out of work when you text me."

"Oh, yeah, it's okay. So, do you have a few minutes?" wondered Indie.

"Yeah, for you, always."

"Well, I know you're busy and there's a lot on your plate," Indie hesitated, "and I hate to even bring this up now, but I need to move forward and make plans."

My heart made its way into my throat as I awaited her next sentence.

"Will you be my date for Helene and Lukas's wedding?"

An audible sigh of relief escaped me, and I couldn't help but laugh.

"Yes, of course. Geez, Indie, you sure know how to scare a girl."

"What? Scare you?"

"Yeah. 'Can we talk' is code for let's break up."

"What?! Oh, god, no! I'm sorry I made you think that! I just know how much you hate weddings and things of that nature, so I thought it would be a big deal."

"Ahh, yes, but I'd go anywhere with you. I'm kind of in love with you."

"You are?"

"Yes, indubitably."

"Wow, you've never told me you love me."

"That is a lie, madame, I told you many years ago," I cooed. Her giggling brought up warm, fuzzy feelings I was still not accustomed to.

"Ok, you're not wrong, but I meant now... the second time around. But I love you too."

"Music to my ears, Ms. Woodley, music to my ears."

"So, here's another kicker: it's on your birthday."

"That's fine. There's no one I'd rather spend my birthday with than you and a hundred strangers."

"Haha, very funny. One more thing, though."

Indie paused and took a deep breath.

"My daughters will be there. I've told them about you."

"Oh, cool. I'd love to meet them."

"Ok, it's just...well, I've never...that is, they've never. Ugh. I've never introduced them to anyone before. This is all new for all of us. They're not nervous, you don't seem nervous, but I'm a wreck!" she blurted.

"Babe, it'll be okay. I'm a little nervous, but it has to happen someday," I assured her. "And, if they're anything like their mother, I'm sure we'll get along fine."

"Oh, I'm so glad you said yes! It'll be great for you and the girls to meet each other. Plus, I'm excited, and a little scared, for you to meet my friends. They are bugging the crap out of me."

"I know that feeling!"

"Okay, babe, gotta run, but I'll talk to you later?"

"Yes, indeed, milady."

Sauntering past Bob into my closet, I perused my selection of tailored suits. I gravitated toward the lighter gray one for wedding attire, but perhaps Indie would like the blue better. I grabbed my phone and texted her pictures, asking for her opinion. Continuing towards the back of the closet, I started thinking about shirt colors. Cream or light yellow would look great with the blue.

"What do you think, Bob?" I quizzed the feline bathing himself at my feet. He returned my vocal expression with some of his own. "I completely agree; the cream with the navy and white polka-dot pocket square."

My phone chirped and Bob and I both rushed towards it.

"Well, good sir, never mind, Indie says wear the gray to go better with her rose-colored dress. I do, however, appreciate your input." I declared to my furry confidant, rubbing his head for good measure.

My phone chirped again, but instead of seeing "First" pop up on my screen as I expected, I saw a notification in a messaging app from Mark.

> **Hey, girl! Haven't talked to you in about a week, but.... big things happening here. **hint-hint** I'll message you later to see how things are going in love-land. lol**

I replied with a shocked emoji face and focused on planning the outfit that would make Indie fall helplessly at my feet. I could not, would not, think about Dubai or what things might be happening there that could affect my life, and the lives of a few other people, so greatly. Part of me was grasping at this chance for promotion, like I had been for years, but, now, there was another part of me, a long-dormant part of me that had come alive. That part had been asleep for a long time, and she wanted a family. With Indie.

Mark stayed true to his word, and I got him all caught up with the happenings in the U.S. He had an official offer for the soon-to-be-open position here in Boston, which meant the offer would soon be sent out to whomever they chose to take his position in Dubai. He kept hinting it would be me. Evidently, those above us had asked him about his thoughts on me and my abilities. Singing my praises, he catapulted me to the top of their short list. While I was grateful, I was also torn. This would be the biggest decision of my life so far. I would be forced to choose between my career and my love. Although Mark had been the one to point out the repercussions my lifestyle may have in an Islamic nation, he seemed oblivious to that fact when it came to conversations about Indie.

Behind his confident, almost macho, exterior, Mark was a hopeless romantic at heart. He seemed to only see the beauty behind the story, not the ugly reality that may be facing me and my love in the very near future. Hanging on every word I said about me and Indie, he seemed more invested in our relationship than either of us did. I didn't have the heart to bring up our impending doom, so I kept it all to myself. I had downplayed the possibility of me actually getting the promotion so much to Indie that she never even mentioned it.

Opening the large window off of my kitchen, I stepped out onto my tiny balcony, inhaling deeply. A small head rubbing on my leg was on cloud nine. Sitting out here was something we didn't get to do very often any more. Car honks cut through the din of the city. Finding this apartment had been luck. If it weren't for Mrs. Stanton, I would never have gotten to live here. It was her sublet, and it was pretty cheap, for midtown. She and Mark, and who knows who else, had all pushed for me to get this promotion. My parents expected constant perfection and upward movement, along with pay raises. So many people helped me get here. Would I be letting them all down if I refused the offer?

The lock of the next-door window made a sound. I was getting company. Closing my eyes, I waited.

"Hey Sammi! Sammi? Are you, are you sleeping? Hello? Henry, grab me that pointer stick," my young neighbor shouted into her window.

The moment I felt a poke at my arm, I yelled out and grabbed the stick reaching through the railing. The startled screams of two young kids brought out my evil laugh.

"This stick is mine!" I teased. "Surrender and I'll have mercy on ye!"

"Nevaaaaa!" Henry shouted as he shot a fake cannon ball my way.

"Are you guys watering the plants?" Mrs. Simons inquired from inside.

"Yes, mom." Jenny returned.

We all snickered and kept the pirate battle going in hushed tones while the children completed their chore. My ship sank, the stick was returned to its rightful owner, and the kids went back inside.

Resting my chin on the railing, I pondered my life. It had always gone in the same direction. I had missed parties, lost partners, ignored my penchant for travel, all to get ahead in this crazy, cutthroat world of high end, commercial architecture. None of it even felt like a sacrifice, before now. I couldn't just give up on everything I worked for, letting down everyone who helped me along the way, just for a chance at love. Could I? What would people think? How would I make money? Where would I go?

Nudging my thigh, Bob brought me out of my spiraling thought pattern. Purring, without a care in the world, this feisty feline calmed me. Bob was ushered inside and the window to the outside world was closed. Sleep was nowhere in the near future for me, so I whipped out my computer and did the only thing I knew to do: work.

Glancing at the clock, I panicked. I had to get up in a matter of hours and pretend to be a fully functioning adult. Shit! I ran to the bedroom, brushed my teeth, and took off my pants. This shirt would be my pajamas for the next few hours. I attempted to check my alarm, and maybe allow for another fifteen minutes of sleep in the morning, but my phone was nowhere to be found. I searched the living room, then the kitchen, my pants, and the bathroom. All of the action had awoken Bob, and he wanted to go back out on the balcony.

"The balcony!" I shouted a little too loudly, startling my furry companion.

I opened the window to the freezing air and saw a few flurries landing on my phone's screen. I snatched it up. Freezing my palms and fingers in the process, I illuminated the screen. Two missed calls and three texts, all from Ali. The sudden overwhelming urge to throw the phone back out the window passed. *Breathe in, breathe out, breathe in, breathe out...*

Clicking on her name, I saw the last message:

I just miss you so much, baby.

Rolling my eyes, I headed for the bedroom. I did not have time for this shit. My phone vibrated in my hand.

"What?" I growled.

"Wow, that'ss kinna rude, Sam. I know yer mother taught you better," my ex-girlfriend slurred into the phone.

"Are you fucking drunk?" I accused. "Are you actually calling me at three a.m. drunk? What are you, seventeen?"

"No, oh baby, I just miss oo. I mish you so much."

"Well, I sure as hell don't miss you."

"Awww, sure ya do. I got a new job lass year—or maybe it was two yearses ago. I moved, ya know. Griff died," she lamented.

My heart softened just a bit.

"He did?"

"Yeah, yesserday."

Sighing and rubbing my temples, I closed my eyes and steeled my resolve.

"Look, Al, I know he was a great pet, and you loved him very much, and I'm sorry he died, but you and I haven't spoken in years. You don't miss me, you're just sad. Go to sleep."

"But I do misss you." she sobbed into the phone.

"Goodnight, Ali."

I hit the small red button on my screen and fell onto my bed. Bob hopped onto my stomach and meowed.

"Hey there. Sorry to tell you this, but your old buddy died." He looked down, like he understood, and then started to lick my hand. I smiled down at him.

"Normally, I find this gross, but you're grieving, so I'll allow it. Now get off, I've *got* to get to bed."

What felt like two seconds after closing my eyes, my alarm blared its annoying sound. I slunk out of bed, trudging towards the bathroom. The half-dead looking person in the mirror brushed her teeth, made herself presentable, and moved on to a sad little bowl of oatmeal in the kitchen. The chime of my phone forced my eyes open.

**Hey, thinking about you. Here's hoping
your day doesn't suck, friend!**

I smirked. If she only knew. I couldn't resist baiting her a little.

**guess who called me drunk
off of her ass last night.**

**No. No. FOR REAL! OMG, you better
damn well have time for a quick phone
call on your way into work. DO NOT
leave me hanging on this!**

Laughing brought some life into my sluggish body. Swiping the answer button up, I started spinning my tale to Jenn.

CHAPTER 19

Indie

"INDIE? INDIE WOODLEY?" a female voice behind me called out.

Turning slowly, I saw a woman who looked familiar waving. I waved back and smiled, still not quite certain of her origins in my life. Taking my friendly wave as an invitation, she was soon hugging me.

"Oh my gosh, it's been forever!"

"It sure has," I replied, still unsure of exactly how long.

"The last time I saw you, you and that Sammi girl were making out after graduation." she teased, nudging me and winking.

Recognition flooded my brain: Angela Tanner, cheerleader at Rickmon High School.

"Hey now, Angela, don't be spreading rumors," I responded, only half joking.

"Yeah, right. I saw it with my own eyes. You two were hot and heavy, I remember that. I know at some point you guys broke up. You married a guy, and she ended up shacking up with that Jenn, umm, what's her name. You know, that girl you used to hang out with all the time."

"Murphy?"

"Yes! Jenn Murphy, that's her. Anyway, how have you been?"

"Uh, I'm good," I started, taken aback by the new information which was thrown my way. Shaking it off, I continued on, "I have twin daughters..."

She cut me off with ease and skill. Yep, this was definitely Angela Tanner.

"Twins! Oh wow, that's got to be a handful for you. I have four now. Natasha is almost fourteen, she's the oldest..." she rattled on for what seemed like a small eternity, but I wasn't too upset, because I needed time to ponder. Sam and Jenn? Why would she not tell me about this? Jenn was my best friend for all of high school. When Sam and I broke up, Jenn kind of just went with her, leaving me behind. I always thought it was because I married Zacariah, but perhaps there was more to it. My mind was spinning, but I kept up the nods and occasional agreeable sounds to look interested in Angela's son's braces or whatever she was babbling about now.

"Woodley?" a man called out.

I whipped around, catching his eye, "Yes, that's me."

I turned back to Angela and feigned sadness. "I gotta go, but it was great to bump into you."

Twirling back around towards the florist, I mouthed 'thank you' to him and his smile widened.

"Just drive your car around back and we'll load up all of the bouquets and boutonnieres. They need to be refrigerated right away, when you get to the venue or wherever you're taking them."

Nodding furiously, I replied, "Yes, sir, absolutely. You have my word. Thank you...for everything."

He chuckled knowingly and went back to work.

Driving as if I had a newborn baby just rolling around in the trunk, I made my way back to Helene's mother's house, where final preparations were in full swing. I couldn't get what Angela Tanner had said out of my mind. Sam talked about Jenn a lot. I know they still talked, and they had visited each other over the years. I hadn't seen or heard from Jenn since just after graduation. My mind kept going back to the way Jenn abandoned me when I married Zacariah. We had been so close the entirety of our high school years, and then nothing.

Did Sam break up with me and then sleep with my best friend? Were she and Sam keeping this from me? Sam had called Jenn her best friend. That hurt a bit, but I decided to be mature about it. People grow and change; that's just part of life. I had lost touch with many friends over the years, but if this was the real reason, how could I trust either of them now?

I had to know. Things had been kept from me my entire life. People always said it was 'for my own good', but it was more for their comfort than my good. Confusion quickly gave way to anger. I would not be misled. I would not allow the wool to be pulled over my eyes. I would find out the truth. I was a grown ass woman, and I was tired of being handled by others because they thought I couldn't handle things myself.

I pulled into the driveway, honking twice. Lukas, Melonie, and Ethan filed out the front door while Sara opened the garage bay door. The massive stainless steel, double door fridge lining almost one entire side of the garage was impressive. Helene had told me her mom used to own a catering business and had extra fridge space, but this was not at all what I was expecting.

Sara beamed at her children, applauding their efforts and care with the floral arrangements. Coming around the side of the car, she confided, "I don't think I'll be able to live without seeing them on a regular basis. A part of me will die." Her smile never wavered.

I hugged her from the side, searching for any configuration of words that could possibly help in this moment. I was so lost in my own anger and grief I couldn't feel empathy for my friend. At least no one was trying to take my children away from me.

"I wasn't even sure they were coming this weekend."

She dropped the happy facade, facing me directly.

"Oh, I had to fight. I may have even fought a little dirty. And I think I figured out why Lisaida is doing all of this now, almost two years after we divorced," she divulged, glancing around and then leaning in closely. "There's a girlfriend."

Jerking back as if I'd been stung by something, I raised one eyebrow and cocked my head to the side.

"Oh hell no." I stated a little too loudly. Reining in my ire, I continued on, "Please, PLEASE tell me Lisaida is not putting the needs and wants of her new girlfriend over what is best for her children."

Sara just nodded in return. My anger over the whole Sam/Jenn situation had found fuel. I kicked the side of my tire as Sara was removing another box of floral cargo from the hatchback of my Subaru. She side eyed me and raised her brows.

"Here sweetie," she cooed as she handed the box to Ethan. She smiled at her retreating son's form, then turned towards me, "What the hell was that?"

"I'm just angry. I'm so fucking angry. People are selfish assholes. I'm so done with the whole goddamned world!" I replied whispering and screaming all at the same time.

"Whoa, hey," she soothed, her kindness driving the tears in my eyes over the edge. "What? Oh my god, what is going on? I've never seen you so... out of control."

My spilled tears escalated to full-on sobbing as Sara hugged my shaking form.

"What on Earth happened at the florist, hun?"

"I think Sam is keeping something from me. Like the fact that she slept with my old best friend in high school after we broke up."

"Oh, Indie, I'm sorry."

I pushed back slightly from her as I chattered on.

"And Lisaida is being a selfish ass! She has no right to put her own needs above Melonie and Ethan's! Kids are human beings, ya know." Sara was rapidly nodding along to my rant. "We should be able to decide what's best for us at some point. And now, I'm an adult. Why would Sam keep this kind of thing from me? I'm tired of people deciding they know best. I matter. Melonie and Ethan matter! YOU MATTER!" I declared before collapsing into a heap on the ground.

Sighing, Sara plopped herself next to me and slung an arm around my heaving shoulders.

"So *that's* what this is about. Oh, sweetie, when are you going to face this?"

"No," I insisted, "that's not what this is about. This is about people manipulating other people. This is about telling the fucking truth." I looked directly at my friend. "Why do people lie so damn much?"

As Sara pulled me into her shoulder, she rested her head on mine.

"I just don't know."

Lukas came around the back of the car, whistling. The abrupt ceasing of the tune let me know he had seen us. Feeling Sara move slightly, I was sure she had shooed him away. We sat on the cold, hard ground for a while, both letting the tears fall. I felt the arm around me tighten for a moment, giving me a reassuring hug.

"Your dad wanted you to know. He wouldn't have said anything otherwise." Sara waited for a response, sighing when she received none. "We are all here for you, no matter what you decide or find out. I hope you know you are most definitely not alone. I need you to promise me you will at least consider getting a test or something. I think this is affecting you more than you realize."

She pulled my tear-stained face up and I nodded.

"Good, now let's get our faces cleaned up. We are a hot mess, my ass is freezing, you still need to meet the newest Amie lover, and Bridezilla may pop out here at any moment."

The chuckle we shared felt good.

"So, there's yet another one? What's this one's name?"

"Veronica? Maybe? I don't know. She is helping, so that's a plus, I suppose."

I stopped her before she rose to her feet.

"Thank you. You are an amazing friend and mom. I am here for you no matter what. I may have some ties to the mafia if you should need anyone taken out."

Her mellifluous laughter filled the air as we got up and walked inside.

"Okay, I was trying not to pry, and figured you'd tell us when you wanted to, but I'm freaking out a bit and need a distraction." announced Helene. "Why were you two crying on the ground last night?" she asked Sara and I.

Sara and I looked at each other and said in unison, "Lukas."

"Yes, Lukas. He told me last night after we got back from my mother's. Now spill." ordered the bride, crossing her lace covered arms.

Amie and Gabriel looked to both Sara and me, confused, but eager. Sara stood, looking at me for some sort of direction, but there was no facial expression I could give that would convey my feelings at the time, so I simply shrugged.

"Ok, so, you all already know Lisaida is being a... well, she's being Lisaida. I made a comment to Indie about thinking that the reason for her sudden behavior regarding our children was being driven by a new girlfriend."

The collective gasp from the shocked crew gave Sara one more chance to seek my comfort level with her story, but I still had nothing to give.

"This upset Indie, a lot. She started ranting a bit about people deciding what's best for other people, especially children, when it is usually what's best for the person deciding." Sara paused, allowing me to chime in.

"I think Sam is keeping something from me. Something happened right after the first time we were together."

Glancing at the faces of my audience, I gathered they would not let that go, so I continued on, after rolling my eyes.

"I heard from someone that went to high school with us Sam and my high school best friend got together after Sam broke up with me."

"Oh, no, no, no, gurl. Heeeell to the no. Got with your bestie?" Gabriel exclaimed, with hand motions to match his excitement.

Murmurs agreeing with him swept around the room.

"Wait, you heard this from someone besides Sam?" Helene inquired.

"Yes. I ran into a busy body from high school at the florist yesterday. She didn't know we were back together; we were just talking about old times." I informed my crew.

"Since that had just happened, I was kind of on edge when Sara shared her news. I just kind of lost it. The kids don't deserve this," my voice trailed off.

Helene and Sara exchanged glances, and Gabriel chimed in. "What the hell was that?" he inquired, pointing back and forth between Helene and Sara.

Looking down at the floor, Sara left Helene on her own. She sighed and replied, "Indie's dad kinda sorta dropped a truth bomb on her on his death bed."

"Helene!" I burst out.

"What? I didn't say what it was!" Helene replied. "Besides, you can't yell at me today, I'm the bride."

"I think you should let it out, Indie. We all love you and are here to support you." Amie chimed in.

"Oh really?" I shrieked, tears streaming down my face.

Feeling arms surrounding my body in all directions, I relaxed and felt the security of my little gang. A few minutes of that much lovey-dovey was about all a girl could take. I straightened up and wiped away the tears, everyone else joining in.

"You don't have to tell us. I didn't mean to upset you. I just meant you *can* tell us, and we might be able to help, or at least make it less of a burden," Amie whispered.

Sniffling, I croaked out, "It's okay. I know. Honestly, maybe you all should know. I hate having secrets. Like I was ranting about yesterday, the truth should be shared. I just can't do it right now." I looked around at the confused faces of my friends and chuckled. "I'm gonna go get my makeup cleaned up." Turning to Helene, then Sara, I said, "You guys tell them. Then I want to not hear anything about it for the rest of the day. After all," I continued, walking out of the room, "we're celebrating today."

Closing the door behind me, I let out a sigh and started down the hallway. My breath caught in my throat. There she was, in a fitted gray suit and light pink button up. The beating in my chest threatened to overpower me. Her smile fell away as she saw my tear-stained face.

Rushing over to me, Sam pressed me for information. "Babe, oh my god, what's wrong. Is everything okay?"

Holding back the flood of emotion was not going to happen with her standing there in front of me, so I let it all flow.

When I finally came up for air, I managed to blubber, "It's just been an emotional twenty-four hours."

"Oh, Indie, I'm sorry. Is there anything I can do? Is it Helene?"

she queried. Her face grew stern, "Is it the girls? Are they okay?"

I waved off her words, "Yes, they're fine. Helene is fine."

I stared at the concern filling her eyes. If I was going to make a life with this woman, I had to trust her. I had to be willing to ask the hard questions.

Inhaling deeply, I asked, "Did you and Jenn ever hook up after high school?"

Shock crossed her face as her eyes closed.

CHAPTER 20

Sammi

COULDN'T BELIEVE what I was hearing. Why in the world was the woman I love standing before me, at her friend's wedding, tears flowing, asking me about eighteen years ago? I had to tread carefully, because, obviously, something had upset her.

"I'm assuming you mean dated or slept together when you say 'hook up', yes?" I clarified. She nodded. "Then no, Jenn and I have never hooked up."

The form before me melted into my arms and started weeping again. "Oh good. I knew you wouldn't have broken up with me and then slept with my best friend."

"What? What gave you that idea?"

"I saw Angela Tanner at the florist yesterday, while I was picking up Helene's wedding flowers. She brought you up and said you and Jenn hooked up after we split."

"Angela Tanner? Angela? Tanner?" I repeated, wracking my memories for some hint of who that was.

Indie nodded at me.

"Angela Tan– wait. Angela from biology? Angela Tanner the gossip queen?" I started to laugh uncontrollably.

"What is so funny?"

"She was hitting on me after you and I broke up!"

"Angela Tanner was...into girls?!?" Indie gasped.

"Well, she was at least curious at that time," I replied, raising my eyebrows suggestively. "One time when Jenn and I were out, as friends, she started hitting on me. Jenn saw my very obvious discomfort and came over. She pretended to kiss me to get that crazy girl to leave me alone. What Angela never saw was Jenn had put her hand over my mouth before she started making out with me," I finished, searching Indie's face for any hint of doubt. Finding none, but still wanting to make sure she believed me, I took out my phone. "Do you want us to call Jenn right now? She will tell you the same thing."

"No, I believe you." A light kiss was planted on my lips, having an instant calming effect. "I love you." Indie whispered breathlessly.

The involuntary shiver made my teasing less effective, but I did it anyway. "I tolerate you."

A nice little slap landed on my arm. Feigning severe distress by limping on my left leg, I walked my girlfriend towards the bathroom to fix her makeup before the ceremony.

"You look amazing."

"Even with the tear streaks?"

"Even with the tear streaks."

"The makeup station is that way," Indie informed me, pointing behind us, "just so you are aware."

"I know." I lied. "I was just taking the long way so I could be arm-in-arm with you a little bit longer."

"Yeah, riiiiight."

Watching Indie stand next to her friend, in front of an altar, fanned the flame that had started months ago. Never in my life had I thought I would want marriage, which is one of the reasons it didn't work out between Ali and me. Her sleeping with other people was the main reason, but even if she hadn't cheated, it would have all fallen apart anyway. She wanted marriage, I did not. It was that simple and, yet, utterly complicated. Sitting here surrounded by strangers, however, I could see myself up there, Indie by my side, pledging our undying love to each other. Amidst my daydreaming and focusing on Indie alone, I decided to take a look around me. Behind Indie and her friends, whom I could only assume were Sara, Gabriel, and Amie, there were a few junior bridesmaids. Two of them looked like sisters, and those sisters looked like Indie. My breath caught in my throat. Mari and Veda. I would be meeting them, officially, in a matter of minutes. My usual confidence in meetings evading me, I began to sweat.

"Dammit," I breathed quietly.

The woman next to me gave me a little confused glance, but I just shrugged her off and gave her a little smile. She went back to watching the scene at the front of the church.

My old enemy, overactive sweat glands, just had to pick today to rear its ugly head. The ability to remain levelheaded and calm during intense situations and important meetings had come about due to necessity. I would never have made it very far if I started sweating like a pig every time a big meeting came up in my firm. This particular meeting was different from board meetings, client meetings, and the like; this was personal. If the twins didn't like me, what did that mean for Indie and I? No mother is going to choose her high school sweetheart over her children. Feeling the panic rising, I focused on my breathing and closed my eyes.

Breathe in, breathe out, breathe in, breathe out...

The sound of clapping interrupted my intense focus, and I started applauding along with the crowd. The ceremony had ended. An air of faux confidence kept things steady as the bride and groom started down the aisle, followed closely by the most wonderful woman on the planet being escorted by a man who looked far too happy to be next to her. Indie caught my eye and smiled brilliantly as I glared at him, instantly changing my face and emotional state. How and why this woman had such a hold on me was a mystery.

At the front of the church, the friend group exchanged a few glances and head nods in my direction. Being one of the only Asians present, they had all quickly deduced who I was. Gabriel and one of the women just smiled knowingly at me. The other woman gave me a little wave, which I returned along with a head nod of greeting. Indie's daughters were staring as well. Seeing my wave and nod, the smiling one gave me one of her own, which I answered with a smile. The other, whom I pinned as Mari, had an expression of stone; completely unreadable. She just stared at me. She was much like the Japanese businessmen that had come through Finnick&Douglas over the years. Placing my palms together, I gave her a small bow. While it was a bit awkward trying to bow in a pew, she repaid my efforts with a slight head nod. Conversations with Indie had told me being acknowledged at all was a very good sign. Everyone was just as Indie described them. I thought I had figured out which friend was Amie and which one was Sara. I couldn't wait to talk to her later to see if I had gotten them all correct.

Slowly, but surely, each row of guests filed out of the pews and made it to the back of the church for the procession line greeting. The one I believed the be Sara saw me first, nudging Gabriel, who, in turn, nudged who I thought to be Amie. Their whispering and smiling caught Indie's attention. Following the gazes of her friends, our eyes locked. She smiled and gave an apologetic look. I waved her off and smiled my most charming smile. Noticing my demeanor change, the three friends turned towards Indie in unison and grinned.

As I approached the bride and groom, nodding, smiling, and greeting, the bride started her usual spiel, but stopped short upon seeing my face.

"You must be Sam!" bubbled Helene.

"Yes, I am, and you must be Helene." Turning slightly toward the groom, I continued, "And you must be Lukas. Congratulations on your wedding, and thank you for allowing me to be a part of it."

"Glad you could make it," Lukas replied then leaned in closer, teasing. "You are quite the topic of conversation, but don't worry; they don't bite much."

I clapped my new comrade on the back, thanking him, before moving on to come face to face with Indie and her escort. I made a show of kissing the back of her hand while looking her, then her companion, in the eyes. Giggling like a schoolgirl, she turned to her friends.

"Guys, this is Sam. Sam, this is Sara, Gabriel, and Amie," Indie gushed.

"Oh, we know." chimed Gabriel, eliciting snickers from the other two. "We've been eyeing her up for half the ceremony already."

His eyes briefly flitted behind me as he caught his breath. I dared a glance and saw a slight man with dirty blond hair and wire-framed glasses smiling sheepishly back at Indie's swarthy friend. No one else noticed.

"Nice to meet you," offered Sara.

"Likewise," I returned.

"Yeah, you're as cute as Indie said you were!" interjected Amie.

Indie's face turned red, bringing more snickers. I replied, "Thank you, but I'm nowhere as gorgeous as this woman," kissing her hand once more before moving on down the line. "I'll see you in a bit, milady. I'm going to go say hi to your daughters now."

Her face contorted. "Oh my god! I didn't think about that! I was going to introduce you at the reception!" Indie panicked.

"Hey, I got this." I winked as I walked away.

Mari's face was still expressionless, and Veda still looked as if she might burst out of her own skin with excitement.

"You must be Mari," I declared, looking Indie's eldest in the eyes, "and you must be Veda," I continued, shifting my gaze to the youngest.

"And you must be Sam," deadpanned Mari.

"Oh my gosh, yes you are!" squealed Veda. "Mom said we wouldn't meet you until later, but here you are!"

"Yes indeed. It is very nice to meet you both, but since your mother had a plan in mind for the three of us meeting, I will respect her and move along. I am eager to get to know you both."

I completed my little speech with a bow, and swore I saw Mari's lip twitch up on one side.

The reception hall was beautifully done. The building itself was well over a hundred years old, and I spent the forty-five minutes before the wedding party arrived exploring and admiring the structure. I found my place card after quite a bit of searching, having begun at the back of the great room. I was just to the right of the bridal table, in the very front. I realized I was sitting with some of the bride's extended family and Kenny. I would have to remember to thank Helene and Lukas for their kindness in sitting me so close to Indie.

A man offered me his hand as he sat in the seat next to me.

"Hello, you must be Sam. I'm Kenny. Helene told me we would be sitting next to each other."

I looked up to see the slight man Gabriel was looking at earlier. I took his hand. noticing his surprisingly good grip.

"Hello, Kenny. It's nice to finally meet you."

"Likewise," he remarked.

"Indie says good things about you. You really know your stuff, evidently," I offered.

"I could say the same about you," Kenny said, smiling. "She is too kind, I'm sure. I seem to annoy her often."

Laughing, I patted him on the back.

"You are funnier than she described. So how do you know Gabriel?"

"Wh-what do you mean?"

"I just saw you two exchange glances earlier and wondered if you were friends with him. Is that how you got the job with Not Your Mom's?"

"No, no. I just applied and got the job. I met Gabriel at Indie's house a few weeks ago when we were going over some business stuff. I don't know him. I mean, I know him, but, well…"

Sweat droplets formed on Kenny's top lip and his breathing picked up.

"Don't worry, I won't say a thing to anyone," I vowed.

He sat staring at the place setting in front of him for a while before replying, "Thank you."

"So, tell me about yourself, Kenny, my man."

The rest of our table filed in, as did the wedding party, and dinner was served. I spent most of the time staring at Indie between bites as she did the same, echoed by Gabriel and Kenny. I chuckled at one point, leaning over to Kenny, asking how the rest of them did not know. The corner of his mouth turned up before he ate another bite of his chicken.

In between dinner and cake, Indie gathered her daughters and headed my way. I stood, meeting them a few feet away from the table.

"Good evening, my love. I know I've technically already met your daughters, but I have been anxiously awaiting our official introduction all day. So, take it away."

Indie's smile almost undid my carefully curated composure. "Sam, this is Mari," she announced, gesturing to the still serious girl beside her, "and Veda," pointing to the giggly teen on her other side. "They told me you were polite in your introduction earlier, but you insisted on waiting for me to be properly introduced." She beamed, mouthing, "Thank you."

Nodding and giving her a sideways grin, I turned my attention to the two youngsters.

"I was sincere when I said I was eager to get to know you two, so, please, ask me any questions and tell me anything you'd like to."

Veda took a deep breath, but Mari interrupted.

"You first."

"That's fair," I replied. "Well, my name is Satomi Nakamura, but my friends call me Sammi and your mother calls me Sam." I started, daring a peek at Indie's angelic smile. "I went to high school with your mom. I'm currently an architect at Finnick&Douglas in Boston. I have a cat named Bob." I continued, pausing briefly as I saw both girls react happily to that tidbit of information. "I have one sister and one brother and," whispering as I leaned in, "I collect antique scissors. Not many people know that. And that's me in a nutshell. Any questions, comments, or concerns?"

Veda breathed in only to be beaten to the punch, again, by her sister.

"Yeah, what are your intentions regarding our mother."

"Oooo, yeah, good one!" Veda approved.

"Well, my intention is to love her in the best way I can, as long as she'll have me." I replied sincerely.

"We'll see." Mari stated before her sister started going full force.

"I'm Veda, and this is Mari, as you know." she started, motioning to the sullen sibling now standing next to her. "I love doing crafts and riding horses. Pink is my favorite color, and I just started high school this year. I have a weird obsession with bones and also love to forage for, learn about, and eat mushrooms." Babbling on, she began Mari's interests, "Mari is, obviously, also a ninth grader. She likes to swim. She's really good, too!"

"Veda." Mari warned.

Ignoring her tone, Veda continued on, "She wants to be a marine biologist someday!"

"VEDA!" Mari snapped. "I can speak for myself, thank you very much."

Veda simply shrugged. "Then go ahead. I'm gonna refill my punch."

She traipsed off towards the drinks table ten feet away.

I smiled expectantly at Mari, but she seemed not in the mood to talk.

"You don't have to say anything more. I'll just nod so your sister thinks you are giving me some good intel. I don't really like talking to people until I get to know them either."

Scoffing, Mari interjected, "She means well."

"Of course she does. She reminds me a lot of my sister."

This piqued Mari's interest. "Are you a twin?" she asked.

"No, she's a year younger than me. Everyone thought we were twins, but I'm sure that's nothing like actually being a twin. She used to drive me crazy, but in a sweet way. I always felt like I had to protect her. She and I get along really well now. She lives in New Hampshire with her husband and two kids."

Mari was staring at me intently. I started to shift my weight and look to Indie for some sort of guidance, but she just stood there.

"You and your sister didn't talk for a while," Mari stated.

"Umm, yes. For two years after she graduated high school, we weren't on speaking terms," I sputtered.

"Nice to have met you, Satomi Nakamura," Mari declared as she excused herself.

Turning to Indie, I asked, "How did she know that?"

"Mari just knows things sometimes. So don't try pulling anything with me, lady," she teased.

"Yes, ma'am!"

"By the way, sexy lady in a suit, happy birthday," she expressed, and kissed me gingerly. "I'll give you your gift later," she teased, linking her arm in mine and leading me towards the wedding party table. "Now comes the really difficult crew. Time to meet my friends!"

"But, it's my birthday!" I argued while faking a heart attack. Being shown no mercy, I was led to the gallows amid Indie's laughing.

CHAPTER 21

Indie

**Zacariah just came to pick up the girls.
I'm leaving as soon as I get done with this
little meet and greet. I'll be there soon!**

> ok. hurry. i need some mouth to
> mouth. i'm fading fast over here.

**Oh, whatever, drama queen.
Gotta jump in the car. Ttyl.**

Locking my front door behind me and throwing my weekend bag into the backseat of my car, I backed out of my driveway, almost hitting Sara.

"Geez, lady! What the hell?!" screamed Sara.

I threw the car into park and opened the door.

"Oh my god, Sara! I'm so sorry! I didn't see you."

"I would hope not! Were you going to leave me behind?" she asked.

"Oh! I forgot to tell you. I'm leaving right after to go to Sam's place for the weekend."

"Ahh, ok. Well then, I guess I'm driving myself," she shot.

"People get a damn girlfriend and no one else matters," Sara ranted, throwing her arms up in the air, before storming off down the road.

Rising from my seat and calling after her to no avail, I retreated to the safety of my vehicle, looked twice before beginning to back up, and sped off.

Walking into the Local Lesbian Leaders' monthly meeting, I went straight to the deserted bar area and ordered a Blanton's whiskey on the rocks. Head in hands, a massive sigh was released into the air.

"Well, we meet at a bar again." Delia prodded, "What's on your mind this time?"

Lifting my head, I gave her a weak smile.

"Just friends being jerks to each other."

"Ahh, yes, I know that well. But...then the friends make up when they both cool down." she encouraged, slugging back the rest of her drink before slamming the empty glass on the counter, motioning for another. "Looks like we both had a sucky day."

"Yeah," I commiserated, "this day has had its ups and downs. Hopefully, it ends on a way better note."

Taking her new glass from the barkeep, she chugged that one as well.

"Yep, I'm kind of hoping that too."

I stared at her loopy expression.

"How many of those have you had already?"

"Umm, that one makes... five. I think."

"Five? Maybe you should slow down a bit, Delia."

"Maybe you should come home with me tonight," she suggested, inching closer.

"Whoa," I cautioned, putting my hand up between the two of us, "I already told you; I'm with someone."

"With-schmith. I promise you I'm better."

"At being creepy? Yeah, yeah ya are," I retorted, Delia pushing closer and closer.

Without warning, Sara was in between us. "Step back," she warned Delia sternly.

"Oh C'mon, I was just tal..."

"You were just leaving. Don't make me tell you again," Sara insisted.

Delia threw up her hands and backed into the barstool behind her.

Sara turned to me. "Are you okay?"

"Yeah, I'm good. Are you? I'm sorry about earlier."

"I know. I'm sorry too. I was frustrated and took it out on you," she admitted. "The court date is set."

"Oh, Sara, I'm so sorry. Do you need money? Character witnesses? Do they even do that for real?" I pondered, shaking my head free of the thought. "It doesn't matter. Whatever you need, I'm here for you."

Her glistening eyes scrunched. "I know you are." As the first tear began its descent, she announced, "Aaaand let's change the subject. So, you're going to Sam's tonight?"

I blushed, "Yes, as soon as this is over. I'm meeting her mom on this trip. Well," I paused, "not really meeting, because we knew each other in high school, but meeting again?"

"Have you told Sam about the stuff your dad said to you yet?"

I rolled my eyes. "No."

"You should tell her. You can't run from this forever. It's affecting you, Indie. You can't seem to see that. I'm worried about you."

The rising indignation faded with her last statement. "I know, and I appreciate you all caring so much. I'll tell her, eventually."

Sara nodded and stared straight ahead. "Wait, wasn't her mom not too thrilled with her sexual orientation?" she questioned.

"Yeah, but, evidently, she came around over the years and is excited to see me again."

"Well, okay then. Good luck!" she cheered. Turning around to face the rest of the room, she sighed and said, "Let's go mingle and be all business-y."

Upon arriving at Sam's, I was greeted warmly by George, then by Bob, and finally by Sam herself. She had the entirety of her apartment decked out in fairy lights. Gasping and shrieking with glee, I hugged her. The playful kissing rapidly turned passionate. She pulled away from me.

"We can't start that yet. My mom will be here any minute," she warned, straightening her shirt out.

"Are you sure we don't have time?" I purred, nuzzling her neck.

The buzzing made us both jump. Sam ran over and pushed the intercom button.

"Yes, George?"

"Your mother is here, Ms. Nakamura."

"Thank you, George, send her up." She turned to me and raised her eyebrows. "This is it."

I took a deep breath in and attempted to smooth out my crazy curls. "I'm as ready as I'll ever be."

"You are absolutely perfect, my love. She is weirdly excited we are back together."

"Well, that's a good thing, I suppose."

We both turned towards the door just as Sam's mother rapped on it. Sam ran over, greeting her mother in Japanese, as usual, and taking her mother's coat. I approached the tiny, but formidable, woman.

"Hello, Mrs. Nakamura. It's very nice to see you again."

She turned to me, and I could see the years on her face, but they had been kind to her.

"Oh, Indie. It is so nice to see you again too! Sam has told me much about you. You have two daughters, yes?"

"Yes, I do, twins. They are turning sixteen soon."

"Oh my, yes, very good," Mrs. Nakamura said.

Sam turned back towards us and grinned.

"Dinner is ready in the kitchen. I made shabu shabu. Shall we?"

Dishes everywhere, Mrs. Nakamura now long gone, Sam and I picked up where we left off earlier. In between kisses, she was questioning me about my day. My breathless replies were mostly ignored, except when I mentioned what happened between Sara and Delia.

Abruptly ceasing the kissing, Sam fumed, "She did what?"

"She was just hitting on me."

"Sounds like she was trying to force herself on you."

"I guess, but Sara stepped in before anything really happened."

"What if Sara hadn't been around?" questioned Sam, indignantly.

"Excuse me?"

"If Sara hadn't been there what would have happened? You told this woman you and her were just acquaintances, right? You told her about you and me."

"Yes, of course I did," I sputtered, feeling accused for no reason.

"I don't want you going back to that lesbian group thing. You need to stay away from her before I have to hurt her."

"Excuse me?" I shot back. "I will do whatever I damn well please. I am a grown woman, and I don't need to be told what to do and where to go and who to talk to."

"What the hell does that mean? You want to go hang out with that woman? Fine! Do whatever you want. I'm getting my shower," Sam shouted, storming off.

"What the hell just happened?" I said quietly to myself.

I went into Sam's bedroom, hearing her turn the water on, and got into my pajamas. I stood there, staring at her bed, unsure of what to do next in this home which wasn't mine. Do I get into the bed of the woman who just shouted at me? It didn't seem right, so I went to the guest bathroom, washed my face and brushed my teeth, and curled up on the guest bed.

I heard the shower turn off and, only minutes later, footsteps coming down the hall. I closed my eyes, not sure what to expect. Sam's warm body molded around mine and her arm encircled me. I turned over to face the woman I loved.

"I'm sorry," said Sam. "That was quite asshole-ish of me. You are a grown woman, and I trust you. It's just a knee jerk reaction that I need to work on."

I stared at her silhouetted face, tracing her jaw.

"Yes, you do."

"What are you looking at?" she asked.

"You," I replied, with a smile.

"Yeah, I tolerate you too," she said as she leaned in to kiss me.

It started as sweet and gentle, but quickly escalated as we both let the tension between us slip away, leaving room for the built-up passion of the last week to rise. We kissed heatedly for what seemed like an hour before disrobing hurriedly and slipping under the warm comforter. She laid on top of me, her wetness grinding into my thigh. I moaned with delight and pressed my thigh into her as her tongue swept lightly across my erect nipple. Nearly erupting with pleasure right then and there, I arched my back, lifting the peak to her. She grinned and made a guttural sound as if she were famished and my breasts were the only thing that could satisfy her.

Her mouth had soon enveloped my entire nipple. She hungrily took it all in before releasing it in order to allow her tongue to play with its summit. She did this over and over, drawing sounds from me I could not control as my thigh became saturated from her own desire. Her mouth released me just as I thought I couldn't take another moment of teasing. My neck muscles loosened, my fingers released their grip on her hip, but only for a split second. My body was soon being ravaged again as she expertly moved her tongue across the other breast's taut peak. I needed her touch like I needed beautiful art and flowers and music. And I needed it now.

I rallied my concentration and started undulating my thigh beneath her wetness. Her expert tongue skipped only a beat as her own moan rose to the surface.

"Indie, I'm *trying* to focus on you," she stated with a mouthful of breast muffling her words.

"I just want to feel you come on my thigh while you suck on my nipple. Please? Pleeeeease!" I screeched breathlessly as the onslaught on my bosom increased in intensity.

We found a flawless rhythm in our movements and soon, I felt her tense while the moans trying to escape her grew in volume, still muffled by my chest in her mouth. Her hips began moving faster and faster until her mouth released both the spire within it and the moans of pleasure that had been held back long enough. Her back arched and her face turned towards the heavens.

"Well, well, madame, I'm so glad you 'came'." I whispered into her ear after her body had fully relaxed and collapsed onto me.

She scoffed at my terrible pun and gave my nipple a quick bite.

"Ack!!" I yelped. My neck quickly lifted my head up to her laughing face. "Not nice, not nice!"

"Nice? Oh, I'll show you nice."

Her devilish smile intensified as she spread my legs further apart with her knee and ran her fingers up and down my slit, careful not to touch the pulsing peak that was much further down than the peaks which had been getting her attention so far this evening.

"Look who's wet and ready for me. Too bad I'm going to make you beg for it."

Two fingers slipped around my opening, teasing. I arched my hips, but she refused to fully enter me or touch the bundle of nerves desperate for her attention. Her mouth adeptly found its way back to the northern peaks. Lips, teeth, and tongue working together, alternating between sucking and nibbling my nipples, while the tips of fingers danced around the southern region of pleasure was driving me insane. I needed the release, not like I needed art, but like I needed breath. I felt like I would soon explode from the built-up pressure within me.

She always seemed to sense when I could take no more. Her two center fingers finally made their way inside of me while the thumb found the pulsating crux just above. My eyes opened wide as I sucked in a huge gasp of air, and I saw her glorious face looking down at me with a lopsided grin spread as far as my legs were. I closed my eyes once again as I felt the heat building in my core. My right hand found her ample hip and I dug in.

"Please don't stop. Please. Please. Oh, god, please don't stop!" I kept repeating through strained breaths.

She happily obliged my request. In fact, she doubled her efforts; going faster and angling the digits within to hit that wonderful spot deep inside.

My entire being tensed with the build-up of rapture before releasing with a yell that could not be contained. My head slammed back down on the bed beneath me, my fingers released her hip, and my legs flopped open. She was still leisurely gliding in and out of me, relishing in the shudders that wracked my body after such a powerful orgasm.

"Holy shit, babe, *that* was amazing. Like for real. Definitely top five."

"Oh really? Well, I'm not quite done yet, so get ready for an encore," she replied with the smirkiest smirk ever.

Her onslaught recommenced. My legs shook as my body tried to fight the pleasure so soon after climaxing, but soon relaxed and allowed the expert to do her work. In less than a minute, I was shaking, once again, as the ecstasy flooded over my form.

My legs snapped shut as I said, "Recovery! I need some time to recover!"

Her laughter pealed through the room behind the scent of sex, but she obliged. I wriggled down the bed a bit lower, looking at her with a new hunger.

"Now it's my turn. Sit on my face, woman!"

Once again, her laughter erupted, but she obliged. My tongue flicked her clitoris and her whole body flinched.

"Pay back's a bitch." I warned.

"Be gentle with me now."

"HA!"

I wrapped my arms around her ass and over the tops of her thighs, pulling her slick center down to my face. I started grinding my tongue directly on the erect kernel of rapture before me. I felt her body start to tense and I immediately stopped. I lightly ran my tongue through her folds and kissed her peak. She laughed and nodded. My tongue began mimicking her teasing as it went around her opening, up one side and down the other. My hands released her thighs and felt their way up her back, down her sides, and across her stomach again and again. Her hips were undulating slightly as if trying to convince me to complete my task, but I was having too much fun teasing and exploring this familiar terrain.

After a few more minutes of torture, my arms wrapped around her bottom and thighs once again and my tongue delved into her cavern. Her grip on the headboard made the wood moan along with her. I angled myself so my upper lip could brush across her clit as my tongue surveyed her insides. I felt the muscles on her inner thighs grow more taught as she matched my rhythm with her movements. Soon she was groaning and shuddering as her passion was finally released.

I kissed those beautiful thighs framing my face and the creases where they met her hips, allowing my hand to meander up and down her backside. Her breathing was returning to normal, but she didn't know we were just getting started.

"Ok, we should probably go to sleep now."

She tried to get off, but I wrapped my arms around her thighs again and pulled her down to me. I had much more control in this position than when she was on her back, and I knew her buttons well.

I pulled her down hard on my face, stuck out my tongue, and ground her swollen clit hard and fast until she came again and again.

"Damn, Indie, I *really* like your brand of payback," she said matter-of-factly as she lifted herself off of my head and laid down next to me.

We were both giggling like school girls. This is why we worked. We were friends before anything sexual or romantic or relationship-y came about. We had been friends before and after we fell in love. This is why she was worth fighting for, why we were worth fighting for. All of the other crap thrown onto us by our past, our own issues and insecurities, society, our families, was nothing compared to what we had. I started to tear up as we were lying there cracking up in the dark, holding hands. She was my Sam and she always would be.

"Are you crying, babe?" Sam asked tenderly.

I smiled and shook my head no as the first tear fell.

"What's wrong? Did I do something wrong?"

I laughed weakly, more tears falling.

"No, it's not you. Umm, there's something I think I should tell you; something that's weighing on me. I don't think it's fair to keep it from you," I confessed.

"Okaaaay," she replied uneasily.

"You remember my dad, right?" Sam nodded affirmatively.

"Well, he told me something on his deathbed. He said to me, 'You always knew. Trust yourself. You were right.' and then he died."

"I'm not exactly sure what that means."

"Ever since I was a small child, I've asked my parents if I'm adopted. I always felt different. I would express this every once in a while, but was always told I was crazy. The last time I asked my mother something to that effect, I was about twelve. She flipped out on me, screaming and flailing about like a madwoman. I never asked again. So fast forward to when I'm twenty-eight and my dad is dying, and think of it in that context." I explained.

"Oh." Sam said, pausing and looking down at the sheet in between us. "Oh!" she reiterated, looking up into my bleary eyes. "So, what did you find out?"

"Nothing."

"Nothing?"

"I had just lost my dad. I was hurting and it felt kinda, I don't know, disloyal to look for that information. He was my dad, no matter what. So I just let it go," I lamented.

"I can see how you would feel that way. And now?"

"And now, I don't know. I feel like there's a part of me missing, but am I ready to find out what there is to know? I haven't even talked to my mother since my dad died and we had our falling out. I have no idea what I'm about to find out. What should I do?"

"I think you already know the answer to that, which is why it's on your mind." Sam softly consoled. "Your dad wouldn't have told you if he didn't want you to find out."

"That's what everyone keeps saying." I sniffled. "The whole friggin' friend group knows now."

"Ultimately, it's up to you. I am here, no matter what you decide or what you find out."

"Thanks, my love. I know you are." I whispered, passionately kissing this wonderful, amazing woman.

Sam

WALKED UP to the bright green door and smiled. A cute ranch style painted charcoal gray with some sort of bright blue, metal, spherical sculpture in front, the house was funky and yet sophisticated. I laughed to myself. This was definitely Indie's house. Pushing the small, lighted button on the starburst metal plate, I heard giggling coming from the other side of the door.

Light streamed out of the house, silhouetting the fine form of Indie Woodley. Grinning like a school girl, I leaned in for a kiss.

"Hey stranger," Indie greeted in a sultry voice.

"Hi, good lookin'," I whispered to my love before turning my attention to the teens on the sofa to our right. "Hello, girls. Mari. Veda," I addressed each girl individually, nodding in their respective directions.

"Hey, Sam!" Veda called. "Welcome to our humble abode!"

"Hello." stated Mari, never tearing her gaze away from the book she was reading.

Indie mouthed, "Sorry," and rolled her eyes. "So, you ready for the full tour?"

"Of course, madame." I replied, bowing. Following her through the modern, yet bohemian spaces, I could barely remove my gaze from her face. Her expression was one of contentment.

"And this is my room," she declared proudly.

Entering the starkly different room, I gasped slightly. The room was almost completely enveloped in white. A couple of light wood side tables flanked the light gray headboard that popped against the white walls. White linens layered the welcoming bed with one pale gray decorative pillow. Walking towards the only other things in the room, a small white cabinet with a wooden vessel on it, I exclaimed, "Well, this is a bit different from the rest of your colorful home!"

Her laugh filled the space between us. "I have some trouble sleeping, so I keep this space free of stimulation."

Wrapping my arms around her waist, I challenged, "So no stimulation at all?"

"Well, maybe some sort of stimulation when you're here."

She came in for a kiss. We got lost in the moment for a split-second before the doorbell rang, ending the bliss.

My girlfriend giggled, "Later, my love," and headed back down her hallway, me following closely behind, pinching her butt the whole way.

Hearing a man's voice, I bristled, prepared to see Zacariah. Turning the corner, I saw the smiling, familiar face of Gabriel and let my guard down. His eyes flitted back and forth between Indie and I as a knowing smile flashed across his face.

"Why hello there, Sam. Good to see you again," he greeted, offering his hand.

I obliged, "You as well, Gabriel."

His attention shifted to Indie.

"Sorry to barge in unannounced, which I would normally neevvvveer do," he began, everyone in the room laughing loudly, even Mari, "but I would simply love to borrow your roaster."

"Sure," Indie agreed. "Why? You havin' a party we are not invited to?" she queried, walking into the kitchen, followed by Gabriel and me.

"Umm, well, not really," he paused, before seeing Indie's raised eyebrow. "Fine. If you must know, I have a date."

"A date?!?" Veda interjected from the living room amidst hooting and hollering from the rest of the ladies of the house.

An over-exaggerated sigh coming from the Latino almost made me feel sorry for him.

"Yes, dear, eavesdropping child, a date," he replied.

Mari appeared at my side in the doorway. "Anyone we *know*?"

"Oh my, look at the time," announced Gabriel. "Gotta run. Gracias!"

Examining Mari's face, squinted eyes, tilted head, raised eyebrow, I wondered if she was more aware of happenings in Gabriel's life than she was letting on. While Gabriel was busy helping Indie get the roasting pan down, trying to avoid further questions, I nudged Mari. Her eyes quickly shifted to me.

Pursing my lips, giving a quick nod in Gabriel's direction, and subsequently raising my eyebrows, trying to figure out if she knew what I knew.

She narrowed her eyes and nodded similarly. Staring at her mother for a moment, she silently beckoned me down the hall.

Once we were out of earshot, she started her questioning, "What do you know?"

"What do *you* know?" I volleyed back at her.

She, once again, narrowed her eyes and I returned the look.

"I know who he's got a date with."

"Me too," I said.

"How?"

"I am a master of observation. How do you know?"

Shrugging she replied, "I just do."

"So, we both know who it is, but neither of us are willing to tell the other person what we know."

I wracked my brain for a way to get this child to trust me. I would simply have to tell her, but in a clever way.

"I hope they have fun o'plenny. Maybe they'll eat some eggs benny. Harm, I do not wish them any."

Her initial confused look gave way to recognition. "You DO know!"

"Yep, saw the way they were looking at each other at Helene's wedding."

"How does mom not see this?" Mari asked excitedly.

Her sudden show of human emotion throwing me off, I stuttered, "I–I don't know. She's got a lot on her plate right now."

"What are you two whispering about back here?" a voice chimed in.

"Nothing mom, just getting to know your girlfriend. You know, making sure she's not a lunatic or something," Mari replied, heading back to her sister and their anime show.

Grinning like the Cheshire Cat, I quietly added, "Yeah, mom, we're just getting to know each other."

The onslaught of playful slaps was interrupted by Indie's ringtone. I made my way to the back of the sofa in the living room. Leaning on it, I started to gather intel on this anime called Sailor Moon. Indie came in, joining me in my angular position.

"I have to go into the office tomorrow," she whispered.

Adjourning to the kitchen, so as not to disturb the adolescents, I asked, "Why?"

"There was some sort of mix-up with some paperwork or something. I'm not one hundred percent sure what's going on. All I know is that the woman we've been dealing with most of the time didn't do something important and now the whole deal is in jeopardy. I feel like she's been acting really weird lately."

"How so?"

"In the beginning, she was very professional, always prompt, and kind of seemed one step ahead most of the time. Lately, it's been the exact opposite. She shows up late for meetings, or not at all, forgets things, and is a bit spacey. Ya know what I mean?"

"Yeah, that's no fun to deal with in business."

"Anyway, I'm sorry, but I have to go in tomorrow."

"That's fine, I'll just go with you."

"Really?"

"Why not? It'll give me the chance to say hi to Helene and Kenny again and see your office. I'll just hang out somewhere else while you guys are doing the business-y stuff."

"Oh babe, that sounds wonderful!"

———————

"Quit it!" Indie yelled for the fifth time since we left her house.

"But I have nothing else to do," I whined, once again putting my hand on her thigh and inching it upwards.

"QUIT IT!" she shouted before giggling like a school girl.

"You like it."

"I didn't say I didn't like it. I said I have to concentrate on driving."

"Fine, killjoy," I teased. "So, wanna get married?"

"WHAT?!?" she screeched, swerving.

"I'm kidding, but kinda serious. I've been thinking a lot about us lately. I want us to be together eventually; like living together, building a family kind of together."

"Oh, yeah, I want that too, but marriage? Marriage is a four-letter word to me. It does not represent anything good, or even tolerable, in my mind."

"I mean, I guess I can see that, but I'm not him."

"I know, but it's just something hardwired into me now. I can't think of marriage in any other context. Being with you for the rest of my life sounds absolutely amazing, but the word marriage makes me want to run far, far away."

"Okay, subject change. Wanna have a baby?"

"What in the actual hell, Sam? What is with you today? A baby? As you know, I've been there done that."

"Yeah, but I haven't."

"Sam, I love you, I want a life with you, and I want to discuss allllll of the things with you, but can we wait until after this meeting, please?"

"Yeah, I guess that's a reasonable request, but now I'm bored again." I stated with a devilish grin.

"Well, it's a good thing we're here then!" said Indie, slapping the roaming hand away once again.

Walking up to the century old building was quite the treat. Staring at the buttresses and balustrades, I tripped on the steps, extracting a giggle from my stressed-out girlfriend.

Rushing towards her and kissing the side of her neck, I murmured, "You are amazing," and relished in the glow warming her cheeks.

The rest of the uneventful climb culminated in a massive, molding laden door. The creaking gave our entrance away. Helene's face brightened and Kenny nodded in my direction. Greetings done and out of the way, the trio set right to work. I meandered around the spacious office over the next quarter hour, taking in all of the tiny architectural treasures. Bending down to admire the intricacy of the inlaid flooring, I heard a voice which made my heart stop. Hidden behind a desk, I dared a look.

"Sorry I'm late, all." Alicia apologized.

Kenny muttered under his breath, "We're used to it by now," and was lightly thwapped on the arm by Helene.

"It's fine," Helene started. "We're all here now, so let's get this show on the road."

Helene shook the latecomer's hand and caught Indie's attention, widening her eyes and mouthing, 'She looks terrible.'

"Yes, of course. Indie," Alicia said, shaking my lover's hand. "Kenny," she continued, doing the same to him. "This is Henry Abernathy, one of our lawyers. He will explain what's going on."

Their meeting officially commenced and I stared at the woman from Goodness Goods. What the hell was she doing here? I couldn't let her see me, but I couldn't very well crouch on the floor for the next hour either. Weighing my options, I slowly stood and walked gingerly towards an empty office. Willing my heart to stop beating at the speed of light, I regained my composure. I had the upper hand here. She hadn't seen me. I would wait and emerge cool, calm, and collected while I watched her falter.

The next hour passed slowly and, yet, more quickly than I would have liked. The meeting attendees began rising from their seats. This was it. I was going out that door to face the woman who cheated on me, broke my heart, and left without warning.

Internally thanking myself for dressing sharply today, I strolled out of the office, smiling, composed, and looking like a million bucks. Alicia busily tried to organize her mess of papers.

I went directly to Indie, placed my arm around her waist, and kissed her deeply, but quickly, as was appropriate for the current company and situation.

"Hello, love," I cooed. "How did the meeting go?"

"It went well, I suppose. Sorry if you were bored."

Peripheral vision works in wonderful ways. It allowed me to see Ali's head snap up and her face go ashen.

"Great, and nope, not bored in this treasure trove of a building."

"Ahh, sorry, my manners," apologized Indie. "Alicia, Henry, this is my girlfriend Sam. Sam, this is Alicia and Henry from Goodness Goods."

"Henry, nice to meet you," I offered with outstretched hand.

"Same to you, Sam." he replied in a friendly, business-like manner. He seemed as annoyed with today's situation as the *Not Your Mom's* crew did.

"Ali, I believe we have met before, but I hope you're doing well," I politely addressed my former partner.

"Ali?" Indie questioned, the whites of her eyes growing larger.

"Uh, yes. I'm okay. Thank you. I hope you are too," she sputtered, throwing the mess of papers into her briefcase. "I really should go. Have a good day, everyone."

As Ali and Henry walked out of the large doors, I had two pair of huge eyes fixed on me and one man who was very confused.

"Who's Ali?" Kenny mused.

"My ex," I replied.

Now there were three pair of huge eyes on me.

"Why didn't you tell me?" Indie asked incredulously.

"I didn't know. She was not working for Goodness Goods when we were together. You called her Alicia, and I never put it together." I informed the wide-eyed group.

Two notification messages rang out in the silent, cavernous room.

Indie and Helene glanced at each other before reaching for their respective phones. Indie's mouth fell agape as Helene announced, "We have to get to Sara's. NOW."

Indie looked up at me with fear clouding her beautiful features.

"What do you need from me?" I asked.

"Can you drive me?"

"And me," chimed Helene. "Lukas dropped me off."

"Of course. Let's go." I prompted, opening the door as everyone filed out. "All of this before 10 a.m. on a Saturday," I mumbled to myself, exiting behind the others.

Pulling into Sara's driveway, I felt out of place.

"Do you want me to stay in the car?" I asked Indie in a low voice.

"What, why?"

"Because this is a friend group thing and I'm not part of it."

Gabriel pulled in right behind us. "Amie must have text him too. Good. I didn't even think about that." she thought out loud, before turning her attention back to me. "No, you can go in. You're a part of this now, whether you want to be or not. But I won't make you or anything."

She exited the car, steps behind Helene.

"Does anyone know what the fuck is going on?" Gabriel went on. "Do we need a doctor, a priest, a bottle of gin? Information, please!"

Helene and Indie both shrugged and rushed inside.

I entered the small, aesthetically cluttered home and closed the stained-glass door behind me. It was a beautiful piece of craftsmanship I would have to admire later. Tissues peppered the living room area rug, in the middle of which sat a sobbing woman. I glanced around a bit more. There were quite a few pictures of Sara and two children. Each one contained smiling or silly faces. I couldn't help but grin. My gaze rested on one that held four people, two grown women and the two, smiling children. I could only guess the other woman was Lisaida. Her shoulder length dark hair fell haphazardly to one side as she leaned into Sara. The picture oozed happiness, in stark contrast to the scene on the floor. Sara was soon surrounded by her friends, consoling and hugging her.

The pain in that space was almost tangible, but so was the love. Focusing on career and gaining accolades and accomplishments had been the crux of my life. I couldn't even recall the last time anyone besides family or Indie was at my house. Sure, the Simons family came over to help with Bob whenever I was out of town, but that was not visiting; that was pet sitting.

Gabriel broke through the wordless noise, "Sara, Amie, someone please tell us what's happening here."

Blubbering, Sara tried to articulate words to no avail.

Amie stepped in, "She had court yesterday."

"What?" Indie chimed in. "I thought that was scheduled for Tuesday."

"It was." Amie responded. "They moved it up and she never told us."

"Sh-she… lied…" Sara managed between sobs. Helene pulled her closer and started rocking her like a child.

Amie continued on, "Lisaida told them Sara was not a fit parent. She lied about things and took some other things out of context, all of which made Sara look unfit in the eyes of the court. She now has supervised visits for the foreseeable future pending a full investigation into her life and her parenting."

"Puta!" Gabriel shouted. "Ella merece morir!"

I knew enough Spanish to understand the death wish placed on Lisaida.

"Why is she doing this?" Helene pondered. "What about what Melodie and Ethan want?"

"The court will interview them, I'm sure. Oh, sweetie, it'll all be cleared up soon," Indie consoled Sara, then turned her attention to Amie. "How long has she been like this?"

"We were supposed to go to brunch this morning. I walked in to find her passed out on the floor, surrounded by this mess," Amie motioned to the floor. "I woke her up and she started bawling again. It looks like she's still in her court clothes, so I'm guessing since yesterday?"

"Let's get some tea on. She needs something in her stomach," Indie suggested, rising up off of the floor.

I walked over to her.

"I got it, babe. You stay here."

"Okay, thank you." Indie gave my hand a squeeze and sat back down.

I entered the kitchen which was, thankfully, very organized. I put the tea kettle on the stove before searching for a tray of some sort. I reached around on the top of the fridge, finding one and pulling it down to me. Pictures floated one-by-one onto the floor. Stooping down to pick them up, I noticed they all had the second woman in them. I flipped through the stack. All of them held happy faces from happy times. In that moment, I understood what marriage meant to Indie.

My phone chimed, interrupting my thoughts. I was heading to Dubai next week. Sighing, I looked at the happy stranger in the pictures. Was she as selfish as I was? Is that what went wrong? What was I even doing talking to Indie about marriage and then contemplating taking a job in a country where we couldn't even date, much less marry?

CHAPTER 23

Indie

"WE HAVE TO DO SOMETHING about this Alicia/Ali thing," Helene mentioned. "Not only is it now extremely awkward, but she's not doing her job. I'm frustrated, to say the least."

"Yeah, I wasn't going to be the one to bring it up, but as your friend and business manager, I agree." Kenny offered.

"Oooh, so you admit you are my friend, Kenneth?" gloated Helene.

"Ugh, fine, yes. We have become friends." he responded, feigning pain as he spoke.

"I get to hug all of my friends," she sang, dancing toward her employee.

"Okay, that's enough. We are talking about a serious matter." I reminded my colleagues. "And *I* am not hugging you." I directed at Kenny.

"Yes, so, I have a plan." Kenny started. "I was talking with—uh, someone last night. Anyway, I think I should call Goodness Goods, as your business manager, bringing up all of the ways she has been completely inept over the last few months, and ask for someone else to take over."

"That sounds reasonable, and simple. I thought it would be more complicated, but I guess it's not." Helene admitted. "Alrighty then, let's go to lunch!"

The Thai place was within walking distance and it was a gorgeous day. With the Alicia fiasco behind us and the promise of chicken pad see ew before us, everyone's mood was lifted.

"So, how's Sara doing?" Helene inquired.

"I went by this morning and she had showered and gotten dressed, so that's a good sign." I informed her.

"That's the first time in a week! Heck yeah it's a good sign!" Helene cheered.

"It's just so terrible. How could anyone do that to a parent as fabulous as Sara?" added Kenny.

"Right? I mean, anyone who has seen her with her kids—wait, how do you even know what's going on?" I asked, perplexed.

"Well, uh, I mean, you guys...you guys talk about things," stammered Kenny. "I-I was there Saturday. I knew something was wrong. I just kinda connected the dots."

"Okay, calm down, I was just wondering."

Helene and I exchanged a glance of perplexity at our lunch companion's sudden uneasiness before I continued on, changing the subject. "So, when is that storm supposed to hit? I've heard it's going to be pretty bad."

"Yeah, I heard that too," added Helene. "Lukas has been battening down the hatches or whatever all damn day."

"I think it's going to start around five o'clock and dump like twelve to eighteen inches by morning. There might be some ice too. You should both fill up your gas tanks, pick the kids up early, and get things around as soon as we're done here," Kenny instructed.

"Oooo, when he's our friend, he gets all bossy!" Helene observed.

Heads turned all around the restaurant to see the cackling women and the man shaking his head.

Things started to get crazy while the girls and I were in line to pay at the grocery store. With three hours to go until the storm was supposed to start, the flurries falling just outside the enormous store windows told a different story.

The parking lot, which was black and mostly empty when we walked in, was now getting whiter by the second and was over halfway full. I joined my offspring in watching our breath cloud the sky and almost fell on my ass in the process.

"It's getting slick, girls, be careful." I cautioned, but before the last word left my mouth, Veda took a tumble, slamming her elbow into the macadam. "Oh baby girl! Are you okay?" I screeched, reaching for my injured child. "Mari, put the groceries into the car. I'll help Veda."

My eldest nodded and obeyed. For all her blustering, she was a softie who hated when people she loved were hurt. Gingerly placing Veda in the front seat and buckling her in, I turned to see Mari standing right behind me.

"It's broken, mom." she stated.

"What? Okay, I'll check it when we get home."

"It's broken," she repeated as she closed the car door behind her.

"Not today, please not today," I pleaded with the sky, snow falling on my upturned face.

We arrived home without further incident. Veda made her way inside and I headed for the ice packs in the refrigerator before going back outside to help Mari with the bags of groceries.

"Mom. It's broken. Please put her back in the car and take her to the ER before it gets worse out. Please." Mari pleaded.

"Mari, we don't know th-"

"MOM! I do know. Call it my gift, call it a twin thing, but something is broken in my sister. Please, just take her."

I reached up to wipe the tear from her cheek. "Okay, ya hayati, okay."

———————

"Yep, I'm at the hospital with her now. She broke her radial head." I explained quietly through the phone.

"Oh man, that sucks," Sam commented.

"And Mari just knew. She insisted I take Veda to the ER."

"That kid of yours is kind of amazing, kind of scary. I've already seen her know things a couple of times now."

"A couple of times? Like when?"

"We have our own private conversations too, ya know."

"Uh-huh. One of you will tell me eventually. So how's Dubai?"

"Same old amazing it always is."

Laughing, I remarked, "Yeah, sure, same old Dubai. I'm shaking my head and rolling my eyes at you, just so you are aware."

"Whatever. I'm too far away to care," she replied.

"Get to work, *ya rouhi*. I'll talk to you tomorrow."

"What did you call me?"

"Ya rouhi. It means my beloved in Arabic. I learned it Saudi, but never had the chance to use it before. I figured it apropos since you are currently in Dubai."

"Ahh, ok then, I'll take that! Goodnight, sleep tight, *yahoo-reet*."

I chuckled, "Close enough. Have a good day, go knock 'em dead."

My smile faded as I looked at the clock. The snow had been accumulating for hours already. The beeping of the heart monitor echoed through the otherwise silent space. Only absolutely necessary personnel were here... and us.

Veda stirred. I was carefully pulling the blanket further up onto her body when the doctor walked in. Seeing the sleeping girl, she motioned for me to come into the hall with her.

"Ms. Woodley, the x-ray shows her radial head is broken, as you know. That's the bad news," she paused, smiling. "The good news is that injury does not require a cast, just a sling. In more good news, the bump on her head is just that, a bump."

"No cast and no brain injury?" I asked.

"Yep, no cast and no brain injury. It actually needs to move during the healing process a bit to prevent it from becoming unusable. If we immobilize it, it may never move again."

"Oh, okay, good news indeed. Thank you very much."

"My pleasure. She can start getting dressed. I'm going to get you all checked out and have someone bring a sling in right away. We are trying to get you guys out of here quickly. The roads are already getting pretty bad. Don't want you to have to come right back!" the doctor jested.

"Definitely not!" I agreed. "Thank you again, Doctor..."

"Fuller."

"Thank you again, Doctor Fuller."

She nodded in my direction before continuing down the hall. Picking up my phone, I let Mari know all the details of her sister's injury as well as our pending arrival back home. The sleeping face was so peaceful, I hated to wake her, but we really did have to get home as rapidly as we could. I touched her good arm, causing her to stir, and told her the bad news and the good news, just like Doctor Fuller taught me. We were both beyond thankful she had worn a button-up shirt that day to school, making the difficult task of redressing a lot easier.

Within fifteen minutes, we were both snug in our warm car, leaving the hospital parking lot. I smiled once again at my snoozing daughter, pain prescription clutched in her good hand. Turning my full attention to the white out in front of me, I pulled slowly out onto what I hoped was the road. Almost eight inches of snow had already blanketed everything in a crisp coating of white and the wind had been working it in every direction over and over. I could barely tell which way was up and which was down. I silently thanked the universe my house was only a mile and a half away.

Inching along, hazards lights blinking, we slowly made our way towards home. By the time I saw the lights directly in front of me, it was too late. I turned the wheel as far as I could to the right. The pressure of the airbag pushed my face as the freezing wind whipped through the car. I couldn't tell where the screaming was coming from. Was it coming from me? *Oh god, Veda!*

Then it all stopped. In an instant, everything was black and calm and peaceful.

CHAPTER 24

Sam

A FEW OF THE PEOPLE in the building were getting to know my face, greeting me the same they had greeted Mark the last time I was here. It had only been three days, but I was already finding my groove. The good feeling faded each time I remembered what I would have to give up to come here.

"Sammi!" Mark called out. "Come on up to my office with me."

Shaking his hand in hello as we entered the elevator, I was still lost in my own mind.

"A penny for your thoughts?" he prompted.

"Ha, be careful what you ask for, Marky-boy."

His expectant expression showed no loss of interest. He and Cass were the closest things I had to confidants.

"Okay, but remember, you asked. And this is off the record." I warned.

His nod and crossing of his heart were enough of a promise to me.

"So, remember that subject we discussed the last time I was here, when we were in the limo? Well, I'm in a relationship, as you know. It's not just any relationship. It's my first love and we are getting very serious."

"Ahh," he said, realization flooding his brain. "Yes, that might be problematic."

"Exactly. I can't move here with this person and I can't move here without this person. It puts me in a bit of a bind. I have been working for this kind of a position for what seems like my entire life, so how can I give it up? But, on the other hand, I've been waiting for In– this person for what seems like my entire life too."

"I didn't realize."

The elevator doors opening put a pause on our conversation. We walked silently, nodding in greeting to those we passed. As soon as we entered Mark's office, he shut the door behind him and continued on.

"I know you know this, but if you refuse, they will blackball you."

"I'm well aware."

"Yet, you're still contemplating it. You must really be in love."

I plopped into the soft chair in front of the span of floor to ceiling windows looking out on the amazing skyline of Dubai.

"That I am."

Joining me, Mark asked hesitantly, "May I give you some unsolicited advice?"

My affirmative nod propelled him on.

"Don't give her up. I was in love before and I chose to keep working my way towards the top, telling her it was for the both of us. I could take care of her and give her everything she wanted if I just kept pushing. Thing is, all she wanted was me. I lost her, got all of the promotions, money, and an office in Dubai," he paused, sweeping his arm out in front of him, bringing attention to the view, "but I would give it all up in an instant to be with Trisha again."

"Wow. Thank you for telling me that. I dunno, I think you might be right. I don't know what I would do without Indie," I confessed. "Her daughter got hurt this morning, or last night. Well, last night their time. She fell and broke her arm or something. I hated not being able to be there. I mean, I know there's nothing I could have done, really, but I would've grabbed Indie some tea from the hospital cafeteria or just kept her company, ya know?"

"Yeah, I feel that. So, when are you telling our bosses? I'm slated to move to Boston in a few months, so I'm assuming they want you to come here around then."

"I have no idea. I haven't officially been offered the job yet, so I suppose I'll just wait until then." I panicked for a moment, fearing I had shared too much. "Please don't tell anyone yet. Please, Mark."

"Nah, I'm good for secrets. Besides, this was a conversation off the record. Business Mark doesn't even know any of this information, but he's about to show up, so let's quit the love talk and handle some business."

"Yes, sir," I agreed, saluting business Mark.

We hit a groove and worked straight through lunch. Mark and I thought similarly enough to understand each other, but differently enough to pick up the other's slack and help each other to view things from a different angle. I found myself wishing we had gotten the chance to work together more.

Stomachs growling, we headed down to the restaurant on the corner. Absentmindedly picking up my phone to check on an email, I saw four missed calls from Mari's phone and a slew of text messages. I opened the first one and started scrolling.

Mom and Veda are hurt. Call me.

**Something is wrong. Mom and Veda are
in danger. Please pick up your phone.**

> Sam, where are you? Mom is in the hospital. She won't wake up. Someone hit her. Please call me.

> There's a blizzard. I can't get to her.

> The hospital said Veda is awake, but mom is still unresponsive.

> SAM CALL ME PLEASE!!!

My breathing came in short bursts, I couldn't get my eyes to focus on any more of the texts. I had to get back to Indie. Now.

Amie and Helene were standing by Amie's car at the arrival terminal and rushed over when they saw me.

"How is she? Any changes while I was in flight?" I asked.

"No, nothing." Helene said.

The luggage was thrown into the trunk and the humans piled into the car. The silence was painful. I hadn't known Amie and Helene for long, but I knew they were never quiet. The tears finally started to spill over as I wordlessly begged for the life of my love to whomever or whatever was out there listening.

"How is Veda? How is Mari holding up?" I sniffled.

"Veda is in a regular room, she's eating solids, and has minor injuries, considering. She was lucky. The police said Indie must have turned the car at the last second so her side would take the brunt of the impact. Mari is a mess. She blames herself, since she was the one who insisted they go to the hospital. She hasn't left Indie's side, except to check on Veda now and then." answered Helene.

Motionless, staring at the trees whipping by, the tears fell. My chest hadn't felt free since I had gotten the news. The life was slowly being squeezed out of me and I was helpless to stop it.

"She knew." Amie muttered.

"What?" I asked.

"Mari, she just... knew," Amie reiterated before bursting into tears.

Helene took over the explanation from that point.

"Mari kept calling all of us thirty minutes before the hospital even called. She was hysterical, insisting Indie and Veda were in trouble. We all told her it would be okay and her mom was probably just concentrating and couldn't get to her phone. She could not be calmed down. That's when Sara suited up in snow gear to walk down there. As soon as she came in the door, the hospital called. It's crazy."

My leaking eyes turned their gaze back to the blur of trees and buildings passing by. Of course Mari knew. I will never question that kid on anything.

It's not so much hospitals themselves, it's the constant beeping and the smells that teeter between chemicals and bodily fluids that is so terrible. The hall stretched on forever. Door upon door flew by, each one looking the same as the last. Placing my hand on the doorknob, I braced myself for the sight of the woman I loved and walked into room 415.

Mari barreled into me. "I'm so glad you're here."

I wrapped my arm around the weeping child and we both walked over to the thin curtain separating Indie from the rest of the world. My heart stopped its onward march. Tears welled. This barely looked like a person, much less my person. What little skin was showing through the casts, pulleys, and bandages was covered in various shades of purple and blue. The ever-present beeping showed her heart was still marching. Willing mine to do the same, I let go of Mari and gave Indie a gentle peck on her forehead.

"I've been waiting for you to get here. Twice a day, I go check on Veda. I'll be right back," Mari informed, showing little evidence of her earlier distress.

I simply nodded in return, never looking away from Indie. The subtle hiss of her respirator kept time with the rise and fall of her bandaged chest. Her left arm was in a cast and hoisted above her like she was waving. My eyes moved on to the bandaged upper thigh and left ankle set in a cast. Caressing her cheek, I noticed the tufts of hair sticking out of her head bandage were crusty with dried blood. The tears that held been held at bay for days flowed freely.

"I'll never leave you again. I will be with you, no matter what that means, Indie, I promise," I cried into the pillow next to her ear. "No matter what."

The heavy chair scraped along the floor, but I didn't care. I needed to be close to my beloved. The jet lag and lack of sleep was beginning to take over. I felt my head bob more than once, but refused to willingly go into slumber. In my dream, Mari was yelling for help. My head bobbed once again, and I realized it was not a dream. Storming across the room and out the door, I went to protect Indie's child in her stead.

"I am not going with you. Let me go!" Mari shouted as she pulled her arm out of her father's hand.

"Mari, sweetie, you need a shower and a good night's rest. I'm just going to take you home for a little while," Zacariah pleaded with his daughter.

"I'm NOT leaving mom and Veda!" Mari insisted as she ran past Helene and Amie into Indie's room.

I put my hand up to stop Zacariah from going after her.

"Who the hell are you?" he asked.

"I'm Sam. You remember me?"

"Oh yeah. Long time no see, huh?"

"Yeah, so anyway. I know you are just trying to be a parent to Mari, but she's not a little girl anymore."

He began to protest, but I didn't allow him to get a word in.

"If you take her away now, you're the bad guy."

Sighing, he dropped his head into his hands.

"You're right. I'm just gonna go. I'm not needed here."

"Don't leave them again, Zacariah. This is being a parent. It's hard and, sometimes, they hate you. Your only job is to keep showing up."

"Excuse me? Don't you fucking tell me what to do! I don't need this shit!" and with that, he stormed off down the hallway full of beeps and nasty smells.

Helene turned to me, "I'm really beginning to like you."

I let out a weak chuckle. "Thanks. Shall we?" I asked, holding the door open for Indie's friends.

Mari, hunched over her mother's bedside with her heaving shoulders looked more like a small child than the young woman I made her out to be to her father just a moment ago.

She turned to Helene and collapsed into her, sobbing, "Don't let him take me away!"

"Oh, honey, no. No one is taking you anywhere. We got you. Besides, if he tries, Sam just might beat him up." Helene joked. "Amie and I are going to get you guys some clothes, snacks, books, etc." she announced, pulling out a pen and paper. "Here," she said, handing it to Mari, "write down anything in particular you want."

She turned to me, "I know you have your suitcase, but if you've got dirty clothes, you can give them to us and we'll wash them for you. Also, if there's anything you need, just add it to Mari's list."

"Thank you. Indie has some good friends," I remarked.

"Yeah, well she is a pretty good judge of character, only surrounds herself with the best people," Helene concurred, winking at me.

"I was just thinking, before we go, do you both want to go down and see Veda? We'll stay here with Indie until you get back," Amie interjected.

"Yes," I responded, "good idea."

"Hey, kid, how are you holding up?" I queried as Mari and I entered the room filled with flowers and balloons. While Veda had a couple of bandages and a cast, she was in much better shape than her mother.

"I'm okay," she winced, straightening up in her hospital bed. "I'm glad you're here." she managed with the utmost sincerity.

Her usually animated face had a somber look, which was only compounded by the pain meds she was being given.

"Me too," I agreed.

"How's mom?" Veda probed.

"No change," Mari replied. "I was just here fifteen minutes ago."

"I know, so was dad. Just wondering." Veda yawned.

"We'll let you get back to sleep. I'm here now and I will be until all of you are right as rain. Just say the word, and I'm here," I assured the sleepy teen.

"Thanks, Sam. You're alright," she slurred, smiling slightly and closing her eyes.

The moment we closed the door to Veda's room, my phone started buzzing. Mark was asking for details. I had completely forgotten to let him know when I landed. I shot him a couple of explanatory and apologetic texts back, almost running smack dab into a nun, and put the phone back in my pocket. Mari opened Indie's hospital room door and the phone started up again. I motioned her to go inside, and hit the answer button.

"Hello, Mark." I greeted.

"Umm, what? This is Ali," the caller replied.

"Ali?" I asked, incredulously. "What do you want?"

"Oh, c'mon, Sammi. You seemed so glad to see me the other day."

"Glad? No. I was civil, because we are both adults in a business setting."

"I know things ended badly, but I have no one else to turn to. I got fired. I'm not in a good place, Sammi. I need your help."

CHAPTER 25

Indie

WHERE WAS THAT godforsaken beeping coming from and why wouldn't it just shut up? Muffled voices were somewhere, but I couldn't figure out where or who was talking. The damn beeping intensified. Whoever those voices belonged to had to hear the incessant beeping. I kept trying to shout, get someone's attention, but my throat wouldn't work. My heart began to race. Someone stop the goddamn beeping! Once again, the annoying sound sped up. This time, the voices seemed closer. Maybe they finally heard the beeping. Mari was there! Oh thank god, please stop the beeping, Mari, please. Was she crying? Shouting, beeping, sobbing, what was wrong?!? I couldn't take it anymore. Willing my eyes open, light blinded me.

"Mom? MOM!" Mari cried out.

I tried to speak, but something was in my throat. Pain was everywhere. Tears streaming down my cheeks, my eyes finally focused and I saw the fluorescent lights, Mari's tear-stained face, and Sam. Mari collapsed onto my chest, heaving and bawling her eyes out. I tried to bend my arm to embrace her, but the pain hit in a new wave.

"It's okay, babe. You're in the hospital. You were in a car accident. You've got some broken bones and casts. You're also hooked up to a bunch of machines and there is a tube in your throat." Sam explained slowly.

The more my head cleared, the more pain set in. Looking away from her face, I started to process what I had just been told. I vaguely remembered snow. I was driving. Why was I driving? My brow furrowed in frustration. My mind was a jumbled mess.

"You okay, babe?" Sam asked.

I nodded the best I could. I felt her gently grab my hand as she patted Mari on the back with the other. She had been taking care of my child while I was lying in a hospital bed. Where was Veda? VEDA!! I was driving Veda! Panic replaced pain as the dominant feeling in my body. I was trying to get up, but could barely move. Hyperventilating, I looked to Sam, imploring her with my eyes to tell me about my daughter.

"Indie? Indie what's wrong?" Sam asked.

"MOM?" Mari shouted as she lifted herself from my torso.

I grabbed Sam's hand before she could run out and get medical personnel. I spelled V-E-D with my finger on her palm.

Her eyes widened as she leaned into me.

"Babe, she's fine. Veda is okay. She's on the next floor. Sara is with her right now."

The relief flooding through me brought sobs that wracked my body. The pain no longer mattered, though. My baby girl was alive. The never-ending beeping had quickened so much, the nurses came running in without Sam's intervention. The pain in my chest kept growing and sharpening. My vision started going black around the edges.

One of the nurses put something into my IV and the world's hard edges softened and faded to nothing.

Muffled noises filtered through the haze. The beeping in the background again intensified with every second. I heard a moan. Was that me? Hands were touching my arms. The voices sounded concerned. I recalled this had happened before, but didn't know when. All of my thoughts felt like they were half formed, moving through honey.

"Mom, we're all here," someone said quietly. They sounded far away. I moaned and tried to turn my head towards the speaker.

"She moved her head!" another voice announced. "Someone get Sam!"

Sam? I knew someone named Sam once. We were so young, so in love. She was my everything for so long. Where did she go?

"Babe? Babe, can you hear us?" a new speaker interjected.

Who were all of these people? Where was I? Why was I in so much pain? Something was wrong, but I couldn't figure out what. The ideas and thoughts swimming through my head were starting to become clearer. I had been in an accident. Yes, an accident, but when? Where was I? This was infuriating.

"Her hands are moving!" a young girl cheered. It was my daughter, Veda.

Veda had been in the accident too! It was all coming back to me. The snow, the car, the lights, turning at the last moment, then nothing.

My eyes shot open. The faces surrounding me were not those I expected. Strangers, with one exception. The face was familiar, but I didn't know why. The beeping was compounded by barking orders from one medical professional to another. Numbers and words I didn't understand were all I could focus on. Maybe I had imagined my loved ones' voices?

The pain in my throat intensified and then subsided. A tube

was floating in front of my face. Had it been down my throat? The bone-dry feeling within my mouth prompted me to attempt to speak.

"Water," I rasped. "Please, water."

A kind, rotund nurse smiled and brought a cup to my parched lips. Gently lifting my head, she tipped a small sip of liquid into my mouth.

"There, hun, drink up. You've had quite the week."

I opened my eyes to see the people I had been dreaming about. There, at the bottom of the bed, behind a slew of strangers, were my family. My weak smile seemed to encourage them.

"Indie. Indie, do you remember me?" the familiar face asked. "I'm Doctor Fuller. I told you not to come right back here. Do you remember?"

I nodded and she continued on.

"You are a very fortunate woman. I know you're still coming to, so I'll be brief. You have some broken bones. You did have internal bleeding. We took care of that, but that is why your chest and abdomen feel sore. You and your daughter should both make a full recovery. I'll give you much more in the way of details once you are fully awake and ready."

She passed a light in front of my eyes while taking my pulse. Squeezing my hand, she turned to my people. "She'll be fine. Let her get lots of rest and I'll be back in a couple of hours to check on you all."

"Thank you so much, Dr. Fuller." said Sam.

After more poking and prodding, the team of people who had worked so diligently, and kept me alive, left the room.

"Mom!" Mari exclaimed, running over and hugging me with a bit too much gusto. I winced, but allowed it, nonetheless.

Veda, was next, being wheeled over by Sam. I teared up at the sight of her. The bruising on her face had yellowed a bit, but it was still there.

She reached out and I grabbed her hand. "I was afraid you were..." I gulped, not able to force myself to say the words out loud.

"I know," she sniffled, "me too. No one would tell me anything about you. They put us in different ambulances and I couldn't get any information. I thought... well I thought what you thought."

"Oh baby, I'm just so glad you're alright," I sobbed as my child became blurry.

Sam was at my side in an instant with a tissue, dabbing my cheeks. I looked at my love, fresh tears spilling over. "I cannot begin to thank you."

"There is absolutely nowhere I would rather be," Sam whispered.

"What in the world?" I asked as we drove up to my house.

I looked, wide-eyed, at the woman driving. She shrugged. "You did this? For me?"

"Well, yeah. I'm growing rather fond of you. It's removable, though, don't worry. The ramp, that is, not my fondness." Sam hesitated, "I didn't drill into your house or anything."

Playfully smacking her arm, I replied, "Yeah, that's what I'm worried about."

Veda may have moved on to crutches, but I was going to be in this chair on wheels for a while. Wheeling up the new ramp and into my abode was humbling. The entire house had been rearranged to allow a wheel chair to have access to everything a person could need on a daily basis.

"Surprise!" the huddle of people hiding in the kitchen shouted.

If I had been standing, I may have fallen over in astonishment. The river of emotion flowing inside started leaking out. Wheeling into the kitchen, I marveled at the sea of balloons framing a banner welcoming me home. Each of these people had come to see me in the hospital, but seeing all of them in one room, supporting my little family was too much for me to process. The ugly crying started and, with it, the aching and stinging. Sam was at my side with tissues before I could even request them.

"So, she's a keeper." Gabriel whispered in my ear, nodding toward Sam. "Wait until you see what she did for you in the bedroom and bathroom." Straightening up his spine, he mumbled, "She's had us in here working like perritos for days. I may never again be the same." His feigned trauma was a bit over the top, even for him.

"Oh, really? You poor thing." I replied with the amount of sympathy he deserved. "But, yes, she is a keeper. So how about you? You've been on a few dates lately. How's all of *that* going?"

The normally cool, calm, collected man shifted his weight and looked away.

"Nothing major to report."

"You liar!" I accused in a hushed tone.

"Shhhhh!" Gabriel sibilated. "I may or may not have some news to report. I can neither confirm or deny such allegations."

"Boy, you better spill, or I'm gonna have to start making some noise and there will be many more people trying to get this information that may or may not exist."

"Wow, who knew a gimp could be so mean. Fine," he caved. "I have met someone amazing. He checks all of the boxes. He even checks a few boxes I didn't know I had."

"Oooo, what's this dream man's name?"

My amigo hesitated for far too long.

"The clock is ticking until the broken lady in the wheelchair yells and gets everyone's attention, just sayin'."

"Ugh, fine." Bending down to my ear, he whispered, "It's Kenny."

"My Kenny?!?!" I screeched.

The room went dead silent. Kenny's eyes were like saucers. Almost everyone else looked slightly alarmed and confused, everyone except Sam. She looked suspicious.

"Your Kenny?" Helene offered me a chance to explain.

Gabriel laughed nervously. "Indie had just asked me who made the seven layer dip. She obviously didn't know Kenny knew his way around a recipe." This statement got everyone laughing again.

"Uh, yeah," I started, side-eyeing Gabriel and Kenny, "sorry for how loud it was. I guess I'm still a little loopy from all of these pain meds."

As Amie and her newest soulmate came towards us, I gave Gabriel a glare letting him know we were not done talking about the news he had just shared.

Amie bent down and kissed my cheek. "How are you feeling, sweetie?"

"Pretty good. I'm just so glad to be home, and alive! I don't even care about the pain right now." I declared enthusiastically.

My eyes flitted to the tall, dark brown woman standing next to my friend. I knew what the answer would be, but I just had to ask. "Who is your friend?"

Amie beamed with infatuation. "This is Ifueko. She is from Africa! I met her while you were in the hospital. She's a doctor."

"Nice to meet you." Ifueko addressed me, offering her hand. "I am familiar with your injuries and am very glad you are feeling better."

"Thank you. It's nice to meet you as well." I echoed her sentiment. "Please, eat as much as you'd like, especially that amazing dip Kenny made," I said a little too loudly while doling out glares to Kenny and Gabriel.

"Thank you. It is good," Ifueko replied.

Amie widened her eyes, lifted her brows, and winked at me as she and her date of the week sauntered over towards the food. I couldn't help but sigh. Seeing this, Sam thought I was getting tired or something was wrong. She rushed over like a mother hen.

"You okay, babe? What do you need. Are you in pain? Tired?"

I knew she was trying to be loving and helpful, so I tried to keep my eyes from rolling. "No, dearest, I'm all good."

"What was that between you and Gabriel?" she pressed.

Giddy as a school girl at the prospect of sharing the mind-blowing information I had just discovered, I whispered, "I'll tell you later."

Smiling and kissing my forehead, she walked over to refill snacks and drinks.

Using what strength I had in my hands, I spun those huge wheels and got myself over to the large wall of windows in the sunroom overlooking the backyard. Mari, Veda, Javi, Helene's children, Cameron, and Lydia were all out there playing some form of softball. Veda was sitting in one chair with her leg up on another as the catcher. Overcome with thankfulness to be able to witness these children playing together again, I started to tear up. Sadness crept in. Life is so precious. While my priorities in life hadn't changed, they felt magnified. Nothing was more important than relationships, especially with your own children.

"Penny for your thoughts?" Helene startled me, interrupting my thoughts.

"Geez, girl, don't DO that! I didn't survive a car crash to be taken down by heart failure."

"You looked happy for a moment, then really sad. What's up?"

"I was looking at our beautiful children. That was the happy part. Then I realized some were missing. Melodie and Ethan should be here."

"You're not wrong. They should be. I hate that Sara is going through this. I hate that the kids are going through this!"

"I have an idea." I revealed, piquing my business partner's

interest. "We are doing well, right? This whole Goodness Goods thing is bringing in lots of money."

She nodded, smiling, cocking her head, and waiting eagerly for what came next.

"I know Sara isn't poor or anything, but Lisaida has family money and she has hired one of the best lawyers in New England. I say we hire Sara *the* best lawyer in the whole damn country."

"Indie Woodley, I like the way you think."

"Oh no, what are you two plotting out here?" Lukas interjected.

"World takeover type stuff, that's all," I replied nonchalantly.

After a good laugh, Helene leaned into her husband's ear and told him our plan.

Lukas commented, "Count me in too. I've got a friend in New York who is some big-wig lawyer. I'm sure he can tell us who the shark is in the waters of family court."

Helene beamed. "This is why I love you," she cooed, hugging him from behind.

"Really, Lukas? This is fantastic!" I squealed.

Sara found her way to our little group and was curious.

"What's so fantastic?"

"That 7-layer dip. Lukas got the recipe from Kenny." I replied.

"Wow, you're really into that dip, huh?"

———————

"You're staying here again?" I asked.

"Yeah, I'm staying as long as you need me," Sam reassured me.

"Well, that's awfully nice of you. What about your job? Bob? Your entire life? You've been here for three days and I know you were at the hospital quite a while before that."

"I mean, I have a lot of vacation days saved up, and it's only been a couple of weeks. Plus, I've been going in now and then, as you know, and doing a lot of work from home. The Simons family next door and George are taking care of Bob, but I could bring him here, if you're worried. So it's all good, babe, don't you fret."

She bounded into the bathroom to get ready, leaving me comfortably propped on the bed. Leaning my head back and closing my eyes, I took a few deep breaths. I loved Sam. I was injured. She was helping to get me to physical therapy, taking care of the kids, cleaning, cooking, making sure I could still run my business, so why did I want her to leave?

Exasperated sighs get the attention of caretakers, so I sat silently. This was *my* house. This was *my* life. I hadn't even invited her to stay or do all of this stuff for me. She had just taken over. Tears began to form. I just wanted to be alone. Hearing her nighttime routine winding down, I feigned sleep.

CHAPTER 26

Sam

"I DON'T KNOW, CASS, she's just been acting weird over the last couple days," I explained.

"But, like, weird how?"

"I can't put my finger on it. She just seems slightly hostile and distant. Do you think the brain injury changed her personality? That can happen, right?"

"I think so. I've heard about that kind of thing, but I'm not really sure how it works or what you're supposed to look for. I think it's amazing; all you're doing for her. She better be grateful."

"No, it's not like that. I know she's thankful for everything, something is just off. I don't know, maybe I'm just imagining it."

"Well, I mean, she did just go through some pretty life altering shit. She was in a huge accident, almost died, and can't walk right now. She's dependent on other people for almost everything," Cass pointed out. I nodded in agreement. "Plus, didn't you say her daughter was with her in the car? That has to mess a parent up. She's gotta be very frustrated. I know I'd be."

"Yeah, yeah, her youngest was in the car. I guess you're right. I would be kinda pissy too," I admitted.

"Just cut her some slack, Sam," Cass concluded. "Ugh, gotta go meet with Mr. Davidson. This is the client that never shuts up, I swear! This fucker can go on for a full hour on the pen he's holding. I know the entire history of the Bic Corporation, in case you're ever interested."

I chuckled, "Thanks, I'll keep that in mind. Have fun!" I called after the retreating figure who was, once again, flipping me off behind her back. Turning attention back to the computer screen, I didn't hear the footsteps coming into my cubicle.

"Satomi, may I see you in my office?" Mrs. Stanton requested.

"Yes, ma'am, of course. Just let me send this email and I'll be right in." I replied nervously.

She nodded and retreated to her corner office: the same office Mark would be taking over in a matter of months. This was it. Either I would be offered a job in a faraway country and have to choose between it and my love, or the decision would be made for me, and I could go home to Indie ready for our future together, slightly deflated for having been passed over.

Pulling into Indie's driveway, I saw Sara's car alongside one I did not recognize. Voices were carried on the wind blowing outside the open window. It sounded serious. Debating whether or not to go in, I grabbed the mail and saw a letter from Zacariah. I wasn't sure any therapy breathing would help me right now. That asshole hadn't even shown back up at the hospital after our little discussion over Mari. He called now and then, but had not once come to see his own daughters. Given my current mental state, taking a walk and letting Sara and Indie finish their business would be the best bet for us all.

Indie's neighborhood was peaceful and well laid out. Mrs. Johanssen across the street waved to me as she was watering her garden. She had organized a neighborhood dinner train for Indie and the girls for the first two weeks they were all home. She could be a little overbearing, but that's just because she cared. I waved back, already feeling my mood lifting.

What if Indie and I lived here together? What if Bob could come and run around in the yard? I had already been here for about a week and things seemed to be going well. Why keep my apartment in the city? Today was a day of changes, I could feel it!

By the time I rounded the corner to head back to Indie's house, I felt renewed. The mystery car was gone, but Sara's was still there. The girls would be home from school any minute, so I wanted to get in there and get a snack around before they traipsed in the door.

The scene before my eyes was confounding. Crying with smiles was not a usual combination, especially with Sara.

"Hello ladies," I greeted, "what's happening in here today?"

"Indie and Helene got me the best lawyer ever. I'm fighting Lisaida." Sara beamed, tears streaming.

"So I heard. Congratulations," I replied before kissing Indie on the forehead. She smiled at me, lifting my mood further.

"Lukas and Sam chipped in some too," Indie interjected.

Sara's gasp caused me a bit of embarrassment. I didn't think Indie was going to tell her. "It was only a little, Helene and Indie are the ones who thought of it and did everything. They're the ones who deserve your appreciation."

"Oh thank you, so much. I am just so overwhelmed! At first, not gonna lie, I was upset, but swallowing my pride is worth it if I can get my kids back," Sara gushed.

I excused myself and started getting some goodies around for everyone. Hearing the door open without the usual chatter was cause for alarm. I walked out to see Mari hand Indie a sealed envelope from the school. Veda hadn't looked up from the floor.

"How could they do this? This could go on their permanent records! Oh my god, I can't even pace. How the hell am I supposed to pace while bound to a wheelchair?" Indie vented.

"Babe, I know you're upset, but I also know we'd have done something like this in high school if a kid tried to mess with my sister," I said, trying to calm her and lighten the mood a little.

"That's beside the point! This is their future! Leaving that kid pantsless to run around the school? Is that really the best way to handle things? I wasn't allowed to go to the principal or the police about what happened, but they can pull a stunt like this? This is some prank their father would pull. What am I going to do?"

"Oh, right, him!" I exclaimed, running out of the bedroom and right back in. "Sorry, in all of the excitement today, I forgot about this letter that came in the mail."

"Great," she stated. "Another letter."

Ripping it open, her eyes went from squinting to saucers.

"He's suing me for fifty-fifty custody! He said he wanted to tell me before the official documents showed up."

"What?!" I exclaimed as she handed over the letter. "That's exactly what it says. Wow."

"I know that's what it says." Indie snapped, tearing the letter out of my hands before crumpling it up and throwing it on the floor.

"Hey, let's look at the bright side; he doesn't have a leg to stand on, you have been their sole caregiver for over half their lives, they are old enough to testify for themselves, and you've got the best family lawyer on the East Coast on speed dial." My points having their desired effect, I continued on. "He's just pissed because of what happened with Mari in the hospital."

"What? What happened with Mari?"

"He tried to force her to leave when you and Veda were both still in there. You hadn't even woken up yet. She freaked out on him. I told him he shouldn't make her because she was scared and he would seem like the bad guy. He got pissed at me, told me I had no place talking to him about his own child, and stormed off."

"Oh, wow. Thanks for sticking up for her."

"Always. These kids of yours are pretty awesome."

My comment made her smile; a genuine smile I hadn't seen in a while.

"Yeah, they are."

"I'm not sure this is the right time for this, but I have been thinking about us a lot lately. Obviously, this accident has brought a lot of feelings to the surface for many of us. I know we've talked here and there about our future, but I was thinking about moving in together in the near future. What are your thoughts?"

"Ummm, I–I don't know. I have been so preoccupied. I haven't really thought about that for quite some time. I just started healing. I don't know."

"It's okay, take all the time you need. I wanted to bring it up, that's all. Just suggested it so we can think and talk and plan. No pressure." I rattled on, once again seeing her stress dissipate. "So, change of subject, what in the world was going on with you and Gabriel the other night? We were so caught up in talking about Sara, I forgot to ask you."

"Oh, yes!" smirked Indie. "Huge news! Guess who Gabriel is dating now."

"Kenny?"

"Yes," Indie remarked, confused. "How did you know that?"

"Oh, I figured it out at Helene's wedding. Then Mari confirmed it the first night I came here."

"You've known all this time? You never told me? You and Mari kept a secret from me?" she rattled on, her voice growing ever angrier.

"Babe, it's not like that. It wasn't my secret to tell, so I kept my mouth shut. As for Mari, she had figured it out on her own because, as you know, she just knows things. She saw me staring at them and came to me. It was the first time she and I connected. Since she hadn't told you, I wasn't going to break her trust."

"Fine," she sighed. "Anything else you want to tell me?" she challenged.

I debated not telling her about Dubai, since her mood was already as sour as a Warhead candy, but thought that may make things worse in the future.

"Yes, actually. I was offered the job in Dubai."

"Wait, what?"

"Well, I told you Mrs. Stanton is leaving, right?"

Indie nodded slowly.

"And they were thinking of me to take over things at the Dubai office?"

She nodded again.

"Well, they have officially offered it to me."

"So you were offered a job that you told me you weren't going to get? A job that you downplayed months ago telling me there was nothing to worry about. Is that why you've been going over there? Did you know this whole time and not tell me the truth?" she shrieked.

"No! No, they just offered it to me today. I was told I was a candidate, but was never actually offered the job. I was pretty damn sure I wouldn't get it, but Mark and Mrs. Stanton really pushed for me."

"So you're moving to Dubai and leaving me? You just said we should move in together, and now you're moving to the other side of the world? What does all of this mean, exactly?"

"This means I was offered a job. This means I want you and I to discuss our future. This means I love you and want to do what's best for us."

She sat completely still for what seemed like an hour. Afraid to frighten her off like a small animal I came across in the forest, I was still right along with her.

"I need to go to bed. I cannot handle anything else right now. I feel like I might either throw up or murder someone."

"That's fair. I'll go get ready for bed," I acquiesced, heading into the master bathroom. My phone dinged. "Hey babe, can you check that, please? It should be right there next to you on the bed. It's awfully late, so it might be my mom or the Simons with an emergency or something."

"Today would be the day for it."

I was halfway through brushing when she said, "Why the hell is Alicia, Ali, or whoever she is texting you after 10 p.m., and what is she thanking you for?"

"Wha–?" I came out of the bathroom, toothpaste dripping down my chin.

She threw the phone at me and crossed her arms. I half expected steam to start coming out of her ears like in the cartoons I watched as a child.

"I oh–nt oh."

"What?" shouted Indie, impatient with my muffled words.

I hurried back to the bathroom sink and spit.

"I don't know," I said again. Opening the text, I relaxed a little. "She's just thanking me for helping her out a couple of weeks ago."

"Helping her out?"

"Yeah, she got fired from Goodness Goods because she kept screwing up. She decided to go into rehab for her drinking problem. She called me one day and asked if I could help her. So I sent her some money, that's all."

"Oh, you paid for your ex-fiancée to go to rehab?"

"Well, not exactly. I paid for her rent for those two months."

"So you paid for your ex's rent?! While I was dying in a hospital bed? Just trying to make sure you had a warm bed to go to if I died?"

"Whoa," I started to explain, but was drowned out by the screaming.

"Get out! GET OUT!! Don't you ever come back here! What the hell else are you keeping from me? You wanna move with your ex to Dubai and keep secrets with my daughter and ex-husband? Well go right ahead! I NEVER WANT TO SEE YOU AGAIN!" Indie railed into me with her wheelchair. "Get out! Get out! GET OUT!"

I backed into the hallway leaving her the space to slam the door in my face. Slumping my shoulders, chocking it up to a lot of stress, I turned to see two teenage girls in their pajamas staring at me.

"You might want to steer clear of your mom tonight and be extra helpful in the morning." I warned.

Both girls nodded.

"I'm going to go sleep at my place. Call me if you need anything."

Upon entering my apartment, I was attacked by the cutest purring cat I ever did see.

"I know, bud, I know. I've been gone for a while." I crooned while petting his ever-moving form. "You should thank Indie. If she hadn't kicked me out, I'd still be gone."

Shutting the door behind me, I looked at the empty space. The dust had little kitty paw prints in it, and the hairballs were rolling around the floor like we were in an old western movie. Being too wound up to sleep, I started the long overdue task of cleaning.

As one a.m. approached, so did the end of the cleaning spree. Energy zapped, I fell onto the sofa. I jumped right back up as my phone started buzzing. Something happened to Indie. I was halfway across the room to my shoes and keys when I answered the call.

"Sammi?" said the familiar voice on the other end.

"What the hell do you want now?" I asked.

"You did-nint ressspond, so I called juu," Ali slurred, failing an attempt at sounding sexy.

"For the love of god, woman, leave me alone."

"Wha-at? Why? You loves meeee."

"No, I do not. I used to. I wish you the best. I hope you find what you need in life, but it's not me. Good bye, Ali. Your number will be blocked from now on. Get yourself together."

I hit the red button on my phone screen and was true to my word. The woman I thought I would spend the rest of my life with was now blocked. The woman I wanted to spend the rest of my life with had kicked me out. And the woman looking back at me in the mirror had just about had enough of women for today.

CHAPTER 27

Indie

Getting up and ready in the morning proved more difficult than I realized without someone there helping. Putting clothing on was nearly impossible, and putting my hair up was completely impossible.

"Nice, mom," Veda said after seeing my state. "You going for a homeless look?"

Glaring at her from the other side of her lunchbox, I raised my eyebrows while tilting my head down. She got the message loud and clear, wiping the smile from her face.

When Mari came into the kitchen, she wordlessly helped me get things around. Neither of us would look the other in the eye. Veda sighed loudly upon slinging her backpack over her shoulder.

"Bye, mom. Love you," she said, running out the front door.

"I love you, too," I replied. "Both of you."

Mari's deadpan stare implied I would receive no such sentiment from her this morning. Huffing, she slammed the door behind her.

Turning around, I looked at the mess in the kitchen. Some things would have to stay on the counter, seeing as how they belonged in an upper cabinet. Thank to Sam's setup, I could easily clean off and wipe down most of the counters and I finagled a way to sweep up. I was feeling pretty proud until I tried to get my green juice from the top shelf of the fridge. Giving up, I rolled over to my computer at the desk Sam put in the corner of my living room and got to work.

Trying to concentrate on this quarter's P&L proved to not be an easy task. Between my body aching and my mind flooding, exhaustion quickly came onto the scene. I shut down the computer and wheeled myself back towards the bedroom. Staring at the towering bed, giving up on getting back into that comfy bed was really the only option. I rolled back out into the living room and shifted onto the sofa. Sleep overtook my broken, beat-up body quickly.

———————

Gasping and almost falling off of the couch, I looked around and instantly relaxed. It was only a dream. Not even noticing the tears were there until feeling them roll down my cheeks, I couldn't seem to will myself to move. When a mind has had enough, it will take a rest, whether its owner gives it permission or not.

Outside the large picture window, the naked trees were beginning to bud with this year's leaves. What did Gram used to say? The only thing that never changes is change itself. Someone else must have said it first, but Gram was the one who drilled it into her children's and grandchildren's heads. Change is good. Change is necessary. Too much change, however, can cripple a person beyond anything they can handle. The tears picked up with gusto, blurring the beautiful budding trees. Was this body unwilling or unable to move at this point? There needed to be a different word for this kind of overwhelm. Overwhelmed just didn't cut it. Crushed? Stretched thin? No word or phrase in existence seemed to be able to encompass this feeling.

Lost in the sea of emotional inundation, the notification sound startled me. Wiping the wet from my eyes, I tried to focus on the screen in front of me.

hey how are you feeling this morning?
girls get off to school ok?

Now came the conundrum to confound the confusion in my already overloaded mind; answer Sam or ignore her altogether? Throwing the phone down on the adjacent cushion, the tears began their descent once more.

She lied. She lied about quite a few things. What else was she keeping from the woman she said she loved? Having been through this before, I had no desire to waste years of my life with someone who would just cheat and lie and try to pull the wool over my eyes about all of it.

Some conviction returned to my tired mind. Sam would be ignored. No, not ignored... not yet. No answer would probably bring her over here immediately to check and make sure nothing terrible had occurred. Reaching for the phone, I sent a short, but powerful, reply.

I'm fine. Girls are good. I don't want to talk to you. I'm very upset. I will not be lied to and kept in the dark by the person who says they love me ever again. I wish the best for you in life. Goodbye, Sam. Enjoy Dubai.

There, it was done. Muting any further attempts of contact from Sam, now was the time to concentrate on more important matters; like healing and getting this business where it needs to be to function without Helene. Tears or not, shit had to get done, and no one else was here to do it. This badass single mother, entrepreneur, and self-made woman had not made it this far just to give up.

———————

Feeling the left headphone abruptly lift off of my ear, I inhaled sharply and started swinging.

"Whoa, woman! It's me, Sara!"

"Oh, sorry." I apologized. "Wait, no I'm not. What the hell? Why did you sneak up on me like that?"

"I'd been knocking for a minute or two. I was worried I'd find you like those commercials where the old lady says she's fallen and can't get up," Sara stated with the straightest face a lesbian can muster.

Laughter burst out between two very dear friends.

"Thanks," I started, "I really needed that today."

"What in the world is going on? Sam text me asking if I could check on you. All she would say is that she was worried about you."

I scoffed at my friend's words, turning back to my computer.

"As you can see, I'm fine. I'm working."

"Hold up, now I know something is wrong. What's going on with you and Sam? Did you two get into a fight or something?"

"Yeah, something like that. I broke up with her."

Sara's face contorted with shock for a good thirty seconds before she could get any words out.

"What? When? WHY?"

"She has been keeping things from me."

"Like what?"

Spinning around to fully face the inquisition before me, I listed Sam's offenses without emotion.

"She lied to me by not telling me about Kenny and Gabriel, which she kept from me along with my daughter. She didn't tell me about a job in Dubai she got. She also decided to help her ex-girlfriend out while I was unconscious in the hospital. You remember Alicia, right?" I felt some of the fire leave me. Slumping my shoulders and pinching the bridge of my nose, I softly declared, "I will not live like that again, Sara. I cannot. No more lying and cheating. Zacariah 'helped' lots of women too."

The tears that had been held back for hours flowed freely in Sara's supportive embrace. She stayed, kneeling, holding her wheelchair bound friend for much longer than could have possibly been comfortable. Once the deluge started to subside, she retrieved a tissue for the sloppy, snotty mess who was her comrade in life.

"Okay, let's start from the beginning. Not to sound like I'm not caring about what's going on with you and Sam, but what about Gabriel?"

"Oh, right. Sorry. I wasn't supposed to say anything!" I shouted, panic setting in. "I promised Gabriel!"

"Hey, hey, calm down. It's all good. So don't actually tell me. I'll guess. Are he and Kenny, you know, like together together?"

I nodded.

"Wow! Right, okay. Well, I'll just pretend I don't know a thing. We're all good."

We sat in comfortable silence, holding hands.

"Are you sure about this? I don't know all of the details, and I am in no way defending her, but it seems like she didn't lie, exactly. Now hear me out," she insisted as I opened my mouth in protest. "I'm on your side, always, but you really love this woman. That's a statement, not a question," she announced when she noticed me inhaling to speak again. "Gabriel's secret was his, right? You felt badly for telling me, so maybe she was in the same boat?"

"Maybe," I acquiesced.

"Okay. Next item: Dubai?"

"That's why she's been going there so often. She was working with the current guy so she would be ready to take over."

"Alright, that's a biggie. And she didn't tell you?"

"Nope, not until yesterday when they officially offered her the job."

"Wait, so she did tell you?" Sara clarified.

"Well, eventually. She had told me it was a possibility months ago, but brushed it off as something that was almost an impossibility. Why was she building a life with me, talking about the future and marriage and living together when she was running off to Dubai?"

"Hmm," Sara pondered. "I'm not too sure on that. I will say, she did tell you as soon as she was actually offered the job. Maybe she was waiting to see if she truly got the job first, before worrying you?"

"Maybe," I admitted. "But she was getting all chummy-chummy with her ex-fiancee while I was in a goddamn coma. She sent her money to pay her bills while she went to rehab."

"Indie, it's her money. She can do what she likes with it."

"But it's her ex who she supposedly can't stand."

"True, but once you have had feelings for someone, you always care. You may not love them anymore, but you still care. I mean, she told you about it, or you wouldn't know, right?" asked Sara.

"No, not really. She asked me to check her text that came in. It was from Ali, Alicia, or whatever her name is. She was thanking her. I asked Sam and that's when she told me. I need to eat."

Sara sat thinking as I wheeled myself into the kitchen to quell my rumbling stomach, which had been ignored all day. I gathered the ingredients to make a couple of sandwiches, and soon a lunch for two friends was all plated up.

"Hey, I need some help in here, please!" I called out.

Slowly walking into the kitchen, and smiling at the two plates of food, Sara said, "Thanks, Indie. So, I was just thinking, if she was trying to hide cheating from you, or even just giving money, why would she ask you to check her phone?"

"I don't know. This all just feels too familiar. I'm not ready. I don't think I can ever really trust someone again. It's easier to be single."

"Yes, it is definitely easier, but when has Indie Woodley ever taken the easy way?" challenged Sara.

"Now." I insisted. "By the way, would you, could you, be a dear, and take me to a meeting at the school this afternoon? Pretty please with best friend sprinkles on top."

Pleading from a crying gimp was hard to ignore.

Being wheeled by Sara down a school hallway felt awkward. Teenagers were staring at the lady with the bruised face and casts rolling around their school. It actually felt like being in high school all over again. Everyone staring while the freak went to the principal's office.

Upon reaching the office, Sara checked in with the receptionist, positioned me as out of the way as possible, and plopped into the chair next to me.

"Well, this is a first in my adult life," whispered Sara.

"Mine too," I agreed.

Both looking toward the entrance, Mari and Veda appeared before us. Rubbing her left arm with her opposite hand, Veda stared at the floor. In stark contrast, her sister looked straight ahead, chin up, defiant to the core.

"Ms. Woodley?" a small older gentleman inquired, flitting his stare between Sara and me.

"I'm Ms. Woodley." I responded. The twins rose, ready to file in after me.

"No, you two wait here," he said to the girls before turning back to me. "I'm Mr. Railey. It's nice to meet you, although I wish it were not under these circumstances."

Following him into his office, which was very traditionally decorated, I noticed he graduated from MIT and wondered why the heck he was in a private school as a principal.

"Now, Ms. Woodley, I'm sure you are aware of the situation which occurred yesterday?" he posed as a question instead of a statement.

"Yes, I read the letter and my children explained in detail."

"Good, so we don't have to rehash all of that before we get to the meat of the matter. What your children did was unacceptable."

"I agree, it was not an appropriate way to act," I concurred, surprising the minuscule man across the desk.

"Yes, well, good. Your daughters will each be receiving a suspension. I'm glad we see eye to eye on this matter."

"We do indeed, so let's move on to the other matter."

"Other matter, ma'am?"

"Yes."

"What other matter?"

"The matter of what this boy did to my daughter."

"Excuse me?"

"Mr. Railey, as I told you just a moment ago, my children explained in detail everything which occurred. At the beginning of the school year, this boy pinned my daughter against the wall under a stairwell, kissing her and putting his hands in places he should not have been touching without express permission. My daughter told a teacher, who didn't seem very concerned. The teacher sent an incident report to this office and, to my knowledge, nothing was done about that incident. That's the other matter, sir."

"That is not why I called you in here today, nor does it excuse the behavior of your daughters."

"You are, once again, correct on both points. We have discussed that already, and I whole-heartedly agree my young, teen daughters should have gone to those with the power to punish this miscreant in a more systematic way. But, oh, wait, they did. So, tell me, Mr. Railey, what do those under oppression do when those in power turn a blind eye?"

"Now, Ms. Woodley, let's not make this more than it is. They are all just children, after all. Perhaps, in this case we should cut them some slack. Boys will be boys sometimes, and I suppose the same sentiment is true for girls," the principal chuckled nervously.

"No. My daughters should indeed be punished. They're really not just children who don't know any better. These are young adults, on the cusp of becoming fully-integrated members of society. This is where they are supposed to learn what is acceptable and what is not. It is interesting, however, to see how quickly your thirst for the proverbial blood of the accused in this matter changed when I brought up the other matter at hand. People, male or female, will rise to whatever standard society sets for them. Since this is the standard you have set for the males at this school, I will be making it my personal mission to have you removed."

"Don't you threaten me!"

"I am not threatening at all. I am simply being completely open, honest, and transparent with you. Now, as the parent of Veda Rufio, I am requesting a copy of the incident report submitted to this office by..." I paused, wheeling backward and opening the door. "Veda, what's the name of the teacher you confided in regarding that incident with Jared?"

"Mr. Coones," Veda replied sheepishly.

"Mr. Coones," I continued. "I'll be awaiting my request in the lounge area just outside your door. I'm injured, as you can see, so please do hurry. Have a nice day, Mr. Railey. You'll be hearing from my lawyer very soon."

Exiting his office, I waved Sara over.

"Please slam the door for me, Sara, dear."

"With pleasure," replied Sara, waving to a shocked Mr. Railey.

Slamming the door with gusto, she turned to me.

"Oh my god, girl! We heard all of it! You are some sort of super hero."

The ladies in the office started clapping quietly. One particularly busty administrative assistant already had the official request form ready for me to sign and a copy of the incident report. Handing them over, she grinned and high-fived me.

The two bewildered teens weren't sure what to do. Veda was in tears by this point and Mari was still trying very hard to be mad at me.

"Girls, grab your things from your lockers. We're going home," I announced.

After the impressionable young ones left the room, Sara spun around. "Are you seriously doing this?"

"When have you ever known me to say I'm going to do something and not follow through?"

"Never. That's why I'm so damn excited!" Sara squealed. "I feel like we should go burn our bras or something," she said, causing me to laugh.

The laughter quickly turned to tears and Sara hurriedly pushed me out of the office. Full-blown ugly crying ensued.

Sara's car felt safe. As she slammed the door, heading back in to find the girls, the phone lit up. Beneath the text from Amie was one from Sam. Only one.

I'm not him.

The dam broke. Tears, sobs, and babbling filled the vehicle. They say the mind can only take so much, and mine had, evidently, reached its limit.

CHAPTER 28

Sammi

Enjoy Dubai? What the fuck did that mean? What did I lie about? I'm not some sleazy asshole running around cheating on her. She doesn't want to talk to me? Did she just break up with me?

I leaned into the wall in the elevator, needing something to hold me up in this moment.

"Hello, Satomi. Congratulations on your job offer," said a voice, pulling me temporarily out of my despair.

"Thank you, Jeff." Years of training from Asian parents kicked in. Never let anyone see how you truly feel.

"I'll be sad to see you go. We work so well together. Our team on the Huntingdon Project was one of the best I've ever been a part of. We were like a well-oiled machine!" he continued on, his voice getting higher with each word.

"Yes, we were. Thank you for your kind words."

"You'll whip Dubai into shape in no time. Not that they're terrible or anything," Jeff backtracked. "Just saying any place would benefit from you being in charge. You are a force, Satomi Nakamura."

Nodding and giving a convincing fake smile, I watched Jeff get off the elevator. Heartbreak is a kind of melancholy which can only be kept at bay for a short time. Feeling fresh cracks in my heart, I stood tall. Damn right Satomi Nakamura is a force. She will not be compared to anyone, especially not Zacariah Rufio. Typing quickly, I hit send, put the phone back into my pocket, and threw myself into work. The ball was now in Indie's court.

With a job as busy as this, thoughts rarely get a chance to creep in. Maybe this is why so many in our modern-day society put everything into work. It's quantifiable, predictable, safe, unlike the human interaction part of life.

"SAM!" shouted Cass.

"Ahh! Oh my god, Cass, what?"

"Don't get pissy with me. I have been saying your name for like a fucking hour now. Where is your head, woman?"

Scowling, I replied, "At work, where yours should be."

"Whoa tiger. I was just surprised to see you here this morning. How's Indie doing?"

"Fine, I suppose."

"You suppose? You have been giving me detailed updates for weeks. What is happening? Am I in the goddamn twilight zone?"

"I think she broke up with me," I stated, throwing her my phone, opened to Indie's text thread.

"Holy shit. What happened last night?!"

"She got mad at me for not telling her about her friends dating, then about the job in Dubai, then about helping out Ali."

"Ali? Where does she come into all of this?"

"She asked for help, so she could go to rehab. I helped."

"Geez."

"What?"

"If you were my girlfriend, I'd be pissed too. You're keeping things from me, moving to a different country, and helping your ex out?"

Spinning around in the desk chair to face Cass, I furrowed my brow and threw my hands in the air.

"Well, then I guess I am just a piece of shit."

Cass gave me a look only she can give.

"Look, I told her about the job as soon as it was actually offered, I couldn't tell a secret that wasn't mine, and I told her everything about Ali when she asked."

"She had to ask? You're royally fucked, my friend. Enjoy the single life," Cass said, as she was walking away. "Call me when you're ready to drink and pick up chicks."

Picking up chicks did not sound appealing. Dating just sucked every ounce of energy from both people involved. It had been years of no dating before Indie, and it'll be even longer after her. The fingers in front of me stopped moving across the keyboard and I looked up. Why not go to Dubai? After all, just like Cass said, I had a single life now. If I wasn't going to be dating anyway, might as well move up in the firm. Ideas flooded the once solely focused brain. Staying with Indie had been the only option, really, but now that option was gone. Pain radiated through my chest at the thought of never being with her again. Maybe Dubai could be the thing to fill up the hole she left in my heart. Begging someone to stick around was not going to happen.

"Ahem." the voice behind me sounded.

My head snapped up. Crazed eyes taking too long to focus in the dim light away from the screen they had been staring at for hours, the figure at the entrance of the cubicle remained a mystery.

"What are you still doing here?" Mrs. Stanton queried.

"Ah, Mrs. Stanton, sorry, didn't realize it was you." I looked around at the otherwise empty office illuminated only by emergency lights. "What time is it?"

"Time for you to go home. I came back to get my computer charger and saw your space all lit up over here in this sea of darkness." she chuckled, shaking her head. "You know, you've already been offered the promotion. You don't need to kill yourself to get it."

Letting out a strained laugh, I relaxed my tight shoulders for the first time all day. "Yeah, I know. Just trying to get a little ahead."

"Go home, Sammi. I'm still your boss, for now, and that's an order." Winking, the big boss lady started walking away.

"Mrs. Stanton," I started, staring at her empty hands, "aren't you forgetting something?"

Laughter bounced around the deserted office.

"Pregnancy brain is a real thing, I tell ya."

She turned and traipsed towards her office.

Packing up my things, I finally looked at the time. Bob may be plotting to kill me by now. Eight p.m. was far too late for his dinner. Nodding our final goodbyes, Mrs. Stanton made her way to the elevator as I tidied up my desk and shut everything down.

The city was alive, but, walking through it, I felt like a zombie. Distraction was a broken heart's best friend. Faces passed by, each with their own story. None of them would miss one architect. None of them would know or care if that architect went to Dubai.

Watching the cabs go by, knowing I should be in more of a hurry, the stroll through downtown Boston continued on. The metropolis had plenty in the way of diversionary tactics to keep just about any mind free of unwanted thoughts.

"Sammi!" someone called. In a city as massive as this, there were many other Sammis. Their names may be spelled differently, but we all recognized the name when it was called. I hoped that Sammi was having a better time than this Sammi was.

"Satomi Nakamura!" the same person shouted.

I spun around. There were not many Satomi Nakamuras in this sprawling mass of concrete and humans.

My eyes settled on Cass, waving violently at the entrance to a hole-in-the-wall bar.

"C'mere!"

"I've got to get home to feed Bob." How was she everywhere at once?

"Yeah, okay, but then come back and have some fun!" she screamed.

Nodding and giving her the thumbs up, I carried on. Random people's stares glued to the only remaining party of the little shouting match, I no longer felt cocooned, but now felt surrounded by this city. Rounding the corner and catching the first sight of home, flurries began to float down.

"Hey, George." I greeted the jovial doorman as I entered, shaking the white from my coat and hair.

"Good evening, Ms. Nakamura. How is Indie doing today?"

The name which usually brought butterflies, landed a boulder in my gut. "She's fine. Healing up slowly."

"Good, good. Tell her hello from her favorite doorman!"

The elevator doors cut off George's smile and showed a disheartened face in their mirrored surface. Everywhere I turned, I was reminded of Indie. She had never been to Dubai, although I remember the exact place I was sitting when I found out she was in the hospital. That particular cafe could be avoided. Dubai was an Indie-free zone. No one there, besides Mark, even knew about her. Mark was coming here, so even that faction of knowing Indie would be gone. The once problematic promotion now seemed like the perfect escape plan.

"Bob, dude, I'm so sorry." Petting the furry head was a bit of a salve to this wounded soul. "You wanna move to Dubai, Bobby my boy?" His purring gave me confidence. "I know you can't understand a word I'm saying, but Indie isn't coming around anymore. Maybe we should just cut our losses, huh, buddy?" Bob stopped moving and purring. He simply stared. Unable to tear my eyes away, they started to tear up. It was like he knew. "Chow time!" I announced, breaking the trance.

Soon, Bob had his dinner of flaked fish in gravy and I had mine. The bread felt like cardboard in my mouth, the meat slimy. Nothing felt right. I threw the sandwich in the trash and climbed out the kitchen window. Night air, even in downtown Boston, can have a healing effect.

I had been engaged to Ali, but was always concerned I wouldn't go through with the wedding when the time came. She asked me one day, I said yes. I knew it wasn't right, but I was going with the flow. If you were together for a couple of years, you got married. That's how it goes. I had kept a part of myself from her. A part which had only ever been for Indie. That long-dormant piece of my heart had awakened with her return to my life and now it ached. Whoever penned the phrase, 'tis better to have loved and lost than never to have loved at all', was a fucking idiot.

After all these years, we finally come back together, and now she wants to just end it? I took care of her children, of her, while she was unconscious. I built her a temporary kitchen set up complete with counter and a little sink with an electric water pump. What about the wheelchair docking station right next to the bed with a railing so she could get herself up and around, if needed. I was willing to give up the greatest thing that ever happened to me. I was willing to disappoint my parents, my bosses, my peers, just so I could be with her. Everyone deserves to be, at the very least, heard, but she was hell-bent on ignoring any communication, apparently.

"Hey, Sammi!" A small voice broke me out of my internal pity party.

"Oh, hey there kiddo. How's school going?"

"Ugh, my teacher is being ridiculous. She wants us to write a three-page book report. Three pages! Can you believe that? We've never had to do more than two before," the Simons' middle child huffed.

"Eh, you can do it. You're a smart kid."

"I just don't know. She even said we're not allowed to just write bigger to try to fill up the lines with less actual words. I think she's a mind-reader."

Trying to not chuckle at a third grader's inner thoughts should be an Olympic sport. I nodded pensively, feigning the sharing of her concern.

"Have you ever written a three-page report?" the child queried.

Not able to contain my chortle any longer, I coughed as a cover-up sound. "Yeah, I have, a few times, actually."

"Really? Wow, you must be pretty smart. The teacher said to do our best and not try to cut corners. Rachel said she's going to just write a tiny bit bigger and try to use a lot of adjectives. I feel like the teacher is being unfair. Maybe if it was a report about Sherlock Holmes and Watson, I could do it, but seahorses? Who cares about seahorses?" She looked me in the eyes and asked, "What should I do?"

Her concern was evident and deeply real to her young mind.

"You should always do your best."

"Ugh, you sound like my parents. I thought you were cooler than that."

Not able to hide the laughter this time, and losing any chance at a future gold medal, I replied, "Your parents just might be cooler than you realize."

"No way."

"Bathtime!" Mrs. Simons called out.

Sighing, my conversational companion rose up.

"G'bye."

"Bye."

Lifting the buzzing little box in my hand, I saw three messages from Cass. Can't a girl just be left alone in her misery? If I ignored her, she would just show up here. Echoing the sighs I had just heard from my young visitor, I untangled my legs and ducked back inside the kitchen window, Bob following closely behind me.

It was a short walk back to the bar, but that didn't stop Cass from texting fifty times during it. As I strolled up to the door, I took out the phone to count her messages. I had to be prepared for the verbal lashing I was about to unleash in jest. Eleven unread messages from Cass and one from First.

> **I know, and I'm not the girl I was almost two decades ago.**

What the hell did that even mean? Of course she wasn't the same, neither was I. Maybe I would have a drink with Cass after all. I needed one after today. Shoving the phone back into my pocket, I reached out for the door handle and a rush of voices and warm air met me on the sidewalk.

"Hey gurrrrl!" Cass shouted.

"Hey Cass."

"C'mere, I got someone I want you to meet!"

"Cass, I'm really not in the mood for that."

"Eh, whatever, just say hi," needled Cass. "It's not like ya hafta marry her."

We walked over to an attractive brunette with sharp facial features in a leather jacket and jeans.

"Sammi, Carol. Carol, Sammi."

"Well, hello. Your friend here has been talking you up," Carol politely addressed me.

"Hi. Yeah, she can be a bit pushy, to say the least," I replied.

"You two chat, I'm gonna go to the little girl's room and then grab another drink. Be back soon!" Cass sang, walking away slowly.

"Sorry about her. She means well is all I can say," I explained to my bar stool companion.

Turning to the newly present bartender, I asked for a whiskey neat. Receiving a slight nod, I looked back to Carol. She seemed to be staring at Cass.

"So, Cass said you're both architects?"

"Yep. We've worked at the same firm for about six years now. She's really talented."

"Funny, she said the same thing about you."

I chuckled. "We both are, to be honest. She is more creative, though. I think she has the makings of being one of the greats. I'm just a really hard worker and good at business."

Glancing at Cass stumbling back towards the bar area, I realized this might be hard for someone to believe.

"I'll go further in our company, but she has more potential to really change the world."

"That's incredibly insightful of you. And here I pegged you for the competitive type." Carol teased, running her finger up and down the back of my hand.

A nervous laugh made its way between the two of us.

"Yeah, well I am, but that doesn't mean I'm delusional or an ego-maniac. I-I should probably go." I stammered.

"But you haven't even gotten your drink yet."

"Yeah, I know. I'm just not ready for whatever this is. You seem like a cool person and I want you to put your time and energy into someone who is ready for you. I literally just got broken up with today. At least I think we're broken up. I'm not even sure," I pondered, looking at the floor.

"I get it. It took me two years to get back out here," admitted Carol, making a sweeping motion covering the lesbian bar scene before us. "It's been quite a while and, let me tell ya, it's a whole different ball game nowadays. Work things out with your girl, if at all possible. You do not want to be out here in these waters, trust me!" she advised before taking another swig of her drink. "So your friend is creative, you say?"

Seeing the two of us laughing together, Cass approached.

"Awww, hitting it off, are we?"

Carol, not missing a beat, grinned at me and turned to Cass. "Why yes *we* are."

Laughing, I said, "Oh how the tables have turned, my friend." to a stunned Cass.

The bartender gave me a crooked smile and handed me my drink. Gulping down the whole thing, I set the glass on the counter with a twenty-dollar bill and stood up. "Goodnight, all. Enjoy your evening."

Carol nodded and Cass just stared, eyes wide and mouth agape.

The cold night air once again did its magic but, this time, I was warm on the inside thanks to the amber liquid I had just knocked back. I pulled out my phone to text Indie, but just stared at it for a while. What was there to say? I had said it all. She had decided she didn't want to see me. What was left?

That final question plagued a tired mind the whole walk back to George and Bob and the Simons family. The only thing left was my career. The only way forward was Dubai.

CHAPTER 29

Indie

"WELL, LOOK AT YOU, walking into mi casa. Walking!" Gabriel exclaimed.

"Yeah, yeah, yeah. I'm a regular Olympian. After two and a half months of physical therapy, I can walk with a damn cane," I replied to his poking, still wincing and going at a speed that would incite pity from eighty-five-year-olds everywhere. "Here are the bagels you wanted."

"Good morning, Indie," greeted Kenny, sitting at the kitchen table in Gabriel's colorful kitchen.

"Hey, Kenny. Still weird seeing you here," I said.

"Right back atcha," returned my business manager as he picked through the bag of goodies I had just thrown onto the table. "So, the meeting tomorrow is..."

"Oh, no," interjected Gabriel. "None of that business shit here in mi cocina! You both know the rules."

"Hey, hey now. I did nothing. He was the one who started it!" I defended, pointing at Kenny.

"Kiss it," Kenny said to us both.

"Is that any way to talk to your boss?" I asked.

"You're not my boss in this *cocina*, evidently," Kenny mocked his boyfriend.

Gabriel stuck out his tongue.

"How are the girls? They excited?"

"Yeah. Well, Veda is excited. Mari is apprehensive, as usual," I informed the men.

"She has every right to be. After how that asshole has treated them," Gabriel fumed, sitting at the table with Kenny and I. "And then the whole 'I'm gonna sue you for custody' thing? Don't get me wrong, I'm glad he's stepping up, finally, but I wouldn't trust him either." Taking a sip of his coffee, he continued, "So what are you going to do with all of your free time, mami?"

"Work," chimed Kenny. "It's all she's been doing since the whole Sam fiasco, coupled with Helene taking her leave."

Now I took the opportunity to stick my tongue out.

"I will work, yes, but I will also relax. The first night they're gone, I'm ordering Thai food and watching The Proposal for the hundredth time."

"Wow, don't go too crazy," Gabriel said sarcastically. "And don't stick your tongue out at me, woman! What are you, five?"

"Says the man who started it." Kenny murmured.

"Ooo, don't make me steal Indie's cane and give you a caning," Gabriel teased.

The two men sat there laughing.

"First, don't you touch my cane," I threatened. "Second, eww, I do not need to hear about anything you two do or don't do or whatever. And on that lovely note, I'm leaving."

Rising up as quickly as possible, I was still the last one who was upright.

"Oh, sweets, don't go. We won't be inappropriate anymore. I promise," Gabriel offered without an ounce of sincerity.

"Even if I believed that, I really do have to go finish packing up the girls." I kissed Gabriel on the cheek and waved to Kenny. "You want a hug, Kenny?" I sang in a child-like voice.

He almost snorted coffee out of his nose. I waved again and scurried out the door like a damaged squirrel trying to escape a predator, Gabriel's eruption of laughter following behind.

"Jesus, Veda, just pack whatever. No one friggin' cares if you wear the pink skirt or the black skirt on Saturday," Mari's voice rang through the house as I opened the door.

Sighing, I turned to see the angry teen standing ten feet away with her arms crossed.

"Go easy on her. She is just different than you."

"Yeah, I'm aware."

"Are you packed?"

"Yeah, been packed for like an hour. It doesn't take that long." Mari answered with a scornful glare.

"Okay," I stated in my best mom voice, "let's go over the list. Panties, bras, socks, pjs, pants, shoes, shirts, chargers, computer, book, cash," Mari was nodding to each and every item, "deodorant, hair stuff, toothbrush…"

The young girl's eyes widened as she ran down the hall.

"There's always something. Mom wins again." I boasted.

Sitting on the sofa was pure heaven. How on Earth was a gimp supposed to make it all the way through an airport? This was going to hurt like hell, in more ways than one. Physically, he would protect them and never let anything happen to the girls, but mentally? That was a whole other story. Sometimes he didn't even mean to hurt anyone, but he was just so self-centered he never even saw what the things he was saying or doing did to those around him.

The arguing down the hall ensued once again. Mari was informing Veda of TSA regulations regarding bottles of liquids and Veda was politely telling Mari where she could shove her three point four ounce bottles.

Sometimes, it's best to ignore the children and let them duke it out. Mommy wouldn't always be there to referee, and they had to learn.

Ignoring the argument, my thoughts turned back to their time with Zacariah. He did seem to be doing better. Maybe it was the judge telling him he didn't have a leg to stand on because he was never around. Maybe it was the near death experience Veda and I had. Maybe it was whatever Sam had said to him when she told him to lay off Mari. I wanted nothing more in that moment than to call Sam, thank her, and ask her what exactly she said to him. Tears started forming without permission, as usual.

I hadn't heard a peep from her in well over a month. I did tell her I didn't want to talk to her anymore, but I missed her. Head and heart were in constant disagreement over Sam. She was probably in Dubai by now, with her new job, so it didn't matter anyway. Fiddling with my phone, I clicked on her name. Her number was right there. Did that number even work in Dubai? One tear made an escape.

"Mom, you alright?" Veda asked softly.

"Yeah, ya hayati, I'm all good. Just going to miss you, that's all." I half-lied to my child.

Sitting next to her emotional mother, Veda hugged me. "Yeah, you cry, Mari gets angry. You guys can be a lot to deal with, ya know," she joked.

I stared at my happy-go-lucky child. "There's more to you than meets the eye, kid. You are amazing. Never let anyone convince you otherwise."

Grinning, she put her index finger up to her lip. "Shhh, don't tell everyone my secret. We'll be okay, though, mom, really. And I'll take care of Mari. All tough on the outside, but she's delicate."

"Yeah, delicate like a bomb!"

The outburst of laughter brought Mari out, looking quizzical.

"You two having fun out here? It's almost time to leave, Veda, go finish already."

"Okay, okay, I'm going. I love you, my older sister!" Veda sing-songed as she skipped back down the hallway.

Mari simply rolled her eyes and sat next to me. "Are you crying, mom?"

"Not really, just thinking and I teared up." I replied, grabbing her hand and stroking the back of it. "I will miss you both, though."

"I know. We'll miss you too, but don't worry. I'll take care of Veda. She seems all sunshine and rainbows, but I know better. Deep down, she's a multi-faceted lunatic."

Seeing both of the girls in a new light today, I released a bit of tension. They will always have each other. "I know you will, and you are absolutely correct. Both of you are not what you seem on the outside."

Winking only caused another tear to fall.

Pulling a tissue out of her pocket, Mari revealed, "I knew you'd cry at some point today, so I was prepared."

She gently dabbed my cheeks and gave a sideways smile that was oh so Mari, but exceedingly rare.

I placed my palm on her cheek, she leaned in and closed her eyes. The hard as nails teenager looked like a small child again; innocent and fragile.

"Let's go, let's go, my people," Veda imitated her mother. "We gots ta leave now. What is taking you so long?" she continued on, goading Mari, whose face looked much less innocent now.

Reminiscing about the 'good old days' before the event that changed American travel, I told the girls how you could always walk with people right up to the gate and wave their plane good-bye. Luckily, it was still allowed for parents of minors, with a special ticket from the ticket counter. After checking luggage, getting my special mom ticket, and refusing a wheelchair escort, the three of us made our way through the Boston International Airport. The moving walkways had always seemed silly before, but that day they were a soothing balm to a broken, tired woman.

As I eased my sore body down into an uncomfortable airport chair, a child pointed out we were only halfway to the gate. Gently encouraging them to shut their mouths and go buy snacks by throwing my wallet at them, I leaned back and closed my eyes.

The head bob jarred me back to reality. I narrowed my eyes. That woman looked exactly like Sam from behind. She was even dressed like Sam in a smart, fitted gray suit. I tilted my head, her ass even looked like Sam's.

"Whatcha doin', mom?" Veda's voice broke through the thoughts of Sam naked in her bed.

"Wha? Oh, nothing, j-just thinking." I sputtered.

"You don't look very good. Your face is all flushed and funny looking. Here," Veda insisted, "drink this water and I'll go grab another one."

She took off before any attempt at arguing could be made. Mari shrugged and sat down next to me, opening her juice and chips.

"She's worried about leaving you alone and you were just thinking about Sam," stated Mari.

"No, I'm not. I absolutely was not thinking about anyone in particular. I was just sitting here resting!" I argued, my voice getting higher with each word.

"Uh-huh. Whatever you say mom. Chip?" she offered.

Veda came running back over. "Mother! Drink that water."

Chugging as much as I could, we carried on through the terminal. We arrived at the gate just minutes before boarding, so our goodbyes were mercifully short. If more time had been available, there would have been a family of women crying next to gate B34. The girls walked out of view past the smiling gate attendant. Her pitying looks made it obvious that she too had children. I watched until the plane was out of sight, and sent a text to Zacariah. Our children were en route.

Turning back to the vast network of hallways, I began another glacially paced walk to get back to my car. Even slower than the first time making this trek, I practically wept with relief when I saw the out-of-the-way chairs I had sought refuge in earlier. Sinking down into the familiar, uncomfortable seat, I closed my eyes and allowed the exhaustion to have its way with me. Wet cheeks and aching leg at the forefront of my mind.

"Indie? Are you okay? What's wrong?" a familiar voice asked.

I thought it a dream, so I smiled.

"Indie! Did you pass out?"

The face before me was beautiful, and full of concern.

"Oh, you. You're here, I thought you were just in my dream. Wait, you're here, at the airport?"

Sam's concerned look deepened.

"What's going on? Do you know where you are? Should I call a doctor or something?"

"No, no, I'm fine, thank you. I'm just aching and tired, that's all."

"Okay, I just saw you over here and you didn't look well. Are the girls here with you? Are you going somewhere?" she wondered, looking around for other familiar faces.

"No, they left."

A fresh deluge of saline poured out of my eyes. Sam was beside me in a second, comforting and hugging me. It felt amazing. Finally finding the strength to gently push her away, I wiped my tears with the tissues Mari had left me, and began to ramble out the thoughts swimming in my head.

"The girls are flying out to see Zacariah. I walked them to the terminal. We barely made it there in time. I'm just so slow. They wanted to get me a wheelchair, but I refused it. I had to sit here on the way. The girls made me drink water. I'm just so tired. There's so much pain still. It just hurts, everything, everywhere hurts. Will the pain ever go away?" I asked hysterically.

"I've got this, wait here. I'll be right back."

She jogged off in her fitted gray suit with her tight ass. So that was her I saw here earlier. Within minutes, she returned with a wheelchair and some all-natural pain pills.

"I know you don't like pharmaceutical stuff, so I grabbed these. And here, more water."

She watched as I swallowed them, tears still flowing.

"So, you're walking now?"

"Yep. Of course, I've got to use my trusty friend here to do so, but it is what it is." I replied, patting my cane.

"And you just put the girls on a plane to go visit their father?"

"Yep."

"And you're here alone, with this bum leg and a cane?"

"Yep."

"Okay, let me text Mark quickly. I'll get you back to your car and then I'll leave you be."

"You on your way to Dubai?"

"What? Dubai? No, I'm here picking Mark up. He flew in today."

"Oh, okay."

So she hadn't left yet. I wondered how long she would stay once Mark was here. How long would she have to be here to show him the ropes? I was sure it couldn't be very long. Tears welled to overflowing yet again. The cracks in my heart that had just barely began to heal fissured back open.

"I can make it on my own now, thanks though."

"Oh no you don't. Sit your ass down, I already told Mark we will meet him at the baggage claim."

She wheeled me through the throngs of travelers. We seemed to be the only two people in the world not carrying bags. Everyone was either coming or going except Sam and me.

"Sam, how did you get back here? I had to get a parent ticket thingy to come into the terminal with the girls."

"Oh, well, let's just say my firm is the firm which does the work on this airport. And let's just say I know a lot of people here. Let's also say I like to abuse my power in this regard every once in a while."

"Of course you do." I teased, looking straight ahead.

If I dared to turn around and see her beautiful smile, I might actually combust spontaneously right then and there.

CHAPTER 30

Sam

STARING DOWN at the top of Indie's head was surreal. I hadn't seen or heard from her in so long and now, here I was, pushing her in a wheel chair through the Boston airport, taking her to meet Mark. My mouth felt like the Sahara all of a sudden. What am I even supposed to say? Hey sorry we broke up? Do you still think I'm hiding things?

"So, I saw your cleaning products in Goodness Goods the other day." It had the lowest possibility of being a landmine of a conversation starter.

"Oh yeah? Yep, everything is all done. The deal went through, Helene is bowing out, and I'm running the show. Well, mostly. She is still helping since I'm kind of broken."

"I'm proud of you, Indie. You did it. You are doing it."

"Thank you."

Mark was waving wildly at the two of us. He approached and reached out to shake Indie's hand.

"Hey there, you must be the famous Indie! I'm Mark. Nice to finally meet you."

"Oh, yes, I–I'm Indie. You must be the famous Mark from

Dubai. Nice to meet you as well." She returned the gesture.

Looking between Indie and I, Mark exclaimed, "I just had the best cheeseburger. I can't wait for some New England clam chowder, burgers, pizza, the whole shebang! So, ladies, where are we headed for lunch?"

"I really couldn't intrude on..." Indie started.

"Nonsense, no intrusion at all! Ooo, let's hit Boston Burger Company? They have milkshakes too. God, it's good to be back." insisted Mark.

"Didn't you just eat a burger?" I said, trying to get him to realize this was an uncomfortable situation to put us all in.

"Yeah, true. Well, another time then. We have all the time in the world I am just so excited. You don't know what ya got 'til it's gone. Am I right?" he answered. Walking towards the parking garage, he kept the conversation going. "I can't wait to get started, Sammi. This is going to be great. You and me, together, as a team? What could be better. This city will never know what hit it. We're taking over. Is your office right next to mine? It should be. That will just save time. What do you think?"

"We can talk about everything like that tomorrow at the office." I over-emphasized.

"Right, right, no work talk. I get it." he agreed.

"Wait, what? You and Sam, here? In Boston?" Indie questioned.

"Yep. You can thank me later," Mark gloated. "She would have been great for Dubai, but I knew Dubai wasn't right for her. Plus, I mean, you are here, so that's obviously very important. I insisted I needed her here and it would be better for the company in the long run if she stayed."

"Excuse me, I need to go to the bathroom," Indie pushed the wheels with her hands, tearing the rolling chair away from me.

"Is she okay?" Mark asked, perplexed with her moodiness and sudden departure.

"No. We are not together. She doesn't know about any of this. We happened to run into each other here at the airport and I offered to help her. She just put her kids on a plane to see their father and she's still healing from the accident."

"Oh god, I'm sorry! I had no idea. When I saw you two together, I thought you had worked things out. I'm an idiot. Here I was acting like you two were a couple and I was the hero in keeping you here."

Mark's head slammed into his hands.

"It's all good. I know you had no idea what was going on," I assured Mark. "I'm gonna go check on her, though. Be right back."

Walking down the long row of immaculate bathroom stalls, I came to the large, wheelchair accessible one and tapped lightly on the door.

"Go away, please. I can make it home on my own from here," sniffled Indie.

"The sucky thing about dating within your own sex is you can't run and hide from your ex in a bathroom. Sorry about that."

"Why didn't you go to Dubai?"

"Mark already told you, he convinced them he couldn't do it without me. They were so worried I'd be mad at staying, so they gave me an amazing office, a raise, and a promotion," I said. "It all worked out splendidly."

"But why? What did he mean by saying I can thank him later?"

"Can you please open the door?" I pleaded. She obliged. Staring at her tear-stained face made me feel angry, relieved, frustrated, sad, and everything in between. No matter how much I tried to ignore it, I loved her with everything I had. "I said I didn't want to run away from you. If I left, I knew there was no way things would ever get resolved between us. I couldn't have that hanging over my head for the rest of my life."

"Sam, I–I just can't. I ca–"

"It's okay," I interjected, "I'm not asking you to. This was my decision for me. I'll leave now, wait two minutes and we will be completely gone from sight," I advised, backing away. "Take care of yourself, please. Know you can always call me with no strings attached, if you should need help."

My legs grew heavier with every step I took walking out of that restroom, as did my heart, but I couldn't impose on her anymore. Her face was full of a pain I knew had nothing to do with her injuries.

"Well, she's cute," Mark said about Cass, who was smiling as we walked by her.

"Well, she's a lesbian, so...yeah." I informed him.

"Are there any straight girls in Boston?!?"

Cackling a decent evil laugh, I responded, "We're taking over!"

"I'm going back to Dubai," stated Mark.

"Oh no you're not," a female voice chimed in.

We turned to see a very pregnant woman, hands on hips, head cocked.

"Good morning, Mrs. Stanton. May I formally introduce Mark Delano, your replacement," I offered.

"Oh, I'm sure I could never replace such an amazing woman, but I will certainly do my best. Congratulations, by the way," Mark complimented, gesturing towards Mrs. Stanton's large abdomen.

"Thank you. First of all, flattery will get you everywhere, but only regarding me. Second, I have no doubt this place will thrive under your direction, sir. I have seen what you were able to accomplish in the Dubai office in such a short amount of time. And with Ms. Nakamura by your side, you will both be unstoppable. From what I understand, you insisted she stay," prodded Mrs. Stanton.

"Yes, ma'am. I have seen her in action and, while I knew she would do well in Dubai, I also knew with both of us working together here, we could really take this company far. She is a force," flattered Mark.

"You have no idea, Mr. Delano. Don't call me when she bowls you over," Mrs. Stanton warned light-heartedly.

"Okay, okay, enough talk about me. Let's get this switchover started before this one pops a baby out in the middle of the office," I prodded.

Day turned into night. Bob was fed and I collapsed on the bed. The next day was much the same, except for one huge difference. A text at lunchtime.

> I wanted to apologize for my little freak out the other day. I was a little emotional, sleep deprived, and caught off guard, seeing you there. Thank you for getting me that wheelchair. I do appreciate you trying to help.

With shaking hands, I typed a reply, fearful this may be the last time I would ever text Indie again.

> it was good to see you. i know things were a little weird and i'm sorry if i overstepped any boundaries. i really was just trying to help.

> I know. Again, thank you. It was good to see you too. I hope you and Bob are doing well.

She was continuing the conversation? Pleading with my heart not to get too excited, I picked the phone back up.

> we are doing pretty well thank you. how are you all doing? are the girls enjoying their visit?

Well, as you saw, I am still healing, but can walk with my trusty cane now. Veda is all better physically. Mari is a bit overly protective at the moment. Yes, I think they actually are enjoying themselves. Are you really not going to Dubai?

that's all great. no i'm not going. mark is here and we just completed the official switchover between him and mrs stanton. she is starting her maternity leave in a few days.

OK

Really? An *OK* was all she typed? The fingers before me wanted to type furiously, explain and ask for the same in return. Sadness quickly turned to grief, which rolled right into anger. Heartbeat thundering in my ears, Cass walked into the newly acquired office.

"Whoa, Sam. Why are you ten shades of red right now?"

"Indie."

"Indie? Like the Indie? Did you see her or something?"

"She just text me. And I saw her a couple days ago at the airport, while picking up Mark."

"Hold up, for real? And you didn't fucking tell me? What the hell, woman? Spill, now," Cass insisted.

"She was there dropping off the girls to fly to their dad's. She's walking with a cane now, but wasn't doing well, so I stopped to help. Mark basically told her I stayed here for her. Things got weird. She was crying. Then today, she texts, but it's still weird. I want a damn explanation. I want her to talk to me," I said, my voice raising at the end.

"That is a lot to take in. So she text you? Like she initiated the communication?" Cass clarified.

I nodded.

"Fantastic!"

"What?" I asked.

"SHE contacted YOU. That is huge progress, my friend. Huge progress. How long has it been? One month, two months? She reached out. She's thinking about you. She's wondering."

The anger dissipated, pesky double-edged hope taking its place.

"You think so?"

"Absolutely. I know you're eager to get her back, but just be patient. I have a distinct feeling it's all going to work out very soon," Cass comforted, before her facial expression shifted. "Even thought that means we can't go pick up chicks together anymore."

"Cass, we never did that and we never will."

"That one night was pretty cool! I ended up hooking up with her," sighed Cass.

"Yes, you told me."

"All thanks to you, my friend. It was such a magical night."

"Yes, Cass, you have told me the details, which I never wanted to hear, let alone more than once."

"She was so imaginative."

"Okay, then, I'm gonna have to pull the whole boss thing. Shut up and get out of my beautiful new office before you darken the shine in here with your tawdry stories."

Cass just grinned and rose up from the chair.

"Yes, madame boss lady. Maybe I'll just write you a first-hand account, so you can read it and get some pointers. Did I mention how hot the sex was?"

Walking slowly towards the door, turning around with every sentence, Cass bowed just before opening the door.

"OUT!" I tried to yell through my laughter.

Work was slowly taking over every second of the afternoon. When a text came through, I didn't even hear it. It was twenty-six minutes later when the notification bubble was finally noticed.

I grabbed my things and bolted out of the office, heading towards home.

———————

Mr. Simon met me at the front door. Behind him, George was keeping guard, eyes darting this way and that, knees slightly bent, ready to pounce.

"I'm so sorry, Sammi. He just bolted. I–" started Mr. Simons.

"When? Where did he go? How long has he been missing?" I pleaded.

"We were just going into feed him, like you asked. As soon as we opened the door, he ran past Jenny and I and ran down the hall towards Mrs. Salzman's," he answered.

"I'm keeping watch, Ms. Nakamura. He won't get past me!" George shouted after us as we entered the elevator.

"You didn't see where he went after that?"

The elevator doors closed and the box we were in seemed to crawl at a snail's pace just to spite me.

"No, sorry, Jenny and I both freaked out and bumped into each other. I knocked her down and she whacked her head. By the time we looked again, he was gone," Mr. Simons explained.

"Jenny hit her head? Is she okay?" I asked, suddenly less worried about my cat.

"Yeah, she's got a little bump, but nothing serious. She's with her mom. She just adores you and Bob. She's been crying for the last hour."

My heart softened toward my small friend. She was so good to Bob, and me. Unlike most of the world's children, she was not a selfish asshole. As the elevator doors opened, I turned right, heading straight for the Simons' door. I knocked and caught sight of Mr. Simons mouthing, "Thank you," as he darted off in the other direction to find the escaped feline.

"Come in," came a motherly voice through the door.

The Simons were much older than me. It had taken them years to have children and they were the most deserving people I had ever met. They took the time to be with their offspring, teach them, and they really cared.

Nodding to Mrs. Simons, I knelt down in front of the sobbing child.

"Hey there, no crying. You can't see if your eyes are all full of saltwater. And I can think of no one better to help me look for that little rascal, Bob, than you. He just loves you."

Turning her tear-stained face up to me, Jenny blubbered, "I-I'm s-sorry, Sam. I-I didn't m-mean to. I'm s-sor-ory."

"Hey now, you didn't do anything wrong. He ran past you. I think I'm going to have to ground him, actually. Now c'mon. We have a furry feline fugitive to apprehend and you are the Watson to my Sherlock."

Still heaving, the child smiled and grabbed the outstretched hand in front of her. Half of the building seemed to be out looking for Bob. There were treats and cans of tuna placed outside of some doors, and lots of random people shouting what they had seen and where. We met Mr. Simons in the stairwell between the fourth and fifth floors.

"There's been a sighting on two! I'm heading down!" he shouted as he jetted past us.

Jenny and I grinned at each other and took off after him. Surprisingly, it was difficult to keep up with the almost sixty-year-old man. Huffing and puffing, we all descended upon the second floor, where a throng of people had Bob cornered. His eyes were darting all over the place, trying to form an exit strategy.

Jenny slowly stepped forward, cooing in her most soothing voice. Everyone was dead still. Everyone except a furry escapee and a little girl. The still teary-eyed child knelt down and called Bob to her. He glanced at the statues surrounding him, and decided she was a safe bet. Rubbing his head against her knee, she scolded him for being such a disobedient boy and then asked him how his adventure was.

The pools in my eyes threatened to spill as anxiety started to take over. I had reached my daily limit of drama. Nodding to everyone to thank them as they said their goodbyes, Mr. Simons, Jenny, Bob, and I headed back up to the sixth floor.

Jenny carefully placed Bob on the floor of my living room.

"He's safe now. Sorry, Sammi."

I waved off her apology.

"Why? Because you took the time to chill out and make him feel safe? He came to you because he knows you'll take care of him. That's a little something I know too."

"Let's go, Jenny, it's way past bedtime at this point," Mr. Simons said softly.

Being slammed into by a child seeking a hug is one of the best feelings ever. As soon as the helpful duo closed the door, the tears started falling. Standing completely still, not heaving or sobbing or even blinking, they still fell. The tiny buzzing of the phone the only noise, I ignored it. It persisted long enough to piss me off. I whipped the phone out of my pocket and answered, not even looking at the screen.

"What?"

"Wow, that's one way to answer a phone. What's got your panties in a bunch?" Cass questioned.

"You do not want to know."

"Okay. Come out for a drink with me. No chicks, just you and me. It's a new lesbian bar I just found; real low-key place."

"You know what, Cass? Among work and Indie and Bob, I've had enough reality for today. Send me the address. I'll Uber over."

"Bob? What the hell happened with the cat?"

"I'll tell you later."

Hanging up, I turned to my cat companion.

"I don't suppose you're even hungry after all those goodies everyone put out for you."

He yawned and closed his eyes. Why couldn't I just be a spoiled housecat: no jobs or promotions to give up, no true loves to lose, no pets to escape, just tuna and naps.

"I think I understand why some people become hermits," I confessed to the sleeping cat.

CHAPTER 31

Indie

"AND SHE WAS JUST MAGICALLY THERE? In the airport?"

"Yep. I closed my eyes for a few moments, and when I opened them, there she was," I told Sara.

"I wish some chick would magically appear when I opened up my eyes from a damn nap or something," complained Sara. "I think a good roll in the hay would do me good at this point."

"Lisaida still being a bitch?"

"Yeah, I think she may have even gotten a promotion in the bitch department. The kids are begging to come next weekend for your birthday party and she refuses to let them. I offered to pick them up right before and drop them off immediately afterwards, but no. She just has to be in control."

"I'm sorry, Sara. I know that means just about nothing, but it's all I've got. God, I wish I could do something." I huffed, slamming my fist on her kitchen table.

"Whoa there, don't be breaking my table."

"Yeah, because I'm just such a big, strong bodybuilder."

One corner of Sara's mouth rose a centimeter. That mouth hadn't made a complete smile in far too long.

"Yes, Indie the Magnificent. Indie the Intimidating! Yeah, that's better. It's got that whole alliteration thing going on."

Both of our phones trilled at the same time.

"Amie or Gabriel?" I quizzed my friend.

"Hmm, this time I'm going with Amie."

Flipping our phones over at the same time, I groaned. Sara's half smile returned briefly.

"She wants to go out tonight. Oh, goodness, her and what's her face broke up. What was her name again?" I asked.

"I think it was Susan or Shannon. I'm pretty sure it started with an 'S'." guessed Sara.

"I mean, I know I want to drink until I drop at this point."

"Yeah, I'm in a similar state of mind. You texting her back or am I?"

"I'll do it," I offered.

"Good, I'm going to the bathroom."

"We're meeting here at eight thirty and heading to Kat's in an Uber." I shouted down the hallway after my friend.

"Oh, my, all three of you here together? Whose life is falling apart this time?" Kat greeted us as we walked in the door.

"Haha, very funny, but joke's on you, because it's all of us," Amie zinged.

"Holy moly! Let me hide the good stuff," Kat teased. "Suzie, hide the twelve-year scotch!"

The confused look on Kat's newest waitress's face was short-lived. Sighing and shaking her head, she came over to our table.

"No idea what that was about, but what can I get you ladies besides a twelve-year scotch?"

"You will do well here, Suzie. I'm glad to see you can deal with our Kat," Sara declared as we all clapped in awe.

"I'll have a whiskey, neat," I replied to her question.

"Blue Moon Lager," Sara said.

"I'll take one of Kat's special double margaritas," chimed Amie.

Suzie walked away and Amie's attention was caught by someone across the room.

"Oh my. Who is that?"

Looking at the woman Amie nodded towards, Sara and I both shrugged.

"No idea, but she's cute, that's for sure. Not that you should be looking, Amie," Sara scolded. "Didn't you just break up with Susan or Shannon, or Sophia?"

"Stacey! Her name was Stacey and yes, we did just break up this afternoon. So what? I'm single now, I can do whatever I want." retorted Amie.

"Amie, dear, we're not saying you have any allegiance to anyone, it just that, well, ummm," I paused, not sure how to delicately put what I was about to say, "you tend to jump from one relationship to another rather quickly. Maybe try something different this time?"

Amie opened her mouth to protest, but shut it as quickly as she opened it.

"Yeah, you've got a point, but she's hot. Oh god, oh god! She's looking at me!"

Three of us turned to look at the dashing blonde woman in a suit waving at Amie. Her grin widened seeing three sets of eyes. It was easy to tell what the topic of our table was at the moment. Blondie rose from her seat at the bar and started walking towards us.

"Well, hello there. I just found out about this place today. So far, I must say," the woman paused looking Amie up and down, "it does not disappoint. You come here often?"

Amie giggled, forgetting all about Stacey.

"Well, I come here quite often. We are friends with the owner, Kat. I'm Amie."

"Nice to meet you, Amie, I'm –"

"Indie?" a new voice chimed into the conversation. I looked up to see Sam, standing next to Blondie.

"Indie?" Blondie asked. "Like *the* Indie?"

"Yes," Sam responded. "Cass, meet Indie. Indie, Cass."

"Wow, this is awkward. Nice to finally meet you. Really glad you are doing better after that crash," Cass offered.

"What are you doing here?" I asked Sam, ignoring Cass altogether.

"Cass invited me out for a drink. What are you doing here?" replied Sam.

"Amie asked us to come out for a drink. This is kind of our spot. That's Kat," I explained, pointing to the woman behind the counter.

"Oh, this is Kat's place? Well, we didn't know that. It is weird being in the same place twice in one week," Sam mused

"Twice?" chimed Amie.

"Yes, we saw each other the other day at the airport," Sam reported, never tearing her eyes away from my shocked face.

"Have a seat, Cass and Sam. There's plenty of room and no use in either of you standing," Sara ordered. "Suzie, bring their drinks over here, please!"

Sara refused to look my way to receive the full extent of the glare she was being given. The organ in my chest was once again pumping much too loudly. Ears ringing, mind racing, alcohol being poured down the hatch. What could possibly go wrong in a situation like this?

"Suzie, another, please!" I called out to the grinning waitress.

If only she knew. This was not a meet-cute, this was the beginning of a disaster. Being not much of a drinker had its benefits: it wouldn't take very long to be drunk enough to not care about this whole fiasco.

"Another?' Sara sideways-whispered into my ear, eyebrows raised.

"You're the one who invited them to sit here," I hissed through clenched teeth in an unnatural smile.

Sara simply shrugged.

Glancing around at the usually low-key bar, questions arose. Evidently every lesbian on this side of Boston was ready for a night out. How did they all find out about this place? This was our place. Becoming more like a whiny toddler with each sip, I finally broke my self-imposed silence.

"So, Cass, how did you find out about Kat's?"

"Online," disclosed Cass. "This place has the best videos! Lemme show ya."

We all crowded around Cass's tiny phone screen. I could feel Sam's breath. Shivers erupted throughout my body. How she could still do this to me, I couldn't understand. Didn't the body know when the mind had been betrayed? What happened to the whole mind-body connection thing?

Suzie and Kat were right there on the rectangular window to social media. Soon, we were all laughing at their witty videos. 'Living the lesbian life' was to be their tagline. As far as business marketing goes, this was a genius idea and great content. As far as me personally, this spelled disaster.

"Why did they go and do that?" I whined. "Now everyone will be here."

Sitting back, arms crossed, everyone knew this was a rhetorical question. I wasn't looking for answers, I was looking to be coddled.

"Oh, hun, you can't begrudge Kat wanting to grow her business, Ms. CEO of her own company," Amie cooed.

"We will always be her favorites!" Sara declared, raising a glass. "To Kat's amazing space for lesbians to cut loose and make new friends!"

"Damn right!" Kat shouted back. "Give my favorites a free round!"

Everyone else at the table raised their glass and took a drink. If looks could kill, they would have all been dead. Attempting to storm off, my knees gave out a little. Sam caught me and we were face to face. The alcohol was doing its job. Closing the two-inch gap, my lips grazed hers. I felt her stiffen, then completely relax. Soon we were full-on lip-locking in the middle of a crowded room. Then, without warning, she pulled back, bruising my ego along the way.

The shocked faces behind us were the catalyst for a new deluge of tears. I limped to the bathroom, sans cane and locked myself in a stall. Clattering noise wafted in, then abruptly stopped. The bottom of a cane and a pair of feet showed up under my stall.

"Thought you might need this," a voice husky with pain stated. "Like I said, you can't hide from your ex in the bathroom when you date women."

I opened the door ever so slightly and grabbed the cane. The camel-colored loafers didn't move.

"Do you wanna know why I pulled away?" Sam asked.

Silence.

"I pulled away because I know you've been drinking and, as much as I love you and love kissing you, I don't want you to hate me in the morning for taking advantage of you."

More silence.

"Okay, well, Cass and I are going to settle up and leave so you guys can enjoy your night. Give me about five minutes and then you can come out. G'night, Indie," Sam said. "We really have to stop parting ways like this."

Tears streaming, my hand over my mouth to keep the sobs from escaping, I didn't say a word. A fresh wave of clattering glasses and the din of merry voices came and went once again. I let the break down have its way with me, weeping shamelessly in the bathroom stall of a bar.

"So you guys kiss, you run off, she goes in, she comes out, you're sobbing, we all go home. Care to elaborate, because we're all a little confused here. Come on, Indie; we are your friends," coaxed Sara.

"The things we miss in lesbian bars!" Gabriel said to Kenny.

Sighing, knowing they would badger and annoy until the whole truth was revealed, I began the story. "I had drunk a little too much-"

"A little?" Amie interrupted incredulously.

"Yes, a little, or a lot, whatever. The point is, I was uninhibited, as they say. When Sam's face came close to me, I couldn't resist kissing her. It felt natural, so that's what I did. She pulled away, I ran into the bathroom and cried. It's not exactly a difficult situation to understand." I recounted.

"Yes, but then she went in with a cane, came out without a cane, and she and Cass left. What was said in there?" Sara prodded.

"She said she knew I had been drinking and didn't want to take advantage," I answered.

"What did you say?" queried Amie.

"Nothing," I admitted.

"Homegirl is spilling her guts, trying to make sure she doesn't do anything to hurt you and you ignore her?" Sara said.

"Yes. I just didn't know what to say!" I rose to my own defense. "I was holding back the river of tears and couldn't open my mouth. Plus, I was heavily inebriated, lest we forget."

"Do you still love her?" Kenny asked, shocking the whole group.

"Y-yes. I do," I uttered. "Love has never been the problem."

"Then go meet her... sober," ordered Kenny. "Go, talk things out, get to the bottom of all of it, then, and only then make your decision."

With a group of friends staring at him, Kenny began to shift in his seat.

"It's the only logical thing to do."

"He's not wrong," Sara stated.

"God you're so hot when you're all logical and practical." Gabriel flattered Kenny.

Rolling my eyes, hating the infallible advice, I picked up my phone.

———

"Thanks for meeting me." I greeted my former lover.

"Thanks for inviting me," she returned.

After profusely apologizing for almost every second of the night before, I recounted the conversation amongst the friend group earlier that day.

"So, you're here to talk things out?" Sam clarified.

"Yes."

"Then what?"

"I have no idea."

"Well, okay then, let's get started."

"Why didn't you tell me the truth about Dubai?" I asked.

"Because it was never actually a possibility, so I didn't want to worry you," Sam answered. "I was kind of hoping I wouldn't get it so I wouldn't have to ruin my career in order to stay close to you."

"You ruined your career?!?!"

"Well, no, not exactly, but I was prepared to."

The quizzical look before Sam prompted her to explain further.

"Mark knew I couldn't leave you. He also knew you and I could never live there. On top of that, he knew I was great at my job. Basically, he insisted I stay on in Boston with him because he needed me there. He convinced them that's what was best for the company. They thought I would be mad, with taking away the

Dubai thing, so they offered me higher pay, a promotion, and all kinds of perks. It worked out very well, if I do say so myself."

"You really would have given it all up?"

"Without hesitation."

Heat flooded my face, but I composed myself and continued on with my line of questioning, remaining logical, as Kenny had suggested.

"Ali?"

"While you were in the hospital, she called me about helping her to pay rent so she could go to rehab. She had no one else to turn to. Her family disowned her long ago. So I paid for two months of her rent. I didn't tell you because, to me, it didn't matter. It wasn't even something of consequence to me. You were in the hospital. What mattered was you and Veda getting well. I wasn't trying to hide it, I genuinely had forgotten all about the whole situation until that night she text me. I'm assuming that's when she got out of rehab," Sam explained, looking me in the eyes the entire time.

"Are you ready to order?" the waiter interrupted our moment.

"Not quite," Sam replied, never unlocking from my gaze. As soon as he walked away, Sam continued on. "I love you. You are the most important thing to me. Nothing else even comes close. I want to be with you, more than anything, but I have a question too."

"Okay, shoot," I cracked.

"Why were you so quick to assume the worst of me and not even give me a chance to explain? You just ended it. You broke my heart."

"I've been lied to for so long. Things could always be explained away if I listened long enough and wanted to believe whatever story was being spun. I'm sorry I hurt you."

"I'm not him, Indie."

"I know, I know. It's just a reaction at this point, to protect myself."

"Believe it or not, that's my first reaction too. I'm here to help protect you. Can you trust me? Can you separate what he did from me?"

Looking up through watery vision, I knew I couldn't hurt her anymore and had to speak the truth. "Honestly, I don't know if I can."

"Well, thanks for the honesty. Let's order and try to enjoy the rest of our night. We both have a lot to think about," Sam concluded.

CHAPTER 32

Sam

THE TEXT THAT WOKE ME UP from my dream of Indie and I in Hawaii was from the only person on Earth I wouldn't get angry with for waking me from such a dream.

> **Please come to my party this weekend.
> It's at Sara's at 7.**

I smiled. She must be nervous.

> **ok but which day of the weekend
> exactly am i showing up at sara's?**

> **Oh, right. Friday. Friday at 7 at Sara's.**

> **ok i'll be there.**

> **Thank you. Actually, can you come
> closer to 6?**

> **yes ma'am.**

Thirty-four hours until I would see Indie. She seemed excited, so that had to be a good sign. She wanted me to come early, after all. I couldn't see her telling me she never wanted to see me again at her own birthday party. My smile faded quickly. What if she wanted us to be friends? That might be why she invited me to come early, to break the news to me and see if I even wanted to stay.

I flopped back down in bed. Yes, that had to be it. Otherwise, she would have wanted me to stay after, maybe even stay over. The girls weren't due back until Monday. We would have had the whole weekend to reconnect. The tightness in my chest became so intense, I thought I might actually be having a heart attack. Bob rubbed his head against my calf.

"Being a human is rough, bud. One of out ten, would not recommend. Be grateful you are a cat," I sighed, petting the ball of fur on the head.

"Daaaaaamn! Well, you've had quite the week. Quite the few weeks. Quite the couple of months, my friend!" exclaimed Cass.

"Tell me about it," I murmured.

"This is some TV reality show worthy unrequited love bullshit right here."

"Glad my love life is so amusing, Cassandra."

"Hey now, don't you full-name me, Satomi. I'm just pointing out the obvious. This story could be a money maker. You should pitch it to Netflix or something."

"Seriously, Cass, what do you think?"

"Seriously? Okay, seriously, I think you need to come right out and ask her. Seriously, I think you're right about the whole friends thing. Seriously, I'm glad I'm not in your shoes right now," Cass said.

"Thank you for your honesty. I guess I need to prepare myself, if that's even possible." My head fell into my hands. This was going to be a fresh hell.

"So, different topic, what's up with Indie's friend Amie? She crazy or no?"

I shook my head and glared at her.

"Really? Really?!?!"

"What? She's cute!"

A cat is no help picking out outfits or giving advice. They are pretty uninterested in anything and everything besides getting a pat on the head or food. Taking his only meow as his opinion, I chose my black pants and a fitted, cream-colored, button-down shirt, with the sleeves rolled up. Casual, but sophisticated.

As I looked at myself in the mirror, I thanked Bob.

"Not bad, buddy, not bad. Looking good up in here, if I do say so myself."

Striking the pose of hands in pockets, one leg forward, torso slightly twisted, no one could argue with the sexiness before them.

"If I raise one eyebrow, every lesbian within the city limits may faint. I must be careful in this ensemble."

The short-lived bravado was quelled by a river of nervous energy. On the precipice of yet another heartbreak, the butter-flies in my stomach were whirling into a tornado. Standing tall, I reminded myself, no matter what happened tonight, Indie was back in my life. If we just had to be friends who go to each other's birthday parties, then it would be enough.

My head started spinning. Friends meant we would eventually date other people. Friends meant I couldn't touch her. Friends meant someone else would be on the receiving end of that smile she made. Running to the kitchen window, I threw it open and took a deep breath of the fresh Boston air in early spring.

"Sammi?" a small voice said.

I stuck my head out the window.

"Hey, Jenny. How are you feeling? Your mom said you had gotten a stomach bug."

"Better thanks. I'm just out here enjoying not being in pain and reading the latest Sherlock Holmes book mom grabbed me from the library. How's Bob?"

"Oooh, nice! He's quite content after his little adventure, and I'm glad you're on the mend, kiddo. I gotta go, Indie's birthday party is tonight."

"Ooooo, Indie. Tell her hi from her favorite Simons!" she teased.

"Will do, now go eat some crackers or something and get lots of rest!"

"Ewww, no more of those tasteless crackers, please."

Feeling a tiny bit better, I closed up shop, grabbed the envelope containing the birthday girl's present, and headed out. I was going to meet my destiny tonight with my head held high and looking amazing. Hand around the doorknob, I hesitated. Should I bring an overnight bag, just in case?

Sara's house looked like something out of a movie. The entire side yard was crisscrossed with strings of lights, beautifully illuminating the round tables below decked in champagne-colored satin tablecloths. Atop each of them was an eclectic, yet classy, bohemian display of colored strips of cloth, flowers, candles, and interesting oddities, most of which I recognized as Indie's collection from her world travels. Bamboo chairs, painted in a black lacquer completed the look.

Walking through the scene was surreal, cameras and boom mics were sure to pop out at any moment as Indie rejected me in the most rom-com way imaginable. Looking up, the splendor continued on into the back yard. A huge fire pit was glowing, the flames dancing long before the party officially started. Flanking it on all sides were chaises, chairs, and settees, all decadently draped in soft blankets. As the eyes kept moving, a large table could be seen, with all of the trappings needed to make s'mores. Three different kinds of graham crackers, too many different kinds of candy to count, marshmallows of all sizes, elegant metal roasting sticks with wooden handles, plates, and tons of wet-naps.

In the middle of the backyard was a click-in-place dance floor, flooded with disco lights. The DJ was just setting up beyond. I nodded to her and she smiled, returning the gesture. Her eyes roamed up and down a little too long. Yeah, this outfit was definitely the right choice.

"Sam! So glad you could make it!" Sara gushed, descending from the house with an arm full of plates.

"Need some help with that?" I offered.

"Oh my god, yes, please." Handing me the plates, she zoomed back into her kitchen. "Just put one at each chair, please!"

Setting a table was as good a distraction as any. Indie walked around the corner of Sara's into the side yard. Our eyes met. She smiled slightly, only enhancing how gorgeous she looked. Her hair half-up, slightly askew, curls framing her face perfectly, makeup expertly applied to be just enough, but not cover her natural beauty, she looked like a goddess. The cream-colored dress was flowy, but hugged all of the right places. Long feather earrings cascaded seamlessly with her hair and bangle bracelets abounded. Mediterranean-style shoes were in her hands as she walked barefoot towards me. The wind blew at that exact moment.

Seriously? Where are the cameras? This has to be staged! I thought, my knees giving just a little. What little bravado the DJ had restored in me quickly dissipated.

"Hey," Indie's voice was soft and husky.

"Hey back atcha. You look amazing. Happy birthday!" I replied.

"Thank you. You're looking quite dashing yourself."

Indie's eyebrows raised just a little, setting my heart aflutter. Then her face dropped, causing the fluttering to crash and burn.

"Thanks. Bob helped me pick out my outfit. He and Jenny both say hello."

Her smile once again brightened everything around me. I got back to my plate setting, both so Sara wouldn't kill me and so my mind and eyes could focus on something besides the woman I wanted most in the world.

"I see Sara put you to work already."

"Yeah. I'm happy to help, though, I'm not really adding much to all of this," I admitted, gesturing to the marvelous scene before us. "This is beyond words amazing! I've never seen anything quite like this outside of a movie."

Walking towards me, Indie divulged, "If you knew Sara a bit better, you'd know this is a cry for help. She is a master at staging houses for sale, which naturally translates into amazing party scenes, but she is doing it to distract herself."

"Still having problems with the custody stuff?"

"Yeah." Indie sat in a chair at the table I was setting. "Lisaida has started twisting half-truths to make it look like Sara is abusive."

"What?!? I may not know her that well, but I have seen her with those kids, and those kids with her, and she is not abusive," I defended my beloved's friend.

"You know that, and I know that, but the state has to do a full investigation."

"Oh thank god you're here!" Sara's voice boomed from behind me. "Here," she said, plopping another arm full of plates in front of Indie. "Start setting these out." The crazed party planner persona paused for a moment. "Happy birthday, my friend. I love you so much."

The two long-time friends embraced.

"Okay, now get your limping ass to work, birthday girl. Just don't overdo it."

"She's quite the tyrant when she wants to be, huh?" I queried.

"You have no idea," Indie responded.

Having broken the ice and joked a little, we worked together, putting a gold-rimmed plate at each seat.

"I'm glad you came early, and not just because now I don't have to do all of this last-minute stuff with only the tyrant to keep me company."

"I'm glad too."

Her face remained turned towards the table. "I guess we should talk before the party starts. That way you can exit before anyone else arrives, if you want to."

I gulped. This was it. This was the end of what almost was. The ringing in my ears intensified and my feet wanted to flee, but felt glued to the ground.

"I'm not abandoning Sara in her time of tyranny."

My attempt at humor was marred by the war within me, but Indie chuckled anyway.

"The other night, you asked me if I could trust you. You made a very good point about me punishing you for what Zacariah did to me. What I allowed to happen for all of those years. I have spent the last however many years, since the divorce, building up defenses so nothing like that could ever happen again. These defenses work fast and hard, without hesitation. They have only been an asset in my life until now. They have kept me safe. No one had gotten in, until you."

Her gaze met mine. The pain inside of her spilling out and running down her cheeks.

The urge to hold her almost overwhelmed me.

"I am not totally unfamiliar with that concept."

"I know I'm not the only one with past relationship trauma. I know you've been hurt too. I know that I've hurt you, for which I am truly sorry."

This sounded like the beginning of a break up speech for sure.

"Indie, before you continue, I wanted to let you know I don't regret any of this. I'm glad we became a part of each other's lives again. I'm glad I got to know you again, your kids, and even the tyrant, Sara. I'm glad I didn't take the job in Dubai and I'm glad I'm here placing dinner plates on champagne-colored round tables. I'm glad we at least had the chance."

"Oh, yeah, I'm glad too. Yeah, at least we had the chance. Will you excuse me for one moment?"

I nodded, continuing on with my job. Sara came out the back with silverware as Indie went around the front of the house.

"So, you two all good?" Sara questioned.

"I mean, yeah, I think so. I am just glad to be back in her life on any level, even if we're not together. By the way, thank you for having me at your lovely home. You really do a bang up job!"

"Wait, what? Not together? She pours her heart out, on her birthday," Sara emphasized, "and you turn her down? After all of that I wanna be with you shit, you turn my girl down?!"

"What? Turn her down? I didn't... she didn't... she never..." My eyes widened as Sara's arms uncrossed.

"What did you two talk about?" Sara prodded.

"I may have thought she was trying to let me down easy and kind of gave her permission to do so, in a round-about way."

"Oh my god. Go find her, now!" the tyrant ordered.

My legs couldn't carry me fast enough. Indie's house was only a block from here, she couldn't have made it home already.

"Indie!" I shouted, running full-speed. My feet left the soft grass of Sara's front yard and hit the unforgiving pavement. "INDIE!"

"What?" I heard from behind me.

There she was in all her glory, holding a tissue on Sara's front porch. The soft grass was underfoot once again. I climbed the stairs two at a time until I reached the confused, slightly concerned, love of my life.

"What's goi–" I cut her off with a deep kiss. I could feel the shock melt away from her body as she leaned in and kissed me back. Arms wrapped around my neck, pulling me in closer.

When we finally came up for air, I had a confession that could no longer be held back.

"I want you, Indie Woodley. I want you in whatever way you will allow. If you say friends, we are friends, but know that I will always want more of you, no matter how much you give. I will never tire of you. I will be here for you, and the girls, always in all ways. I am yours, whether either of us like it or not. I will protect you from anything and everything in any way I can. I trust you. You are who I have wanted to be with since I was seventeen. I don't want to do life without you ever again."

Her smiling, tear-stained face looked up at me.

"Ditto. Do you remember what I told you when we first started talking again, about the dream that prompted me to reach out to you?"

"Yeah."

"Well, I didn't tell you everything. I told you I had dreams for a couple of weeks and the people changed each night. Most of the people changed each night. There was one person who was always there. You were always right there next to me, smiling. It's always been you, babe, and it always will be."

"We can be buried together like the Egyptian pharaohs in a huge pyramid I design!" I exclaimed.

A make-out session was in full swing on Sara's front porch. Behind me, cheering and clapping ensued as Sara, Gabriel, Amie, and Kenny all spectated from the corner of the house.

"Now, get your asses down here and everybody help me finish up!"

The tyrant's momentary bout of the feels was waning, but I didn't care.

The evening was as amazing as the surroundings. I met so many people from Indie's life, at her side. My hands barely left her hand, her waist, or her hip all night. Dancing, drinking, laughing, and eating some fantastic food, courtesy of the tyrant, filled a perfect evening celebrating the life of the one I held most dear. I even saw the DJ living her best life, getting a few phone numbers. By midnight, everyone except the core crew was gone.

"A sparkling success, as always, Sara, dear. To Sara!" Gabriel complimented, raising his glass.

"Hear, hear!" we all chorused.

Sara turned beet red. "Thank you all. I could not ask for a greater framily than you crazy lot!"

"I think I'm going to take a break from dating," Amie blurted out.

"What? Really?" Indie gasped.

I had only known Amie for a short while, but she had had more relationships in that finite amount of time than I had in the last two decades.

"I gave up dating for many years. Best thing I ever did. It got me ready for Indie." I declared.

"Exactly! Call it a mid-life crisis, or whatever you want, but I'm ready to get to know me. I haven't been single for more than five minutes since I was fourteen years old. When that comes along," Amie gestured towards Indie and me, "I want to be ready."

"To Amie!" shouted Kenny.

"Hear, hear!" we all chorused once again.

"Alrighty, as much as I love you all, I need sleep." Sara yawned. "Be back here at nine a.m. to help with clean up, though, or I will hunt your sorry asses down! Framily or no framily, I will end you!"

"Sam will protect me," Indie gushed.

Between the laughter and fake retching sounds, everyone said their goodbyes.

"Where is your car?" Indie asked.

"About a block away, down this side street," I answered, surprised and disappointed she wanted me to leave.

"Do you want to sleep at my house tonight? No kids for another two days. We can just walk around naked the whole time," Indie enticed.

"Except at nine a.m. tomorrow morning."

"Yes, except for then."

"Of course I want to be naked with you all weekend. Let me just grab my bag out of my car."

"Oh, so you packed a bag? Thought I just couldn't resist you?"

"I packed it because of wishful thinking," I attested, pulling her in close for a kiss. "It was actually a last-minute decision I decided two seconds before heading out the door. OH! That reminds me, your gift!"

I ran to the car, grabbing my bag and the envelope.

"Ooo, good things come in small packages," Indie sang as she opened it.

A small tube fell into her hand.

"What is this?"

"The literature and instructions are inside. It's a DNA kit. I ordered it for you months ago. You deserve to know who you are."

Fresh tears welled up in her dry eyes.

"Thank you."

Her kiss was passionate enough to obliterate any sense or logic I had. She was everything in that moment. We were all that mattered.

"Ready to go spit into a tube?"

Indie grinned, grabbing my hand. "I thought you'd never ask."

THE END

Indie

"WHERE YOU GOING, BABE?" Sammi croaked.

"Just going to the bathroom," I whispered as I kissed her warm cheek, etched with pillow lines.

"What time is it?"

"It's 4:37."

The small icon on the top of my phone screen was unfamiliar. I clicked on it and gasped, shaking my half-asleep girlfriend awake.

"Sam, SAM!"

"Whaaa?" whined Sam.

"My results are in! Oh my god, I can't even look. What if I was adopted? What if it's all a lie? What if my dad was crazy and I am his? What if I'm some weird thing I didn't even think about?" I peppered the groggy girl next to me with my whirling thoughts.

"I'm up, I'm here."

Her hand found my shoulder and pulled me in close.

"Let's look together."

I nuzzled in and clicked on the icon. We both gasped.

"I'm Egyptian?!?"

"I guess so. Wow, yeah, I can see it." Sam stated, looking at me as if it was the first time she had ever seen me.

"Oh my god, Sam. There's more. Like there's more of me. I think these four people are my half sisters."

She showed me the pictures on her screen. "Holy shit, babe! They look just like you!"

"I know!"

"Well, this is going to be quite an interesting day."

Sam motioned towards the bathroom.

"Let's not start it by you actually peeing your pants."

ABOUT THE AUTHOR

Bᴇᴋ Mɪɴᴀ, author of *Indie's First Love*, lives in Richmond, Virginia with her four children. She is a former high school English teacher, world traveler, and lover of the written word. This half-Egyptian, half-Swiss, American born chocolate lover almost never turns down a cup of hot tea and relishes in rainy days, good books, and trying new food and experiences.

She firmly believes that anyone can do just about anything at any age or stage of life, so she became a writer and a yoga teacher in her late thirties and continues to find new and interesting paths to venture down in life!

Sneak Peek into Book Two

SARA'S
SECOND CHANCE

CHAPTER 1

"AND, THROUGH HERE, IS the rec room, den, whatever you'd like to use it for," I informed the couple walking along behind me.

The young, newlyweds seemed quite enraptured with this home: their twenty-seventh showing in the last month. Hopefully this house was 'the one'. Hopefully, these people would just buy something already so I could get my commission check to keep fighting Lisaida. It would also help not to be constantly surrounded by the lovey-dovey, overly affectionate, blissful couple almost every day of the week.

"Oh, sweets, this would be perfect for our children! We could have an office are over here," the young woman said to her beloved as she swept her arms over towards a little alcove to the left. "That way I could keep an eye on them while I'm grading papers and doing lesson plans."

His hearty laugh reached his eyes. Maybe they were the real deal. Maybe these two would make a happy family. Probably not, but it was kind of nice to have a glimmer of hope that not everyone would be as miserable as I was.

"That sounds perfect. I love you, sweets," he cooed.

"I love you too!" she exclaimed, clapping and hopping in her excitement.

I almost threw up in my mouth but successfully kept my eggs and toast at bay.

"Great! So, are we ready to put in an offer?" I inquired.

"I think so," the young husband replied. "You have kids, right, Ms. Willis? Don't you think this would be a perfect place to raise them?"

"Yes, I do, and, yes, I do."

The door swung shut. I was alone in the perfect house for the perfect family. The tears started their slow descent down my cheeks, splashing onto the perfect floor in the perfect house for the perfect family. Their offer was a little low, but would probably end up working out in the end, after a counter offer or two. After wishing them gone for so many weeks, I was a bit sad to see them get their happy ending and go off without me.

I stood there for a long while, my mind full, but somehow void of coherent thought. The ding on my phone broke through my stunned stillness. I had to get this offer in. I had to try to give someone else some goodness in this world.

I glanced at my phone and saw an email. I had a new caseworker through child services. She had to come tour the house and interview me. *Fantastic.*

The house was clean and I was as put together as I could be, at least on the outside. As I opened the door, a stunning woman stood in front of me. Her wild, curly hair was the same color as Indie's, but shorter. Her smart suit somehow looked casual and dressy all at the same time, like she just belonged in it; a second skin. In the boardroom or at the beach, it would look natural on her.

"Sara? Sara Willis?"

I nodded.

"Good evening. I am Cecelia Campbell and I am your new caseworker."

"Nice to meet you," I replied with very little enthusiasm. "Come on in."

"Thank you. I know you've been through some of this before, and I apologize for the inconvenience of having to start over from scratch with a new caseworker, but I promise you we are doing our best for you and your children."

I scoffed and she pretended not to notice.

"It's not the first time, and I'm sure it won't be the last." I replied. "Coffee, tea, water?"

"No, thank you. May I see where the children sleep?"

"Of course."

I led her down the hallway filled with pictures of Melonie and Ethan. She seemed to be covertly trying to study them.

"Beautiful children."

"Yes, they are. Thank you."

"Neither of them are biologically yours, correct?"

I spun around so quickly that I almost hit her nose with mine.

"No, they are no biologically mine, but we both know that biology isn't the most important thing in life. Otherwise, you wouldn't have a job investigating biological parents to see if their children need to be removed from their care."

I spun back around, seething.

"Biology isn't everything. This is Ethan's room and over there is Melonie's." I stated, pointing to the two doors in front of us respectively.

The woman who was now on my last nerve calmly entered Ethan's room, jotting down notes as she went around the room. She stopped at his mirror where he kept a few post-it notes that I had left for him over the years. Funny quips, inspirational quotes, declarations of love for my child. Her eyes lingered for a moment.

"Biology may not be everything, but it is something, Ms. Willis."

The rest of the visit was infuriating in a way that I had to try desperately hide. How dare this woman come into my home so coolly, so calmly and try to tear me apart quietly. I had to seem collected and in control of my behavior at all times, but her very presence made it almost impossible. She just got under my skin.

I took out my computer and decided to focus on work after she concluded the interview. The counter offer for the young newlyweds had been accepted. I smiled for them as I looked at the reflection of my own weary face in the screen in front of me.

I may never get a happily ever after, but I'm going to do my best to give someone else a chance to get theirs. Unlike Ceceilia Campbell, I am going to give people the benefit of the doubt.

Angrily typing on my keyboard, I answered the seller's realtor, somehow thinking I was 'sticking it' to the infuriating woman who had just left my home. She may suck the life out of people and tear them down, but I was not that kind of a person. I had a heart, unfortunately.

I saw Indie walking up the driveway and slightly panicked. Had I forgotten something? She looked so… intent, focused, and just a bit frantic.

Opening the door, I smiled weakly as her head shot up.

"Well, the results are in. I'm not who I thought I was. I'm not sure who I am. Did you know that I am descended from the Pharaohs for god's sake?"

"Oh, um wow. Well, that is certainly interesting. Care to expound, milady? I would love to hear about anything other than my problems and my new caseworker."

Indie stopped short and gave me a huge hug.

"I'm sorry Sara. I was so wrapped up in myself that I forgot. You okay?"

"Girl, that was NOT a dig at you. I was for real. I don't wanna talk about it, but yeah, I'm ok. Now spill. This has been brewing for forever and I am totally here for it!"

I guess my new caseworker was right. Biology is something. I hated this new revelation and how much it colored my cheeks in anger towards the heartless person who was, unfortunately, in a position of authority over me and my children.

"I already text Gabriel and Amie and Helene. They'll be here momentarily. I don't feel like going through all of this four times more than necessary."

I pushed the curtain aside to see Amie and Gabriel walking up Cary St. from their respective directions. Helene would take a bit longer, since she lived a whole ten blocks away.

"I guess it's time to put the kettle on." I said, trudging into the kitchen.

On the counter was a small business card for a family counselor specializing in non-biological families. *Who the hell did that woman think she was?* I was losing what little control I had left when the crew began to file into my house.

"The party can start, the Gay-briel has arrived!" said Gabriel, snapping his fingers as he walked past.

I smiled in spite of myself, put the water into the kettle, and the business card into the trash.

ACKNOWLEDGEMENTS

MY FOUR, beautiful, amazing, silly, intelligent children are some of the best people I have ever had the chance to know. Adia, Raine, Amaris, & Aveon; I am truly honored to be your mother. You are all way too cool for me, but I'm glad you put up with me anyway.

I wouldn't have had the raw material to even write this book without the love story that I have lived with you, Jess. You were my first love, and now that we're old, I'm beyond thrilled to be loved by you again.

I appreciate Rachel Robson, my editor, for working with this first-time author and being so patient as I underwent so much upheaval in my life, dropping the ball a few times in the process. You fell in love with my characters as much as I did and helped me get their story out.

I could not have done any of this without you, Debbie Rasmussen. This book would be nothing more than a manuscript without you holding my hand every step of the way during the formatting, publishing, and a million other things. Thank goodness for Author Ready!

Thank you so much, Raine Matos, for the gorgeous cover art of Indie and Sammi! I'm so glad you stuck with me through the "that's not quite the right shade" and various other small things that I kept throwing at you. It turned out so well and captured the characters perfectly.

The final stage of making all of these random words into an actual book was handled so well, I barely even had to lift a finger. Francine Platt, Interior designer for a book was not a title I even knew existed before you came along. Thank you for handling my baby so well.

Stephanie Faye, not only do write wonderful books but you are a true friend. Thank you for showing me that it's all possible. My dream has come true because I saw you do it first.

Jeannie, girl, where do I start? You have been there since we were small children, always loving, supporting, and telling me harsh truths about myself. My growth would never have been this amazing without you. You are family in every way and I don't have the words to adequately convey to you how I feel.

Thank you to my mom and dad. They are both gone and will never see this book, but they helped mold me into who I am. The good, the bad, and the ugly of me will forever be tied to these two imperfect, loving people.

And last, but not least, a shout out to my bazillion siblings (seventeen at last count), friends, family, teachers, co-workers, and every random stranger I've ever met. Each of you beautiful souls all around the world have made an impact, and I'm so very grateful.